THROW OUT THE WATER

THE WATER

A Novel

Kevin Corley

Published by Hard Ball Press, 2016.
Information available at: www.hardballpress.com
ISBN: 978-0-9862400-1-0

Cover art by: Patty Henderson,
Book design by D. Bass

Dedication

For
Darcy and Dylan Brown
and
Henry Brown

Special thanks to the following historians without whose help this book would not have been possible.

Chuck Martin of the Christian County Coal Mine Museum in Taylorville Illinois

Greg Boozell at www.minewars.org

Rosemary Feurer at http://www.motherjonesmuseum.org/

The late David Thoreau Wieck for his book <u>Woman from Spillertown: A Memoir of Agnes Burns Wieck</u>

*"If history were taught in the form of stories,
it would never be forgotten." ~ Rudyard Kipling*

*"We always carried water. There was an area in the
bottom of the miner's bucket that we put water. That's
how we carried our water to drink, and the top was
where we had our lunch. If the miners had some kind of
grievance, one of them would say, "Well, what are we
going to do?" So they'd throw the water, and if it would
stay up in the air, well, we'd go ahead and work. If it
came down and hit the ground, we'd strike.
Jesse Lake Interview, 1986*

THROW OUT
THE WATER

A Novel

Kevin Corley

1933

"I heard Sam Vacca broke your nose." Archie Norton set the bag of explosives gently on the backseat of the Model A Ford and cast a quick glance at Kieran Phelan.

"No, it was the old Vacca bitch." Phelan was already behind the wheel and getting irritated by the Chicago thug's constant jabber.

"The one that got kilt in Tovey the other night?" Norton jumped into the automobile and stomped snow off his over-sized feet onto the floorboard.

"Which way to the bridge?" Phelan asked. The Vacca family was a touchy subject, especially since no one but his wife Felina knew he'd been the one to pull the trigger and kill Angeline Vacca. Felina hated the wops more than he did. When he came home from the January third gun battle at the central Illinois mine and told her he'd shot the old biddy, she was so elated she'd ripped off his clothes and promptly provided him with the blood lust that always followed a good killing.

"Drive out east of Taylorville, and we'll circle back on the dirt roads toward Pawnee," Norton said, his bushy eyebrow arched. "That way if anyone sees us leave town, they'll figure we're headed toward Pana."

Normally, Phelan wouldn't have asked advice of someone as squirrely as Norton, but since this was their first assignment together, he wanted to size up the thug. Besides, the man seemed a little slow in the head.

"You still pals with the Shelton boys?" Norton asked when they finally left the city limits.

"Nah," Phelan said. "Them boys ain't got a chance now that Henry Horner is gonna be governor. Horner can't be bought. He's gonna get them boys—unless they get him first." He was proud to have been a member of the notorious gang from southern Illinois, although the Sheltons had kicked him out of their mob for botching the Kincaid bank robbery.

"You think they'll get the governor first?"

"Probably not." Phelan downshifted into the curve. "Bernie Shelton's got the guts, but he's just a dumb ox. His brother Carl's the one who calls the shots, but he's too affable. I reckon their days are numbered."

"So what's you gonna do?" Norton asked. "Capone gone—the Sheltons and prohibition on the way out?"

"Unions are where the money is." Phelan smiled. "These Illinois unions are run mostly by reds. They's communists and socialists who think rich Christians would be willing to share their loot. They don't got the stomach for violence theys self." His smile broadened. "That's where I come in. That's my line of work."

"Ain't that what got the Sheltons in hot water? I heard they kilt that union guy down around St. Louis."

"Sure did." Phelan laughed. "Big Carl tried to bribe a fella named Oliver Moore with thirty G's so the Sheltons could take over the Boilermaker's Union. When Moore turned it down, he got filled with twenty-seven machine gun bullets right in front of union headquarters."

"So that's why you're doing this job for the United Mine Workers?"

"Hell of a deal, ain't it?" Phelan nodded as he turned the automobile onto a backroad and circled back toward the Midland Bridge. "Blow up a bridge and blame it on the Progressives. Hell of a deal!"

"Why are the Progressives and United Mine Workers feuding?" Norton, short even for a short person, straightened in the seat. "They's both coal miner unions, ain't they?"

The Progressive Miners of America had formed a few months before. "Yeah, but the Progressives think Lewis is on the take."

"Lewis? John Lewis? The president of UMW?"

"One and the same."

"Is he? From who?"

"Supposedly from the coal companies."

"Is he?"

"Hell, I don't know and I don't care." Phelan sighed. Norton asked too many questions. "Long as I get mine."

When they reached the mile-long bridge that spanned a wooded valley, Phelan drove up an old fishing lane and parked between a clump of tall trees.

"Ain't nobody ever fishes here," Phelan said. "The runoff from the coal mines has kilt every fish in this area."

"Why do you suppose fishes die but miners don't?"

"Men have lungs," Phelan said. "I suppose lungs can filter out the coal dust."

"Oh, yeah, I hadn't thought of that."

"Now, run this wire from here down to that first pillar on the trestle." Phelan pointed to the pillar. "I'll get the dynamite and be right there."

A half hour later, two charges were hooked up and ready to be detonated from the wires that ran to the plunger box near Phelan's automobile.

Norton stretched onto his toes so he could look Phelan—not much taller—in the eye. "You think that's enough dynamite to bring down the whole shebang?"

"We don't want to bring down the whole bridge. We want the railroad to be able to fix it quickly so the coal company won't lose business."

"Oh, yeah, I forgot." Norton pressed his lips together and surveyed their work. "Can I push the plunger?"

"Sure, Archie."

A man in a striped railroad jacket walked out onto the bridge. He paused for a moment, then reached into his shirt pocket, took out tobacco fixings, and began rolling a smoke.

"Do it now, Archie," Phelan said quietly, a smile on his face.

"I don't know," Norton whispered. "I ain't never kilt nobody before."

"Ah, ain't nothing to it." Phelan leaned toward the shorter man. "Now, knocking a man unconscious without killing him, now that's an art form. It ain't like you see in them movies where the fella wakes up after twenty minutes, shakes his head and goes about his business. No sir, I've seen fellas who get knocked out and then dies in their sleep two nights later." He blew out a long breath and smiled. "Now push the plunger, Archie."

"Maybe you'd better do it."

"Archie," Phelan took the short man's large hands and guided them to the plunger handle. "What kinda gangster are you? You a chicken, Archie?"

The railroader took a few steps to leave the bridge. Phelan placed his hands on top of Norton's and forced the plunger down.

Instead of one detonation that was supposed to knock the end supports down, there was a series of explosions that lasted almost a minute and ran from their side of the bridge all the way to the other. The railroader flew high into the air as if from a circus cannon. All around the flying man sailed thick wooden ties and long pieces of iron railroad tracks. The sky filled with debris that for a moment almost shadowed the valley, then fell to the ground like starlings swarming gracefully into a corn field.

Wood and metal pieces crashed all around the men. Phelan dove under the car and covered his head. When Norton tried to squeeze in next to him, Phelan kicked him away.

After several long minutes, the sound of bridge fragments falling from the sky stopped—except for the occasional rubble released from strained tree branches.

"What the hell was that?" Norton slid out from under a fallen log and scampered on all fours to the front car door. He sat up and brushed himself off.

Phelan crawled out from under the car and looked across the now almost flattened valley. Trees and bushes were lying on their sides as if blown over by a tornado. Lumber and bent iron and steel lay atop one another in a twisted clutter.

"Look at them fellas skedaddle." Phelan pointed to where a half mile away several men were hightailing it up the hill toward a pickup truck. "The Progressives must've already had the bridge loaded and ready to blow. Our charges set theirs off."

"Why there ain't nothin' left of that bridge but toothpicks," Norton said.

"Help!" A voice above them shouted. "Get me down from here."

Phelan and Norton looked up. The railroader dangled precariously from thin branches atop a high cottonwood tree.

"Well, it would appear you ain't no murderer yet, Archibald." Phelan knocked debris off the hood of his car and then jumped in the driver's seat. "Let's get the hell outta here."

* * * * * * *

Bullo Vacca was walking home with a large group of men after a late afternoon UMW meeting.

An explosion shattered the silence, followed by another and another and another. Even after the blasts ended, the ground continued to tremble.

"Midland Bridge?" someone asked.

"Somewhere around there," someone else agreed.

Most of the men scattered quickly to find vehicles that could motor them to the scene.

Bullo and a few others, including mine boss James Hartman, shook their heads and continued to walk toward their homes. Word around town was that Peabody Coal Company, with the help of the UMW, would dynamite something and blame it on the Progressives. That strategy had worked several months earlier when they had blown up their own UMW headquarters—and a few minutes later carefully blew out the front end of the newspaper office. Miners were accomplished with explosives, and it was no accident the printing presses in the back rooms were not only undamaged, but had been left running. Within an hour, a special edition of the newspaper was on the street, its headline blaming the Progressives for the bombings.

Undoubtedly, this night's bombing was another planned assault to be blamed on a rival.

"Don't leave your houses 'til morning, boys," Hartman told Bullo and the other half-dozen men who had chosen to continue walking to the safety of their homes rather than rushing off to see the spectacle of the destruction. "It's going to be a noisy night, I'd reckon."

A few of the men nodded and took the next street toward their houses.

"I reckon I might as well drag the bathtub in from the smokehouse," someone muttered.

"Hell, I just leave mine in the house," another miner said. "My kids are so used to sleeping in it they don't never ask if they can sleep in beds. Our house has so many bullet holes, my wife wants to board up the windows for winter."

Bullo lived across the dirt road from Hartman and his sixteen-year-old son, John. The boy had just started in the mine a few months before, about the time the trouble began. The sounds of explosions and gunshots had been commonplace since September, when most of the Christian County miners split from the UMW to form the fledgling Progressive Mine Workers of America.

"Pa," John said, when the other men were far enough away to not hear, "I still don't understand why John Lewis sided with the coal companies. He's the president of the UMW. What for's he doing that?"

"Well, son," Hartman answered in a tranquil tone, "Lewis understands that the American economy is suffering. Illinois miners get paid a lot more than workers in other states. Lewis knows that if we don't take a pay cut, the coal companies will just go to the other states and we'll all be without a job. Understand?"

"I guess I do." John's eyebrows arched upwards in the middle. "But why do we get paid more than the other states?"

"We, well," Hartman stuttered a moment. "'Cause folks here have got the United Mine Workers to help them."

Bullo liked the Hartmans. James was a widower, and he and his son had been neighbors with the Vaccas for over ten years. He didn't blame James for taking a job as mine

boss when the trouble began. Those who had chosen not\
to break ranks understood that the UMW was simply protecting the workers' jobs, although Bullo did question why
the union didn't accept the job-sharing idea the Progressives had suggested. It wouldn't be so bad to take a pay
cut if miners could work fewer hours a day or fewer days
a week.

Arriving at his street, Bullo saw the lights were on at
Vinnie and Sam's. His own small home between his brother and father's houses was dark. Giant oak trees adorned
the back yards, but to the south lay a large field. Though
barren for the winter, the field would be known throughout spring and summer as Angeline's garden—his late
mother's pride and joy.

He nodded to the Hartman men and stepped over a
snow pile toward his brother's home. He opened the un-
locked door and went in. His wife Mary Kate was cooking
with her sister-in-law Sam in the kitchen. The boys wres-
tled upstairs, and his father, Antonio, sat alone in front of
the fireplace, looking up at him.

"The bridge?" Antonio asked.

Bullo nodded. "Most likely. Although Jack Stanley's
house hasn't been bombed yet this month."

"Well, maybe they'll leave the poor fellow alone," Antonio said. "He didn't ask to be the president of the Progressives. You'd think that blowing up his front porch and then
his outhouse would be harassment enough."

Bullo didn't want to talk politics. If not for the murder
of his mother, his father would most likely have stayed in
mining and become the president of the Progressive local.
Then it would have been Antonio Vacca's porch and outhouse that would have been blown up.

"Is Vinnie awake?"

"Well, he is now," Antonio said harshly. "I'd 'spect that

explosion rattled him out of any good rest he was gettin'."

Bullo guessed that the tension in the room with his father would be nothing compared to what would be in the bedroom with his seriously ill brother, so he sat down in a chair next to the fireplace. Vinnie was even more an advocate of the Progressives than their father. They had made peace with Bullo only after the death of Angeline. Many families in the community were split over the mine war, but Angeline Vacca had instilled such a strong sense of family in her loved ones that it would survive even her passing.

"Saw you walking home with the Hartmans," Antonio said. "Guess he's set himself up pretty good with the company."

"I like James," Bullo said slowly so his irritation at his father's criticism wouldn't show. "His son is all he has left in this world, and I can't blame him for taking care of his own."

Antonio stood, walked to the big front window, lit a cigarette and stared out at the moon-bright night. Across the road, James and his son walked out of their house and to the woodpile. They had a coal-burning stove, but coal was scarce since the strike, and many folks had converted to wood. James loaded his son's arms full of firewood. Antonio wished he had taken Angeline's advice years ago and gotten out of mining when the getting out was good. Now he had lost many good friends—like James Hartman—and if he didn't bite his tongue, he could lose Bullo also.

The young Hartman boy was walking into his house with the armful of wood when an automobile roared down the street between their houses. James Hartman heard it too, and turned toward the road, his own arms also full of firewood. The first bullets splintered the logs in front of his chest, knocking the mine boss backwards, although he somehow stayed on his feet. Then with the next shots, the back of James Hartman's head opened and spit blood like an angry geyser. The truck was out of sight before his legs finally buckled and he fell forward into the snow. Bullo was out the door before his father could move. By the time the stunned Antonio was recovered enough to follow, even Sam had shot past him carrying a dishtowel. Antonio tripped on a snow bank and fell twice before he could finally reach the scene. By then, Bullo was trying to prevent the hysterical John from diving on top of his father, an action that would have prevented Sam from wrapping her apron around the dying man's head wound. Though his eyes had rolled back, James began to gasp. Sam had to resort to one hand in front and the other behind his head to try and hold back the bleeding. The end for James Hartman came with a loud, ghastly expulsion of air and white spittle and blood flowing from his mouth.

As Bullo released his hold, the boy fell on top of his father. Sam was covered in blood from her face to her knees. Mary Kate was suddenly at her side, wrapping a blanket over her sister-in-law's shoulders. Neighbors were now filing out of their homes.

Antonio looked back toward his house. His three young grandsons watched the scene from the big window. *They are good boys*, Antonio thought. They stayed put, as he was certain Mary Kate had ordered them before she ran outside with the blanket.

Then he felt Bullo's eyes upon him. The shock in his oldest son's face was slowly turning to anger. Antonio had seen that defiant look in his fellow miners' eyes every day for over thirty years—but their anger had changed little. Feeling sick at his stomach, then dizzy, he took a step forward to maintain his balance. Still, his foot slipped a little. The warm blood still oozing from Hartman's head had made the snow around the dead man's body slushy.

Bullo took his arm and led him back toward the house. "The governor will be sending the National Guard again," Bullo said.

Antonio's tongue almost lashed. True, his son Bullo would be safer if the Guard returned, opened the mine gates, and delivered miners to and from work. But his other son, Vinnie, and the Progressives would have something to say about that. Thousands of picketing Progressives had successfully kept the coal mines shut down since the big gunfight at the Tovey Mine two weeks before. Dozens on both sides were wounded and two Progressives died, including Antonio's own beloved wife, Angeline, who was killed by a stray bullet when she walked out onto a porch to see what the trouble was.

Antonio and Bullo stopped for a moment once they were across the frozen road. They looked at the three boys' faces staring at them through the frost-trimmed window. Bullo's sons, twelve-year-old Willie and ten-year-old Tony had their arms around their seven-year-old cousin Sid.

"Bullo," Antonio said quietly, then lowered his head and put an open palm over his face. "I'm so tired, Bullo. It's never going to end." After a long moment, he raised his head to the sky and whispered, "Oh, Angeline, will our grandchildren still be fighting this war when they grow up?"

2

Sunrise the next morning found Margaret Eng leaning far out the second floor window of her sister's apartment so she could better see the National Guardsmen putting up tents on the street below. Big snowflakes floated softly from a cloudy, gray sky.

"Why are they making those poor soldier boys bivouac on that cold, hard road?" Margaret asked her sister Angie.

Angie stood on a chair behind her sister. She searched the soldier's faces with a pair of field glasses. "Where did you learn a word like *bivouac*?"

Tall, pretty and blond, Margaret was in her first year of high school, but hardly the student her older sister had been. Angie had recently returned from Illinois State College to take over the teaching job in the one-room schoolhouse in Hewittville. The previous teacher, old Mrs. Foster, had skedaddled town after her neighbor's house was bombed a second time.

"Why, I heard your general fella call it *bivouac* when you was nursing him." Margaret stretched her neck to watch a particularly well-built young guardsmen heft a tote bag onto his broad shoulders. "Do you see General O'Sullivan yet?"

"He's a private, not a general." Angie hopped down off the chair and put the binoculars back in their case. "And no, his Chicago regiment doesn't seem to be here this time."

"Papa says his regiment got sent home because they wouldn't follow the Peabody Coal Company orders and be mean to the Progressives." One of Margaret's hands suddenly slipped from the icy window ledge.

"Oh, would you quit gawking at those soldiers before you fall on one of them?" Pulling on her sister's skirt, Angie roughly reeled her back into the room and slammed the window shut.

"I can think of less pleasant ways to meet my demise." Margaret went back to work on the sour dough she'd been kneading before the troops had burst noisily into town in their military trucks and jeeps.

Angie admired her pretty sister's confidence with boys. She herself was less assured of her own comeliness. She liked the fact she was named for her mother's best friend, Angeline Vacca, but she sometimes felt that while she may have been blessed with her godmother's maternal nature, she also seemed to have somehow taken on her plain looks. Angie's eyes watered when she thought about Aunt Angeline's body lying at that very moment in the cold hard ground of winter.

Sensing her sister's sudden melancholy, Margaret quit kneading the bread dough and wiped her hands on her apron. She knew that Angie had taken a liking to Michael O'Sullivan, though they had only spoken for the few hours he had lain in the bunk bed of the Vacca home recovering from the effects of a tear gas bomb. Margaret hated to admit it, but it was probably due to the effects of the gas on the soldier's eyesight that he had an opportunity to get to know her sister on a personal level before actually seeing her. O'Sullivan didn't seem dissuaded, though, when later that evening, his eyes finally recovered enough to get a good look at the spunky college girl. Still, the post had been mute for over a month with news from Private First Class Michael O'Sullivan.

"I miss Aunt Angeline," Angie said.

Margaret put her arms around her sister. Then they cried.

* * * * * * *

Little Sid Hatfield Vacca had a major crush on the teacher of his one-room schoolhouse. His love, and he was certain it was forever love, was complicated by the fact that Miss Angie Eng might be related to him. He wasn't certain, though. All he knew for sure was that his Grandmother Angeline was Angie's—or, as he had to call her at school, Miss Eng's—godmother. Lately he had been asking various adults a lot of questions about laws concerning the marrying of kin, but so far had received confusing and sometimes conflicting answers.

"In some places, folk marry their cousins," his mother had stated when he probed for information one evening during supper. She was used to little Sid asking questions that required complicated answers.

"Folks around here frown on that sort of behavior," his father said. "There's laws against marrying cousins until they're two or three times removed."

"That's silly, Vinnie. How do you remove a cousin?" Sam asked.

"W...well, I...I don't rightly know," Sid's pa had stuttered, "but I'd 'spect a priest could explain it."

Now, Sid stood under a baron elm tree waiting for Miss Eng to ring the school bell to signal that lunchtime was over. He wanted to be the first in line so he could impress her with his good behavior. While waiting, he watched as his classmates took turns running toward and then sliding on an icy slope that went from the dirt road down to a frozen creek. Most of the grade school students were so accomplished at the slide they were able to stay on their feet all the way to the end of the creek bed.

The road in front of the schoolyard dead-ended into the entrance to Peabody's Number 58 Coal Mine, where close to one-hundred Progressive picketers talked in groups while sipping coffee. Several of the miners were enjoying watching the kids slide, laughing when one of the youth fell, and then cheering when one of them completed a slide to the far end of the creek.

Sid was torn between showing off for the miners or for his teacher. He was considering taking one more run at the slope when he heard a loud shout from the coal miners. Three large, green, military trucks suddenly roared across the railroad tracks toward the company gate and the striking miners. There was a blur of activity as picketers, who had been taking turns sitting in automobiles to keep warm, quickly reinforced their blockade with extra men. The two dozen children who had been playing in the school yard ignored their teacher's fruitless ringing of the school bell and remained at the edge of the road to watch the action.

Sid locked his hands behind his back and walked dutifully toward the schoolhouse porch. Miss Eng, though, surprised her favorite pupil by ignoring his well-mannered behavior and joining her children in front of the dirt road. A miffed Sid followed her.

The students, mostly from Progressive families, booed and jeered as two dozen guardsmen filed smartly from the back of the three trucks and formed ranks six abreast, their rifles at their side. Many of the striking miners reached inside their coats, and Sid caught glimpses of hammers, metal pipes and even the handle of a revolver.

Standing behind the first row of guardsmen, Sherṛiff Watson shouted into a bullhorn, "I have a court order here stating that all picketing of these here mines are ruled un-awful. I mean unlawful." The sheriff's face turned red as he tried to continue over the miners' laughter. "That means y'all need to just get on home before you get arrested."

"By whose authority is our picketing un-awful, Howard?" one of the miner's shouted, bringing forth more laughter.

"Why, by mine, of course. I'm the sheriff. And it's pretty clear that you boys are in the minority on this thing. Folks around these parts stand behind the United Mine Workers."

"How much did Peabody Coal Company pay you to say that?"

"Now, don't go accusing me of malfeasance, fellas. I'm just trying to do my job. If some of your boys hadn't blowed the Midland Bridge and killed James Hartman yesterday, the governor wouldn't have called out the guard again."

"What about the murder of Angeline Vacca and Vincent Rodems?" someone yelled. "The only thing the governor did after that was have the guard try to stop folks from attending Angeline's funeral. Hell, he even had airplanes buzz the cemetery to disrupt the service."

Sid's stomach went real hollow when he heard his grandma's murder mentioned. He thought of her body lying in the ground. Now his nice neighbor James Hartman had been killed, too. He felt Miss Eng's hands on his shoulders and the bad thoughts went away.

Some of the rear guardsmen backed away from the conflict and hurried behind a house across the road. A moment later, they ran between that building and the next one. With their backs to the closed and locked mine gate, the striking miners were effectively cut off to their front and left. Only the school yard offered an escape, and that was filled with children crowding up close to the road. Little Sid Vacca seemed to be the only one who understood this. Grandpa Antonio had once used his toy soldiers to show him how his regiment had outflanked the enemy during the Spanish-American War.

Sid reached up and tugged on Miss Eng's skirt. She immediately pushed his hand away.

"Miss Eng!" Sid said loudly, but his voice was drowned when picketers on the road began shouting. Guardsmen were raising their guns to their side and fixing bayonets.

But Miss Eng's eyes were set on a giant of a man who had emerged behind a National Guard truck. Sid recognized him as the man who had been in his grandparents' house the night Angie came home from college last fall.

"Angie!" Sid shouted as loud as his little lungs would allow, "The guardsmen are surrounding our men!"

* * * * * * *

At just over six and a half feet tall, Corporal Michael O'Sullivan was accustomed to viewing the world over the top of other people's heads. As soon as he got out of the military truck, he spotted Angie Eng struggling to hold back a crowd of angry grade-school children. Many of the students were picking rocks from the ground and packing them inside snowballs.

Having just arrived in Taylorville that morning, O'Sullivan was not prepared for the melee before him. Many of the guardsmen wore ill-fitting uniforms and struggled to fix bayonets on their rifles. He suspected they were hired gunmen brought in by the coal company to bully and harass the Progressive community. The regular guardsmen wouldn't have the stomach for such atrocities. Just that

past November his own Chicago Company had openly re-
belled against the orders of coal company officials and had
been deployed back home. Had it not been for his father's
political connections, Michael O'Sullivan would not have
been reassigned to a different company and given a pro-
motion to corporal. All this because he had become smit-
ten by a tiny, rather plain-looking schoolmarm named Angie Eng.

One of the coal miners stepped in front of a young
guardsman. "My name's Jack Battuello," he said, "and you
may not know this, but you and I are part of a brother-
hood. Do you know what you boys are doing to us? You're
taking bread out of our mouths, and you're supporting the
coal company that would enslave us." Battuello's eyes never wavered from the man's. "Now gimme that rifle, son."

The young guardsman handed the rifle over as if he
were giving stolen apples to his father. Lieutenant Sebuck,
the commanding officer on the scene, immediately rushed
forward and grabbed the rifle from Battuello.

"Arrest this soldier!" Sebuck shouted.

Two officers grabbed the young private and pulled him
toward one of the trucks near the rear.

"Now, don't you boys go poking those miners with your
bayonets!" Sheriff Watson warned by shouting through his
bullhorn. "You hear me?"

As if his words were a signal, several of the guardsmen
wearing the ill-fitting uniforms lunged out with their weapons, two of which effectively drew blood with their jousts.
The screams of outrage from the miners were followed by
more lunges and more blood as strikers who were huddled
together in tight quarters struggled in vain to avoid the
sharp blades.

The professional guardsmen were slow to take part
in the attack. They started to move forward, but changed

course when the cold stings of rock-covered snowballs struck their faces. The school children's expert aim with their aerial assault was all that prevented a complete massacre of the striking miners. Even the company thugs who were dressed as guardsmen fell back to avoid being pummeled by the rocks, which by now were no longer disguised as snowballs.

The picketers holding signs took advantage of the lull and stepped forward to block the bayonets and provide cover to their comrades seeking escape.

With the mine gate locked behind them and guns and bayonets on all sides, the miners had but one avenue for retreat. The icy slope the school children had been enjoying was suddenly filled with grown men sometimes running but mostly sliding on their stomachs and backs down the hill and into the frozen creek bottom. For several minutes the strikers ran away from the gate while screams and shouts erupted from the National Guardsmen as they grabbed and detained as many of the wounded and those wielding picket signs as they could.

Once on the far side, the Progressives huddled together in an angry mass. A few picketers holding handguns were quickly told by their leaders to put their weapons away.

"Wait 'til we tell the boss we got those big, tough coal miners to skedaddle!" one of the company thugs shouted.

"Yes," yelled Angie Eng, "and don't forget to tell him how you big, tough Chicago gangsters were sent packing by a couple dozen grade school children."

Miss Eng gave a glare towards O'Sullivan. Turning to her students, she shouted, "Now back into the schoolhouse we go! We need to learn how to make slingshots for our next defense of our liberties!"

Her students cheered and followed the little lady who was not much taller than some of them.

Kevin Corley

* * * * * * *

Over two hundred women packed the high school gym that evening for the emergency assembly of the Women's Auxiliary. The only men in the room were the principal, Harry Kroll, and Dr. RJ Hiler, who walked in just as the meeting was getting started.

"Ladies, ladies!" Lena Eng shouted above the din. The faces of most of the women in the room were sullen and anxious. "Why don't we start the meeting by letting anyone who has a concern have one minute at the podium? Then we can address the issues one at a time. Mrs. Wilson, would you go first please?"

As Elizabeth Wilson walked to the front of the room, the gym became quiet except for the squeaking of the rickety wooden chairs and an occasional cough.

"What am I going to do?" Tears rolled down Mrs. Wilson's cheeks. "My husband was one of the men wounded and arrested this morning. I don't even know how bad he's hurt."

"I just left the jail, Elizabeth," Dr. Hiler interrupted. "Jay is doing fine, as are the others. None of the men were hurt badly, thank God."

Many of the women in the room crossed themselves, and Mrs. Wilson, hand clenched to her mouth, hastened back to her seat.

With an angry scowl, an older woman hurried uninvited to the podium. "We need to get these men to forget this union business and go back to the mines!" She spoke so loudly the women in the front rows sat up in their seats. "This socialistic idea of getting the company to let the miners work fewer hours so more men can have jobs is crazy. All job sharing means is that we'll all starve together."

"Not if no one takes a pay cut!" someone in the back row shouted, and then added, "Why should the coal company be getting richer while our men are dying down in those hell holes for a few dollars a day?"

No sooner did Lena's raised hands get things quiet than another woman shouted, "How are we going to survive? This strike could go on for years!"

The room was again thrown into pandemonium. Just when it appeared that order would not be restored, Sam Vacca stood and walked to the front of the room. When the crowd saw her, they slowly began to quiet. Years before Sam had earned the respect of the entire community when she risked her life by crawling through a narrow hole in the mine to save her husband, father-in-law and two other miners trapped by a cave-in. The girl from the mountains of West Virginia was not wearing a dress, as were the other women in the room. Her slim body was concealed by the baggy bib overalls that everyone knew she preferred, and a bright red bandana was tied neatly around her neck.

"If folks could survive in West Virginy during a strike with nothing but a mountain to live off of, then our Progressives shouldn't have no problem getting by in Illinois." Sam Vacca spoke so quietly the room became hush as the women leaned forward to hear her confident and reassuring words. "Why, we've got better soil for gardens, orchards and livestock. There's plenty of hunting and fishing, and even wild berries for collecting. Some of our menfolk can go find work in Chicago or St. Louis." Sam lowered her voice even further and added, "And, of course, there's always gonna be a strong demand from the Shelton boys for those good spirits you Italians make."

"Sam Vacca!" Mary Kate hissed. She stood, hands on hips, but a wry smile lit her face. "You aren't suggesting that we finance our strike by selling bootleg liquor to the same men who tried to rob our Kincaid Bank? Why, you yourself shot at them that day."

"Why them boys ain't no different than any others," Sam said firmly. "Quite a few of our own like to whoop it up occasionally."

"Maybe Sam is right," Angie Eng said when the laughter subsided. "But we'll probably be able to sell it legally. Prohibition will most likely be gone when Franklin Roosevelt becomes president in March. At least he says he'll get rid of it."

"Not if we Christians have anything to do with it!" yelled one of the women.

"Well, I've been a Christian for near a hundred years," a woman named Borgononi said in a strong but crackly voice, "and I figure that as long as I follow the commandments, the good Lord will take the time to explain these other sins when I have my meeting with him on Judgment Day."

A loud commotion erupted from both the front and rear entrances. Several women jumped to their feet and screamed. Others ducked low in their seats as if they were being fired upon. Over a dozen National Guardsmen rushed noisily into the gym and took up positions in front of each of the four exits. While they didn't carry rifles, they each had one hand placed on the pistol in their holsters.

Lieutenant Sebuck and two of his officers went straight to the front of the room. He did a double take when he saw Sam Vacca standing in front of the podium.

"Corporal O'Sullivan, arrest this—" Sebuck's face turned bright red as he stuttered to finish his sentence, "w-w-woman!"

"On what charges, Lieutenant?" Michael O'Sullivan asked. He remembered seeing Sam the day he was in the Vacca house recovering from injuries received during a gas bomb attack.

"Why, instigating a riot, of course," Sebuck said. "You can see by that red scarf that she's a c-c-communist."

While everyone in the room seemed to be watching O'Sullivan, only the angry eyes of Angie Eng troubled him.

"I don't much know what a communist does," Sam said, "but we wear these bandanas in West Virginy to show we're union folks. That way we know who not to shoot when the trouble starts up."

"Sam, hush!" Lena Eng said, then turned quickly toward the Lieutenant. "She doesn't mean that!"

"Arrest this anarchist, Corporal!" Sebuck's voice was so commanding, O'Sullivan found himself stepping forward and taking Sam's arm.

Dozens of women in the room rushed the podium, shouting insults at the uniformed men. Lacking company thugs to bolster them, the bewildered guardsmen retreated a few steps, leaving their commanding officers to fend for themselves against the chaos of the angry tirade. Seizing the opportunity, O'Sullivan pulled Sam toward the exit, a task he found much more difficult than he would have thought, considering the slight build of the young woman.

"Run for it!" O'Sullivan whispered.

Sam gave him a bewildered look, then bolted up the steps from the gym, rushed through the long hallway, out the front doors and into the night.

3

"Sam, you have got to quit wearing that damned red scarf around your neck," Antonio scolded.

Vinnie's wife had been breathless when she entered his home and related the story of the National Guardsmen breaking up the Women's Auxiliary meeting.

"Well, some folks wear 'em on their arm," Sam said. "Would that be all right, Papa?"

"No. Don't you understand that red is associated with communists and socialists?"

"I reckon I am a socialist, Papa."

"Sam," Antonio said quietly. He had learned to speak to his daughter-in-law in the same composed manner he once had to his late son Filberto, who had also been a free thinker. "Did I ever tell you the story of how my Angeline and her brother Vincent came to be in this country?"

"Why, no, Papa. You haven't."

"Their mother and father had to leave Italy because the government and the church didn't like their socialistic views. They were friends with a Russian woman named Anna Kuliscioff, and they all worked for a socialist newspaper called *Critica Sociale*. This Kuliscioff lady was one of the first women to graduate with a degree in medicine, and she believed that women should be equal to men, including having the right to vote. The government didn't like that idea or her socialistic views. The Catholic Church sided with the government. People died, Sam, and while our grandparents fled to America, Anna Kuliscioff stayed and fought."

"Did she win, Papa?"

"Well, yes, indirectly, I suppose. In 1925, the women in Italy got the right to vote—but it was two years after she died." Antonio rubbed his big right hand over his clenched left one. "It seems that every generation has to fight for some new freedom. There's always someone who wants to beat the other fellow down and make himself feel superior. I don't know if it will ever end."

"I hope it does." She placed her hand on her father-in-law's shoulder, an unusual gesture from Sam, and it startled Antonio. "I surely do hope that our coal miners will get back their sense of independence before our children and grandchildren become too comfortable with this here capitalism thing. And I hope it ends in your lifetime, Papa. I don't want your grandsons to have to fight the battle like you and Mama have."

Antonio lay his head against Sam's shoulder and cried. "Oh, my dear Angeline! I miss her so. Please be careful, Sam. We can't lose you, too."

"I will, Papa," Sam said softly, "and I promise that I'll only wear my red bandana when this is all over."

"I'm sorry, Sam. For asking you to—"

"That don't make no never mind, Papa." Sam undid the knot on the red bandana, then held it out to her father-in-law.

Antonio didn't take the small piece of cloth that meant so much to his son's wife.

"Keep it, my daughter. Put it in a drawer. Maybe someday we'll all wear one."

* * * * * *

With the National Guard keeping Progressives away from the mine gates, United Mine Workers were brought back to work in the Christian County mines. While much of the Hewittville Mine still hand-loaded coal, two work areas featured newly composed crews of fourteen miners who worked four chambers at a time.

One chamber had timbermen in charge of sounding the tops and propping as needed. When they were done, they went to start another chamber, while a second crew came in and laid rail tracks. They then brought in a ferocious looking, saw-like machine to undercut the six-foot-high seam of coal just above the rocky ground. After this was completed, that crew followed the timber men, who by this time had finished the second chamber. That's when the third crew, the drill and blast boys, came in. Using electric or sometimes the old hand-cranks, they would drill a hole six feet into the face of the coal, load it with explosives, then light it and get out. After the explosion and the dust had settled, the fourth crew came in with the big Jeffry 44A loading machine.

Peabody Coal Company had kept it a secret that previous year when the first two 44As were brought to Christian County and assembled by the Jeffry Company technicians. The mine boss took Bullo Vacca and four other men down into a chamber and told them that they had ninety days to learn everything there was to know about the machine. There was no manual and no instructors to help them. If they mastered the machine, they would be paid eight dollars and seventy-five cents a day to be operators in either a day shift or a night shift. In less than a month, they had the loading machine operating efficiently. The Vacca team was fortunate enough to draw a day shift.

As his crew readied the big 44A to be moved along the

tracks into the new chamber, Bullo carefully placed his un-gloved hand on the ceiling to sound the top with the flat of a pickaxe.

"What for are you doing that?" James Cheek asked. He was nicknamed "High Pockets," and was one of the few experienced men brought in from a southern Illinois mine. "The prop men already sounded that top. As fast as this new loading machine works, we'll be in and out of here before those timbers start buckling."

"Do you know those prop fellas, High Pockets?" Bullo asked as he continued checking.

"No, of course not. They just started last week."

"So you trust your life to someone you don't even know?"

"No, I reckon not." Cheek followed close behind his loading machine boss, then added in almost a whisper. "Ah, hell, Bullo, I'm so disgusted with this place I'm ready to go join the Progressives. At least they'd like to get rid of these damned machines."

"The machines are here to stay," Bullo said. "You'd might as well get used to them."

"What about this dirty air we're a breathin'?" Cheek asked. "Why don't the UMW do something about that? Hell, at least when we hand-load, our lungs stay cleaner than with these infernal machines."

Bullo couldn't disagree with that point. The company doctor, RJ Hiler, had risked his career just the previous spring by complaining to the Department of Mines that the machine operators were getting sick from breathing the soot. When the loading machine was in operation, the air was so thick a man couldn't see his own feet. It was im-possible to generate lighting good enough to do their work safely. The dust sometimes got so bad men would leave the work area to cough up a thick, green, slimy vomit.

After initially firing Doc Hiler, the coal company received unexpected pressure from legislators, so they brought him back with the understanding they would improve circulation. They promptly sank air shafts and started making larger work chambers that could better accommodate the new technology. They had figured out that the old hand-loading mine chambers were too small for the machines and much too small to accommodate good air circulation.

"The UMW could do something about it if they didn't have to spend all their time and money fighting the Progressives," Bullo said. "John L. Lewis knows these machines are coming whether the miners like it or not."

"Yeah, but look at how many miners will lose their jobs."

"It won't cost miners their jobs," Bullo said, spinning toward and then glaring at his partner. Shaking his head, he turned back to sounding the top. "Hell, half the miners are ready to retire anyhow. The company just won't hire anyone to replace them."

"I've heard that," Cheek said, nodding. "I think they call it attrition, or something. But that still means less miners."

"Yes, fewer miners, but better wages for those who learn the skills to run the machines." Bullo moved to one last corner of the room. "Wouldn't it be better to have one thousand well-paid miners than five thousand destitute ones? So, let's get the UMW to focus on getting the company to clean up this air and do a better job training our workers so these damned tops won't be crushin' our skulls."

Bullo tapped the flat of his pick on the top and a chunk of rock three-foot wide and several hundred pounds crashed loudly to the ground. He turned his head toward Cheek, who swallowed hard, grabbed up a pickaxe and began sounding.

"High Pockets!" a miner named Henry Runnels shouted from behind the loading machine. "The section foreman wants you to help clear the old chamber."

"That's another reason I liked the hand-loading days," High Pockets mumbled. "We worked at our own pace and were paid by the ton we brought out. Now they drive us like slaves for a measly, flat wage."

High Pockets left the room. Bullo directed the dirt gang to clean up the rock fall so the timbering crew could reinforce the top with another prop. A few moments later while he was checking the loading machine, a terrible sound erupted that no coal miner ever wanted to hear. The rock fall in the old chamber was so immense the miners would have felt the vibration even if the loading machine had been operating. Bullo grabbed the arm of one of the inexperienced men who was about to instinctively rush to the aid of the other miners.

"Not yet," he shouted to his crew. He turned to an older miner. "Phone the mine office. Tell them what happened, and have them reverse the main fans."

There would be zero visibility until the dust cloud from the rock, dirt and loose coal settled. Bullo's instinct told him that a fall of this size could be the first of several.

"Push the loading machine out of the way so the rescue squad can get their equipment through!" he barked at the men.

"You're not going to just leave them there, are you?" one of the miners asked. "I'd have been in there too if High Pockets hadn't told me to wait while he checked the room."

"Did anyone else go in with him?" Bullo asked as he began counting the men.

"Just Henry Runnels," another miner said.

All the men were accounted for except for the man Bullo had sent to phone the surface. All the men in his crew were miners who'd been brought in since the Progressive strike began. None of them had more than two years' experience, and none of them probably knew the two men in the chamber were most certainly already dead.

William Stork, the mine boss, was at the scene even before the rescue team. He had a frantic look on his face as he ran up to the section foreman. "Did the fall damage the machines?"

"No, the machine was already out of the chamber," the foreman said.

The mine boss's face relaxed. "Well, what are you men waiting for?" Stork shouted. "Back that loading machine out of here before we get another rock fall."

None of the men moved.

"What's the matter with you men?" Stork asked.

"Two miners got buried in the fall, Mr. Stork," the foreman said, his voice cracking.

"Oh, well, I'm sorry about that, men." The mine boss removed his cap and crossed himself. "But what's done is done. Now let's get that machine out of this area before we lose . . .anymore lives."

As he retreated from the chamber, Bullo thought of the words that his father had heard from his own mine boss over thirty years ago after a similar accident. "We can replace a miner, but, by God, mules cost money!"

* * * * * * *

It was well after midnight when Bullo walked into his father's house. Mary Kate and Sam immediately rose from their seats to comfort him. Mary Kate hugged her husband and held onto him until he reached up and gently pulled her hands from his shoulders. He had to be strong. She would urge him to tell her everything, would want him to completely share his feelings. Of course, he would not. That was not what a responsible husband did.

"I need to see Vinnie." Bullo gave his wife a reassuring kiss, but didn't feel it was really necessary. She understood the Vacca men were the ones he'd want to talk to about the tragedy.

His father had left that morning with his friend Joe Harrison, concerning a business opportunity in the little town of Herrick. Antonio wasn't expected back until the next day, and though they had made several phone calls, they were unable to get hold of him.

"Vinnie waited up as long as he could, Bullo," Mary Kate told him. "Doc Hiler stopped by when he left the mine yard. Vinnie had a fever again, so Doc gave him something to make him sleep."

Bullo hung his head. Unable to hold back, a flood of tears fell onto his wife's shoulder. Sam turned toward the window. When he was finally able to get his sobs to stop, Bullo straightened his shirt collar and sat in his father's rocker. Mary Kate dropped onto the floor beside him. He allowed her to rest her arm and head on his leg.

"Henry Runnels was a single man, but James Cheek had a wife and six children," Bullo said finally, his voice breaking as he spoke.

Sam turned back toward him and sat in her sainted mother-in-law's chair. She pulled the blue apron—the one Angeline had always worn—off the back of it, and, as each family member often did, caressed it on her lap as she rocked. Coal miners' wives knew when to give their men space, when to hold them, and when to speak after mine deaths. They'd had plenty of experience.

Every year at Christmas, Angeline Vacca had placed small candles on the fireplace mantle—one for each man who had died in the Christian County mines since Antonio began working there in 1900. On New Year's Eve, at a few minutes before midnight, she would light each and say a prayer before putting the candles out. Just a few weeks ago, there had been one hundred thirty-six candles on the mantle, as well as another fifty-four for the miners who'd died that Christmas Eve at the terrible Moweaqua Coal Mine disaster in nearby Shelby County. Like most mining wives in the community, Angeline and Lena Eng had attended almost all of the funerals.

Mary Kate and Sam had been the ones who boxed the candles up on the morning of the third of January, not knowing their mother-in-law would be killed that night during a mine battle between the UMW and Progressives. Now Bullo, Mary Kate and Sam were all looking at that mantle, wondering how many more new candles they would need at the end of 1933 to join the ones they would have for Angeline Vacca, James Cheek and Henry Runnels.

"James was talking to me about joining the Progressives just a few minutes before he died," Bullo said, one hand on his forehead and the other holding that of his wife. "I argued with him, told him the United Mine Workers would make things better. He was arguing for job sharing, wages by the ton, and he was cursing the machines. Sam, why is all this so hard to understand?"

Mary Kate felt Bullo's hand tighten slightly around hers. She wanted desperately to comfort her man. As she waited for her sister-in-law to gather her thoughts, Mary Kate prayed that Sam would be able to provide the comforting words she could not.

"It ain't just about machines and wages and working hours, Bullo," Sam said in a slow, melancholy voice. "Coal mining is a way of life. Communities and families and friends—we're all one. Why, back home in West Virginy, mountain folk always stuck together, even before the coal mines came. That's how we survived. Then our men went to work mining, and they saw a chance to give their families a better life." Sam looked down at the apron as if memories were coming out of it. "We started getting electricity and riding on locomotives and automobiles, and the whole countryside would stop and look up when an airplane passed over the trees. We liked our old life in the hills, but we liked being part of those new things, too. Our men and women believed that our families would always be together because the young'uns would learn to mine too, and it was a good way of life."

The mountain girl's smile faded, replaced by sadness. "But then the coal companies started bringin' in folks from other countries, folks who would work just as hard for lower wages. That meant our boys had to work for less, too. I remember how my Pa used to fret when he couldn't provide for us girls. It seemed no matter how hard he worked, he never had enough to pay for the company house we stayed in, much less to get food and supplies from the company store." Sam put her head back and closed her eyes. "Then after Ma died, he just gave up. Took to drink and never was the same again."

Sam reflected for another moment, then opened her eyes and smiled at the in-laws that she loved so dearly. "No, Bullo, unions and coal minin' ain't just about havin' stuff. It's about kin helping kin and friend helping friend." Then she seemed to catch herself and added, "I'm sorry, Bullo. I shouldn't talk so much."

Several moments of silence ensued.

"Bullo," Mary Kate finally said. She wanted to be part of the healing for her husband. "My father always took pride in bringin' up sixteen tons of coal a day. If the company was honest and didn't dock them, miners were rewarded for working hard because they were paid by the tonnage."

"Yes," Bullo said, "but they also took days off whenever they wanted and often left the harder-to-get-coal in the chambers."

"But wouldn't paying machine operators for the tonnage brought up give incentive for them to work faster and more efficiently?" Mary Kate asked.

The sudden flare in Bullo's face said she should have remained quiet. "Yes, but the company can get the same or better profits by hiring efficiency experts to get the miners to work faster," he said loudly.

"Whip them slaves!" Vinnie shouted from the bedroom doorway.

Mary Kate and Sam jumped up and helped get Vinnie to the couch.

"I thought Doc Hiler drugged you?" Bullo asked.

"I spat it out," Vinnie said. "I knew you'd be coming home and would want someone to argue with."

"I ain't in an arguin' mood, Vinnie," Bullo said, but his expression said otherwise.

Vinnie's drooping eyelids indicated he was in a near hallucinating frame of mind. "At least it was two scabs that got kilt today," he said. "I'd hate to think of one of our good union men dying down there."

"They weren't strikebreakers! They were United Mine Workers!" Bullo shouted, then stood and walked to the door. He suddenly turned back to Vinnie and added in a calmer voice, "For Mama's sake, I will not fight you."

"For Mama's sake," Vinnie said, his bloodshot eyes looking hard at his brother, "I will not kill you!"

4

Sam Vacca was so mad at her husband Vinnie she swore at him in Italian. At least it might have been Italian, though she wasn't really sure, since she had never spoken that language before. They were swear words, though, of that she was reasonably certain. She'd heard her mother-in-law Angeline, God rest her soul, use the words on her own husband on at least a dozen occasions over the ten-odd years Sam had been blessed to know her.

The first time had been back in 1921, when Vinnie brought her on the train from West Virginia to the coal mining town of Hewittville, Illinois, to meet his family. Vinnie and Sam had thought it would only be a visit. Angeline, though, had ordained that a house be built for them right near her own and next to that of her other son Bullo, his wife Mary Kate, and their two children. Angeline was determined to keep her family together. When Vinnie got mad at his mother's manipulations, Antonio, his father, put his foot down and told Angeline to let the newlyweds make their own decisions. That was when Angeline had hit him with the Italian expletives. She never knew Sam and Vinnie heard her shouts through an open window on the second floor of the house. She also didn't know that Sam's love for the little Vacca matriarch had begun at that moment.

Now Sam was using words she didn't understand so

her seriously ill husband would know his mother's spirit was alive and well. "Bullo doesn't deserve to be treated the way you treated him last night."

"He's a damned scab." Vinnie gave one cough as punishment for each word.

"He's the sole provider for his family right now," Sam said. "And with you sick I intend to provide for my family. I *will* take over Mama Vacca's garden this spring and I *will* accept the job at Shorty Robert's fillin' station," Sam said sternly. She lowered her voice and said softly, "At least until you get back on your feet."

Vinnie was wheeling from Sam's colorful trimming. He fell back on the bed, too weak from squirrel fever to voice a strong objection. The events since his mother's death had been more than even Vinnie's strong constitution could endure. Dr. Hiler advised that recovery from this form of typhoid could take as long as six months, and even then he should expect relapses.

Sam's offer to work didn't surprise Vinnie. It wouldn't even have bothered him—if not for the coal mine war. "The UMW and the coal company have brought in more thugs," he said quietly. "The Progressives don't have a Sid Hatfield to do their fighting for them."

Sam knew it was true. The miners had formed the Progressive Miners of America last September when UMW president John L. Lewis sold them out to side with Peabody Coal Company. The miners in Illinois were a tough lot, but no match for gangsters from Chicago and southern Illinois who killed for a living. Sid Hatfield had been a sharpshooter with nerves of steel when he and other miners faced down a dozen Baldwin-Felts detectives in Matewan, West Virginia, back in '20, leaving nine of the thugs lying dead in the street. The following year, however, Sam and Vinnie had been witness to Hatfield's assassination as he walked up the courthouse steps in Welch. They had named their son after the fallen hero of Matewan.

Sid was playing with blocks of wood at the foot of his father's bed. His uncle Bullo had cut the blocks from two-by-four boards, and his cousins Will and Tony helped Sid paint them a variety of colors. They were Sid's favorite toy.

"Will you tell me the story of Sid Hatfield again, Papa?" Sid asked. Putting down his blocks, he leaned toward the bed and rested his head on his father's foot.

His mother gently put her hand on little Sid's curly hair and tried to smooth it into some sort of order. "You need to get over to Aunt Mary Kate's and let her trim that yeller bush on top of your head."

"Are we friends with Uncle Bullo again?" Sid asked as he put his blocks back in a wooden box.

Vinnie's eyes began to water and he was having trouble staying awake. Being from West Virginia, Sam was very familiar with this form of typhoid and knew what a long haul the couple were in for. That's why it was important for her to be the bread winner until her husband recovered. She wished she could go down in the mines as she had back home during the Great War, but times were changing. Though women now had the right to vote, that didn't mean their men were ready to share their responsibilities. Sam ran her hand through her husband's hair.

"Ask Mary Kate if she can stop by later and give your father a good trimming, too." She said. "And see if they would like to have vittles—I mean *dinner*—with us? Tell 'em I've made neck bones and greens."

Little Sid had been taught to follow adult directions on the first command. His mother had not answered his question except to tell him to invite Uncle Bullo's family to have eats with them. He knew that was all the answer he would get. Sid was glad his father was friendly with Uncle Bullo again.

Little Sid threw his coat on and went outside to find his cousins making a snow fort. "My papa and yours ain't feuding no more," he announced, then plopped down on his knees in front of them. It was a sad looking fort because the snow was too light and fluffy. "You could sprinkle a little water on the snow and get it slushy," Sid advised. "It would pack better."

Willie was twelve and Tony ten, but they knew to listen to their younger cousin. Their Granny Vacca had always said that little Sid was as smart as his Uncles Filberto and Libero had been before they died in the Spanish Flu epidemic of 1918. Willie especially liked Sid, even though he wasn't as mischievous as he and Tony.

"I heard Mama yelling at Papa one night for being mad at his kin," Willie said as he spit three times on a small ball of snow and began working it in. "She said Granny Vacca would rather die herself than have her family fightin'. Then Granny got shot and kilt and I thought Mama'd say I told you so, but she didn't." Willie held up the snowball that was now packed tight and firm.

"I miss Granny Vacca," Sid said, ignoring the snowball.

Willie and Tony exchanged glances. They both sat right in the snow on either side of their cousin. They didn't put their arms around him because their Granny Vacca had told them that Uncle Vinnie and Aunt Sam showed their love differently than most people. They sat quietly and waited for Sid's sadness to pass. After a few minutes, Willie thought he saw a tear drop from his cousin's eyes, but when he looked, little Sid was spitting in the snow.

"I wonder if steam from an iron would work better," Sid said thoughtfully.

When the boys walked in the house, Mary Kate yelled at them for tracking snow. With the ire of the red-haired

Celtic woman that she was, she smacked all three of them on their bottoms with her broom before using it to brush their legs and feet. She swept the snow into a small pile on the wooden floor.

"Now get a towel and wipe up that mess!" she said sharply.

Willie and Tony hurried into the kitchen for a towel, but Sid got down on his knees and rolled the snow into a ball with his hands.

Mary Kate watched him as he held the flakes away from his body and slowly walked toward the roaring fireplace, all the while packing the snow as if it were the most important thing he'd ever done. When her sons came back and toweled off the floor, they joined their mother and watched their cousin.

"He's studying the best way to make snowballs," Tony told her as if it were a completely normal behavior.

Sid suddenly lofted the packed snow into the fireplace and wiped his hands on his britches. "Ma wants y'all to eat neck bones and greens with us tonight."

Mary Kate smiled. Sid liked to country talk like his ma, even though he could use more multi-syllable words than most adults.

"Did she invite Grandpa Vacca, too?" Tony asked.

Sid thought a moment before answering. "He's kin, ain't he? Want me to go fetch him?"

"No," Mary Kate said. "You boys can bring in some firewood while I go next door."

Mary Kate took her coat off the hook on the wall, removed her apron and hung it where the coat had been. She followed the boys outside, and when they scampered off toward the woodshed, she turned and trudged through the snow to her in-law's house. It was smaller than her own, and much smaller than Vinnie and Sam's two story home, yet, she thought as she opened the door without knocking and walked in, it was filled with more love than any house she had ever known. For it was in this home that Antonio and Angeline Vacca had raised their four sons, only to have the youngest two die before they were fully grown. The room was warmed by a large fireplace. Two empty rocking chairs faced it, one of which had a familiar blue apron lovingly draped across its back.

Seeing her father-in-law was not in the kitchen or his bedroom, she walked into the room her husband and his three brothers had once occupied. Antonio Vacca sat on one of the two bunk beds that almost completely filled the little bed chamber, leaning forward and holding his head in his large and powerful hands.

Although he had not looked up, he was aware of her presence. She wasn't invading a private moment. The Vacca family love had no closed doors.

"Sam wants the family together for dinner at her house," Mary Kate said.

"She's not feeding us possum, is she?" Antonio asked, still not looking up.

"No," Mary Kate smiled. "Neck bones and greens."

Antonio raised his head and laughed. "You know it'll be cooked in possum fat, don't ya?"

"Yes, and I'll tell you the same thing Granny Vacca would say. 'You don't ever talk bad about my little girl Sam.'"

* * * * * * *

At seventy-four years of age and despite legs that allowed him limited mobility, Shorty Roberts enjoyed life more than anyone Sam had ever known. Like her, Shorty claimed the eastern mountains as his home, though he couldn't describe exactly where in them he hailed from. "I be from up big Smoky way," Shorty would tell new customers when they inquired about his drawl.

His home in the back of the filling station was filled with charcoal drawings, mostly of men down in coal mines, as well as a few oil paintings of mountain landscapes he remembered from his younger years. Shorty especially enjoyed it when Sam let young Sid stop in at her work. The old man often painted as Sid sat beside him and colored.

"I just got me a little tab left to do, then it'll be all did," Shorty said when he saw the young boy with his mother one day.

"I'd like a twofer when you're done, Mr. Roberts," Sid said politely.

"Why, what's a twofer, Sid?" Shorty asked when he approached the candy counter.

"Twofers are two horehounds for a penny," Sid replied, holding out an open palm containing a penny.

"Now where did you get a penny, young man?" Sam asked her son. She had just walked in with a box of soda empties.

"W-w-why," Sid stammered. "Why, I found it along the railroad track when we were huntin' coal, Mama."

A car pulled up to a gas pump and honked. Sam gave her son a frown and went to wait on the customer.

"You storied to your Mama, didn't you, Sid?" Shorty said.

"Well, I didn't want to tell her I sold old lady Borgononi a box of apples."

"Where for did you get a box of apples?"

"I picked them off the ground in Mrs. Borgononi's yard."

"So you sold that poor old lady her own apples?"

"Pretty smart, huh?" Sid said proudly. "I want to be

rich someday. I'm going to see the elephant."

"That's good, Sid. Just remember not to let that ol' elephant step all over you. You knowed it was wrong to sell that old lady her own apples, didn't ya, son? Now you hear me well, young Sid. Don't ever do nothin' to cause your Ma to lose the apple in her eye."

On most days, while Sam pumped gas, changed oil and did basic maintenance on automobiles, Shorty made charcoal drawings while his friends sat arguing politics or occasionally exchanging notes on the latest talkie down at the picture show.

One bright morning, Vinnie was among the six men gathered, along with his brother Bullo and Harley Eng, both of which had come along in case anyone gave Sam a problem. They were mostly leery of the National Guard jeeps and trucks that stopped twice a day for a fill up. While she didn't wear a red bandana, Sam did wear her coveralls and her husband's short-billed cap, her blond hair tied up in a ponytail. Vinnie was afraid one of the guardsmen from the scene at the high school might recognize her and try to make an arrest.

"You fellows know the only reason I'm not staying with the Progressives is because I'm ready to retire," Old Homer Keel said meekly. "As long as I stay in good standing with the UMW, my wife will receive death benefits when I pass."

For several moments, an uncomfortable silence ensued. Vinnie knew the old miner was looking for forgiveness. Homer's wife had been nagging him for weeks to go back to the United Mine Workers. Several family members on her side worked for Peabody Coal Company. Vinnie wished the conversation would have stayed on the subject of the latest Jean Harlow movie. But here it was, and he wasn't surprised when his own brother was the first to chime in.

"Ya'll are cutting off your noses to spite your ugly faces," Bullo Vacca said. "You know damned well the Progressives are gonna wind up settling for five bucks a day. Then you'll be no better off than if you'd stayed with the UMW."

"Well, at least we'll have our pride that we didn't bow down to John L. Lewis and a company that's getting rich off our backs," Vinnie replied.

"The American economy is in a bad fix right now, fellas," Bullo said. "Ain't that right, Harley?"

"Companies are made up of stock holders," Eng agreed, "and if they don't make a profit with one business, they will simply sell and go to a different one. Very few coal companies made a profit last year. Buying stock is a gamble. You can lose everything overnight. I'm proof of that."

Everyone knew that Harley Eng had lost his fortune practically overnight in the stock market crash of '29. They respected him, though, for getting up early the next morning and taking a job at the coal mine.

"That's right," Bullo said. "If you think stockholders can do otherwise, why don't you miners put your assets together and buy your own coal company? Then you can pay your workers as much as you want."

"How could we compete against other companies?" Vinnie asked.

"You couldn't," Eng said. "Coal is only selling for a little over two dollars a ton right now. Besides, with everyone buying natural gas and oil, demand for coal is down. You would have to control all the coal production in the United States to set a high enough price to make a reasonable profit."

"But if you think the company is making that much money," Bullo said, "why don't you go ahead and try?"

"We need to reach the laid off UMW workers, then

maybe—"

A military jeep pulled in front of a gas pump, followed by two National Guard trucks. A dozen guardsmen filed out of the back of the trucks and began lighting up cigarettes.

"F-f-fill'er up, son," Lieutenant Sebuck said from the passenger seat without looking up from the papers he studied.

Sam recognized the soldier who was driving as Corporal O'Sullivan. She gave a nervous glance toward her husband, who was watching from inside, pulled her cap down over her face, and lifted the nozzle from the gas pump.

When she approached the jeep, the young corporal jumped gracefully from the driver's seat and stood between her and the Lieutenant. He pulled a cigarette from his shirt pocket, and as he lit it, he looked directly at her face with a nervous smile.

A few minutes later, Sam moved to replace the hose, and the Lieutenant spotted her.

"T-t-that's that anarchist that got away that night at the school!" Sebuck shouted.

"She does look a little like her, Lieutenant," O'Sullivan said calmly. "But no, I don't think so. The girl that night was much prettier than this dirty, little tomboy, don't you think?"

Sebuck squinted, studied the girl for a long moment, then turned back to his paperwork. "I s-s-suppose you're right," the Lieutenant said as he began chewing on a pencil tip. "These d-d-damned hicks do all look alike. Move on, Corporal."

O'Sullivan glanced at the soldiers, who were busy climbing back into the trucks. He quickly pulled a paper from his front pocket and handed it to Sam.

"Put the fuel on the State of Illinois' tab," he said gruffly, then swung into the driver's seat, started the jeep, and drove away.

When the other trucks disappeared out of sight, Sam looked at the paper the corporal had handed her. It was addressed to Miss Angie Eng.

* * * * * * *

"I don't want to read anything from that...that green-belly," Angie said that evening when Sam brought the corporal's note to her apartment. "He was with the sheriff when they arrested our boys, and then he broke up our auxiliary meeting."

"And he's only been in town for a few days, and he's already kept me from being arrested twice," Sam replied.

"That's probably only because our family helped him last fall," Angie said.

"Well, why don't you read his letter so you can be sure?" Margaret said.

"You read it, Sam." Angie turned toward the window and watched the hated guardsmen talking around campfires on the street below. "Then throw it away if you want to."

"Well, I don't think I should be the one to read it," Sam said as she studied the letter. "Since I don't write so good, I'm always afraid I'll put down the wrong words, and since I don't read good, I'm afraid I won't rightly understand the person doing the writin'. No, I think it's best if I just talk to folks so I can see their eyeballs when they're trying to tell me how they feel. I've found that eyeballs are easier to understand than readin' and writin'." She handed Margaret the note. "I'd spect it'd be okay if you read it, bein' how you're her sister and all."

Margaret was excited to be included. She quickly

opened the note and began reading aloud.

> *Dear Miss Angie,*
> *I'd spect that if you don't like me you could give this letter to my leutent and I'd be cort martaled for frat-rinizin with the enemy.*

"Oh, my goodness," Margaret said. "He can't spell no better than a fifth grader."

"Just go on, Margaret," Sam said.

> *I came back to your town cause I wanted to see you agin. My Pa is a aldrman in Chicago and he got me resigned to this unit. I know the risks of doing this but I just had to see you. When you was takin care of me I got to know you real good and I liked what I saw even though I was blind at the time.*

"Oh, that makes a lot of sense," Margaret said.

"Just keep going," Sam said.

> *When you talked to me I feeled like I'd always knowed you. I can't explan it but I think I undrstand you better than I do anybody else. I'm sorry I'm so tall and hope that won't put you off.*
> *Wishin you and yours well,*
> *Michael O'Sullivan*

"Why, that boy writes real pretty," Sam said. "I almost feel like I can see his eyeballs in those words. I'd say one thing's fer sure, Angie—that boy's stick floats with yours."

Angie remained standing with her back to the two girls. When Margaret stepped toward her sister, Sam touched her arm and motioned for her to stay back. Several minutes passed, during which Angie took occasional deep breaths. Finally, she turned toward the girls, tears in her eyes. "I know it's crazy," she said with a sob, "but I'm in love with a National Guardsman. Oh, girls, what am I to do?"

5

Kieran Phelan watched as Felina ran her hand lovingly through the corpse's bloody hair. He was used to this type of behavior from his wife, but it was lately getting more bizarre than even he could stomach. Felina had insisted he bring the young bootlegger's body to the cabin and lie it on the bed next to them while she and her husband committed themselves to some carnal pleasure. Had it not been for her fervent ardor after a killing, Phelan would have objected. They had enjoyed a fine romp while the dead man's head danced merrily to the music of the bed springs. The opus was made complete by Felina's operatic squeals and the loud percussion of the headboard keeping rhythm against the wall.

"He was a handsome boy, was he not?" Felina asked when the sonata was finished and they enjoyed a shared cigarette. She had taken to speaking in a manner that she considered sophisticated, annoying her husband to no end.

"If I'd knowed you was going to fuss over his good looks, I'd have placed my shots better." Kieran wanted to say something more sarcastic, but decided to refrain in case his pretty wife wanted a second round.

"Do you think rigor mortis will set in before morning light?" Felina lifted the dead man's arm, spooned her naked body beneath it, and lay her head on the still slightly warm chest, where just an hour before a heart had pumped blood.

Phelan rolled over on his side, his back to his wife. He didn't want to see what else she might do.

By the time Felina awoke the next morning, her husband had disposed of the corpse. He didn't offer any explanation and she didn't ask. It was as if it had never happened—except that Felina was in a much better mood than usual.

"What do you suppose the Shelton boys will do when prohibition is repealed?" Felina asked when they were on their way back to Taylorville in their Chevy.

"Well, they still got their gambling houses and whores to make money, I suppose." Phelan steered around a large pothole. "I don't imagine the government will be objecting to those vices for quite some time. That's why we need to buy that tavern in Taylorville. We bring a few whores up and set up some crap games, we could make a fortune."

"I liked prohibition," Felina said in a wistful voice full of nostalgia. "It won't be fun anymore if boozing is legal. I wish that Italian had killed Roosevelt instead of shooting the Chicago mayor. Do you think the Shelton boys hired him?"

Phelan had to think about how to answer. Two weeks ago on February 15, Giuseppe Zangara had shot Mayor Anton Cermak and four other people as the mayor was shaking hands with Franklin Roosevelt. Cermak was still in critical condition in a hospital in Florida. Phelan's fear was that Felina would run off with Bernie Shelton if she thought him powerful enough to try to get a president assassinated.

"Nah, most likely he was hired by Frank Netti. Netti's been running the Chicago outfit since Capone got sent to the joint. I'd suspect that Zangara would've kilt them both if he hadn't been so short. They said he had to stand on a wobbly chair to see over the crowd and get the shots off."

"I'd sure like to get in Zangara's cell for a night." Felina playfully twisted a long strand of blond hair around a middle finger. "He looks handsome in those newspaper pictures."

"That little runt ain't no bigger than a ten-year-old." Phelan steered the vehicle into a filling station and took his jealousy out on the car horn by honking it vigorously. "Doubt if he'd be able to please you."

When the slim attendant reached his car window, Phelan rolled it down only a crack. "Four bits," he shouted, and then added, "and for ten cents a gallon, you'd damn well better get these windows good and clean."

"Kieran," Felina said, "look who's sitting on that porch."

"By God," Kieran said, "a union meeting. Vinnie Vacca, Harley Eng, Ray Tombassi, and I'm sure the other two are Progressives, too."

"What you going to do about it, Kieran?"

Phelan was slow with an answer. "I still got some powder left over from the Midland job. Reckon it wouldn't take much to light up a place filled with gasoline."

Felina slid over next to her husband and kissed him hard on the mouth. Phelan hoped his wife wouldn't want him to bring home the bodies left over from the explosion.

* * * * * * *

In the weeks following Michael's letter, Angie spotted him only sporadically and never had an opportunity to speak or even pass him her seventeen page response to his note, which she carried with her constantly. Sam worked at Shorty's filling station from sunup to well past sundown every day except Sundays. Lena and Margaret Eng delivered Progressive families beans, coffee, bacon and sugar three days a week, and milk and bread every day. Sid Vacca walked with several other children along the railroad tracks, picking up coal that had fallen out of bouncy railroad cars, then delivered it to homes of Progressives. He hated that his cousins Will and Tony couldn't join him simply because their father had stayed with the UMW. Sometimes, though, they would accompany young Sid fishing and let him keep everything they caught, even though they knew it went to the Progressives. Bullo and Mary Kate never commented when they saw their sons come home empty-handed except for their cane poles.

Antonio Vacca was retired, but he too stayed busy. Leal Reese, the attorney for the Progressives, gave his clients a forty-acre timbered lot, and Antonio took charge of a cutting crew, the wood to be used by the striking families. Extra lumber was sold off and the proceeds used for oil and gasoline for the cause.

On days when Vinnie was strong enough, he joined a soliciting committee and visited local farmers. They arranged for members of striking families to help feed livestock and mend fences and barns. They did all this in exchange for what food the farmer could give to feed the Progressives.

While days were busy and mostly quiet, the darkness of nightfall almost always brought the sound of gunfire and an occasional bombing. Neither side being overly bloodthirsty, outbuildings and porches seemed especially threatened.

Sam Vacca worried the filling station was a ripe target for an aggression, being that it had become a hangout for the PMA members. Barely a day went by that Shorty Roberts, a retired miner himself, didn't have half a dozen strikers sitting around his porch or dining room, smoking and talking union.

Sam also recognized that Shorty was having a rough winter. The country's economic depression seemed as bad as it could be. Few people could afford automobiles, much less gasoline to run them. Matters were made worse by the National Guard vehicles drinking up fuel on credit—credit Shorty and Sam suspected the State of Illinois would likely never pay back. Still, the feisty, old gas station owner never missed giving Sam her wages, even when at the beginning of March his health began to decline. When the old gentleman developed a fever and chills and was too weak to walk from his office rocker to his bedroom, Sam decided to take matters into her own hands.

"I'm fixin' to get shed of some of them chores first," Sam said one evening as she closed up the station. "Then I'm goin' to fetch Doc Hiler."

"I won't have no flatland doctor pawing around on me," Shorty said from his office rocker. "Sam, you know us hill folk don't take to being fussed over."

"Doc Hiler's been practicing medicine for near on twenty years," Sam argued.

"Well, that's good," Shorty said, pulling his afghan up to his neck. "When he's had enough practice and gets really good at it, maybe I'll let him work on me."

Sam did something she had never done before, not even with her husband. She allowed another human being to see a tear run down her face.

"Somethin' has got to be did and did now." Sam said slowly.

"Oh, fiddlesticks, Sam, go on and fetch your old doctor friend then."

Sam held out her hand. "We're going to shake on that before you crawl fish's out."

Shorty struggled to extend a weak hand. His eyes met Sam's, but before they could shake, the room exploded.

* * * * * * *

"I've never seen anything like it. The building was lifted off its foundation by the explosion and when it came down, the bushes were inside the house."

Sam heard every word the man said, despite her ears feeling like they were stuffed with cotton balls. It seemed as if it were only a second ago she was extending her hand to Shorty, but now she was lying on her back looking up at a starless sky filled with black smoke. She turned her head to her left. Dozens of men stood fifty yards from the filling station and watched two cars burn. The building wasn't on fire and was somehow still standing, its walls tilted inward at the top like an Indian teepee.

Someone touched her hand. Doc Hiler gently felt up her arm, did the same to her other arm, and then both legs. Sam looked to her right.

"I'm feared my big mouth has got us into a whole big heap of trouble," Shorty Roberts said. He was also lying on his back, his face turned and looking into hers. "Someone sure had it in for me."

"Oh, it ain't no such thing," Sam said. Her head had a terrible pain, so she closed her eyes for just a moment. "You're the best old boy there ever was."

When she opened her lids again, she was staring into Shorty Roberts' lifeless eyes. Then she fell back into a deep sleep.

* * * * * * *

For the next week, Antonio had his hands full keeping a still very sick Vinnie calm. One minute his son was wiping his wife's head with a wet cloth, and the next he was trying to find his shotgun, which his father had deposited at Harley Eng's house.

"I'll kill those Peabody thugs!" Vinnie would shout, and then fall back into the lower bunk where he'd slept as a child. Sam lay in and out of consciousness in the other lower bunk, the one once occupied by Libero. Sid slept above her, where his Uncle Filberto had once dreamed of talking movies and other inventions.

The first day that Sam awoke feeling better, she heard loud claps of thunder along with wind and sleet hitting hard outside the home. She smelled cigarettes, and then noticed a cloud of smoke hovered above the bunk beds. A voice she hadn't heard in several weeks spoke loudly from the living room.

"I would be in favor of unions," Joe Harrison said firmly, "if they weren't run by communists, socialists, anarchists and gangsters!"

"If it weren't for them," Antonio said in an equally loud voice, "we wouldn't have a chance against the UMW, the coal company or the corrupt politicians!"

Sam smiled as she imagined her father-in-law waving his hands to make his point. She also knew that her usually docile Uncle Joe would back off now that he'd said his piece. Having worked together in the mining industry since the turn of the century, Antonio and Joe's friendship would survive even this controversial issue. Then her husband's voice entered the conversation louder and more determined than either of his elders.

"You both say all the time that every generation has to fight for their freedom! Used to be white men with property, then it was all men regardless of property, then it was blacks, then women. Well by God, now it's time for laborers to be free of cruel, selfish, money-hungry capitalists who get rich off the backs of us working men and women.

If my generation don't win this fight now, then our children and grandchildren are gonna still be fightin' to make a living long after we're gone! I'm sick o' hearing these rich bosses tell us that we're lucky to have a job. Hell, we work ten times harder than any of them just to put a few measly crumbs of bread on our children's plates, then when we get sick or get old we lose *everything*, while the capitalist passes his fortune onto his children and them to their children. I say, end this now!"

For several minutes, Sam didn't hear anything but the rocking of Antonio's chair, then another familiar voice came, speaking quietly.

"I know what you're saying, Vinnie," Dr. RJ Hiler said. "My Carmela died at Ludlow, as did two dozen others, fighting for exactly what you are saying. All I can tell you is that none of those victories for freedom as you described them have happened overnight. Each of those gains required several generations of work. I know it's hard to understand this, but this world has made more achievements in freedom since July 4, 1776, than it did for the entire millennium of mankind previously. Why, just in your father's lifetime, our unions gained minimum age for workers and worker's compensation as a result of the Cherry Mine Disaster in '09. They got improved work conditions and eight-hour work days as a result of tragedies like Ludlow. And I believe that with Franklin Roosevelt in office, he will do more to help the common laborer than any American president in history."

"But why are you so against unions, Uncle Joe?" Vinnie asked. "Don't you think it would be better if all businesses were controlled by labor?"

"Vinnie, I think you are forgetting that socialism and communism, just like capitalism, all have one unflattering quality in common."

"What is that, Uncle Joe?"

"They are all run by humans," Joe said.

Harley Eng's voice came next. "Vinnie, if we divided all the riches in the world equally among all our people, within one hundred years, ninety percent of the money would revert right back to those who were better educated and worked harder. Would you want to get paid the same as a man who forsakes an education, refuses to get any job training and still expects to be paid as much as you?"

"So we base wages on job skills and performance then," Vinnie said.

"I agree with that," Harley said, "but then you're right back to capitalism."

From the silence in the room, Sam knew that Vinnie and even his father were hard put to come up with an answer. She slowly rose from the bed, wrapped her robe around her shoulders and, making a last second decision, went to the dresser and removed her red bandana from the top drawer. It was tied neatly around her neck when she startled the cigarette-smoking men by entering the room.

"It's all right to use this red bandana to keep my neck warm on a cool evening," she asked meekly. "Ain't it, Papa?"

Antonio stood from his rocker so Sam could sit next to her husband, who occupied the chair their sainted Angeline had used. The men sat quietly for a few moments, smiling and letting their loving eyes admire the mountain girl, Vinnie's eyes a brighter twinkle than anyone's.

"I've been listening to you menfolk talk, and I sure know y'all put a lot of thought into your words," Sam said. "Vinnie and me, we don't hold much in the way of formal educates, but I'd 'spect I'm mighty proud to have worked the three-foot mine in West Virginy with my Papa during the Great War, and, of course, Mama Vacca sent Vinnie to work when he was a young'un, mostly to keep him out of trouble, I'd 'spect."

As Vinnie blushed but nodded, everyone took a moment to reflect on Angeline Vacca.

"I sure would like to understand all those high faluttin' words you fellas been usin'," Sam finally said. "Uncle Harley, do you think these fellas called *capitalists* are good men?"

"Well, Sam," Harley said. "I can't say all of them are, but most of the ones I've met are pretty decent fellas."

Vinnie coughed, and Antonio turned his head and looked in the fireplace.

"Well, what do they think when they go down in the mines and see how hard the men are working?"

"Sam, stockholders and mine owners don't go down in coal mines."

"Oh." Sam squinted.

"Honey," Dr. Hiler said, "people with money are just people."

"Oh," Sam said again, nodding slowly. "I imagine they're real nice folks."

"Of course, Sam," Harley said, "but when they join a stock company, well, they have to consider the profits of the company."

"I see," Sam said, "so is that when the company's profits becomes more important than the fella doing the work?"

Harley opened his mouth, but stopped and looked at Doc Hiler, who kept silent.

"People keep saying this red thing around my neck stands for something called socialism." Sam pulled her feet up in the rocker and covered them with a small quilt. "Hell, I don't think I hardly even know what that word really means. I suppose that to a wife it means she doesn't have to worry that when her man goes off to work he'll be crushed to death by a rock because the company used cheap timber to improve their profit. Maybe to us women, socialism means that our men'll make enough so that his kin don't go hungry. Myself, I think that fancy word means that the fella my man labors for'll respect his work enough to treat him fair when he's sick or hurt or dying. A man that lives his whole life making a livin' with his muscles ain't askin' for more than a fella who makes his livin' with his brains. Our boys just want to have a decent life—want to leave a little something for their wife and babies when they're gone."

The men sat, thinking, weighing Sam's words.

"You're right, Uncle Joe," Vinnie added. "Unions, socialists, communists, capitalists are made up of human's all right, and there's good ones and bad ones on all sides. But ain't big businesses and companies something a lot different than a mere human? It seems they're more like machines that add profit and subtract workers."

Little Sid stayed that night at Bullo's house next door, which worked well for Vinnie and Sam, who enjoyed their first healthy evening in quite some time—to the point that Vinnie fell asleep with only his night shirt on, and Sam with nothing but the red bandana around her neck. They were still spooning comfortably in bed, a pleasure they rarely partook of, when the distant sound of an explosion woke them. Having fallen asleep in his rocking chair, Antonio yelled through the bedroom door for them to stay put and he'd go find out what happened.

A second, much louder explosion came thirty minutes later. Vinnie and Sam were dressed and heading out the door when Antonio returned.

"They blew the porch off George Howsham's house," Antonio said. "The explosion a few minutes ago came from the mine superintendent's house."

"It's our boys getting revenge for them killin' Shorty, ain't it, Papa?" Vinnie asked with a wicked smile.

"Yes." Antonio locked the door and pulled down the window shade. "Now, get back to bed, both of you. I'll not have harm come to anyone else in this family."

With lowered shoulders, Vinnie and Sam dutifully followed instructions, though they left the bedroom door open. This time they also left their clothes on, and, without a word, lay in separate bunks.

"Feels like we've done this before, don't it?" Sam whispered, pulling her quilt up to her neck. Two rapid gunshots echoed in the distance.

"Think it'll ever end, Sam?" Vinnie asked. "Think any of this will ever make a difference? Make things better?"

"It'll make a difference," Sam said, her voice strong enough that even her father-in-law could hear from the next room. "Maybe it's like Doc said. His wife and those other folks who died at Ludlow, Sid Hatfield, and our boys kilt up on Blair Mountain." Her voice cracked a little as she added, "and Mama Vacca. They each made a dent, only a dent, Vinnie, but I b'lieve they did make a difference."

6

As she walked past the Old State Capitol building arm-in-arm with her mother and sister and surrounded by several thousand women, Margaret Eng thought of the many important moments in history that had occurred on the streets of Springfield, Illinois. The victorious election of Abraham Lincoln as the nation's sixteenth president, his famous farewell speech at the Great Western Railroad Station in February 1861, and then the mournful return of his body to the city in 1865. Ironically, despite the great man's legacy toward creating racial harmony, Springfield had also been the site of the 1908 race riots that left much of its black citizens' part of town in ruins. The only good thing about that riot was that it led to the formation of the National Association for the Advancement of Colored People, an organization whose successes were just beginning to come to fruition.

Margaret hoped this day's march on the state capitol by the Progressives' Women's Auxiliary would be an equally historic moment. The founder of their movement and leader of the throng, Agnes Burns Wieck, was a woman Margaret greatly admired. Wieck had been the march's primary organizer and motivator. The pleasant-looking middle-aged woman was barely five-foot tall, with black hair, brown eyes and freckles that stood out playfully when she laughed. Her tenacity in championing socialism seemed unbounded—and even a little frightening to most of the other women.

Sam Vacca also idolized Mrs. Wieck, and, despite a noticeable limp, struggled to walk beside the great woman. Like most of the ladies in the march, Sam wore a white coat and a white nurse's cap. At the suggestion of Agnes Wieck, the only ones wearing black were the women who had suffered the recent Moweaqua Christmas Eve Disaster that killed fifty-four miners.

"I'm sure glad you were able to join us, Sam," Mrs. Wieck told her as they walked. "I saw that building you were in. It's amazing you survived."

"Yeah," Sam said, a little short of breath after so much bed rest. "I figure I got more luck than a rainbow full of shamrocks."

"Well," Mrs. Wieck said, slowing a moment to give Sam and many of the older women a chance to rest. "We are going to win this war, Sam. One day labor will win over corruption. We have reliable men and women on our side."

"You sure wouldn't find no fussin' from folks around these here parts." Sam's awkwardness with words caused her face to turn as red as the bandana she wasn't wearing. "Reliable-some-ness is an important trait among coal mine folk."

"Sam kicked a company thug once during the West Virginia strike," Margaret told Mrs. Wieck in an effort to rescue Sam, "and when the Shelton boys tried to rob the Kincaid bank, she stood right in the street and shot it out with them."

"Oh, my," Mrs. Wieck said, "weren't you afraid of being hit?"

"Nah," Sam said, as she hushed Margaret with an open palm. "I figure either a bent rifle barrel or bad shooting was the Shelton boys' problem. Weren't nobody in no real danger."

"Sam's just modest, Mrs. Wieck," Margaret said. "She's the darling of Christian County."

"Why ain't you just crammed neck-high with personable-ness today, Margaret?" Sam asked. "Anyway, I do appreciate you, Mrs. Wieck. As long as these here mines are run for profit alone, our boys will pay for it with their health or their lives."

"Well said, Sam," Mrs. Wieck said. "Now, let's get on with the fight!" She began a chorus of "Solidarity Forever":

It is we who plowed the prairies, built the cities
where they trade,
dug the mines and built the workshops, endless miles
of railroad laid.
Now we stand outcast and starving mid the wonders
that we've made,
But the Union makes us strong!

Ten thousand women sang in unison as they rounded the corner onto Capitol Avenue.

* * * * * * *

"I'm looking for an Elliot Ness to take down the Shelton Gang and clean up southern Illinois," Governor Henry Horner announced to the two men sitting in leather chairs in front of his cluttered desk. Each of them smoked one of the governor's favorite cigars while they sipped coffee.

"Oh, hell! Ness had to use tax collectors to take down Capone." The cop named Joe Schrader tapped his shoulder harness, which held a pearl-handled pistol. He smiled. "All I need is this."

Horner wasn't sure he liked or trusted Schrader, who

seemed more interested in his stogie than talking strategy, but Claire County Sheriff Jerome Munie, the third person sitting in the room, trusted the man, and that was enough. Horner only wished the two policemen would *smoke* the expensive cigars and quit chewing on them.

"Shoot first," Officer Schrader added, "and ask questions later."

"Maybe." Horner lifted a set of bulky instruments from his desk. "But these will help—two-way radios."

"Ya think we can talk the Sheltons to death?" Schrader laughed.

"It will allow you and your deputies to stay in touch with one another on the backroads that the gang travels," Sheriff Munie said. "They would be useful if one of your men gets out-manned and needs some back up."

Schrader leaned forward in his chair and inspected the radios. The word was that Munie was a straight shooter. The sheriff had reportedly turned down a hundred dollars a day bribe to leave the Shelton family's crime syndicate alone.

"Governor," an immaculately dressed aide interrupted from the doorway. "The Women's Auxiliary just rounded the corner and are coming down Capitol Avenue."

"Well, good, right on time." The governor checked his pocket watch. "I like punctuality. How many are there? Two, three hundred?"

"Uh, w-well," the aide sputtered. He was a young man and, like the governor, new to his position. "I think you'd better see for yourself, sir."

Horner walked to the window, followed by his two untouchable lawmen. The capitol lawn and every street leading into the Illinois State Capitol building was filled with over ten thousand sign-carrying women. When they saw the governor standing in the window, the women began a chorus of chants.

"Down with Lewis's pay cuts!"

"Down with dictators!"

"Down with Peabody!"

"Down with the state militia!"

Schrader spit a wad of chewed cigar into his coffee cup. "Wanna use one of them fancy radios to call for backup, there, Governor?"

Agnes Wieck stood on the capitol steps, a megaphone aimed at the window in which the governor stood.

"We have come to seek redress from the oppressive and intolerable conditions in the coal fields of Illinois!" Wieck shouted. "Dare you fail us now, Governor Horner?"

"Oh, shit!" Sheriff Munie said under his breath. "We'll leave you to your constituents, Your Honor."

As the officers quickly departed, Horner put on his best baby-kissing smile and made a little wave to the mob below the window.

Agnes Wieck looked nervous as a crew of men set up a microphone on a stand next to her. After a moment of adjusting the shrill feedback on the sound system, one of the men gave her a nod, and Wieck started her speech over from the beginning. She spoke as slowly and clearly as she could, although she appeared to have trouble compensating for the echo of her own voice that followed each word. The crowd of women did not seem dissuaded by the technical issue and hung on every sentence their leader spoke.

"It is well for the state that we have come while we still have faith in government, for that faith has been terrifically shaken during the past year. When it was no longer possible for our men to have a voice in determining the condition under which they worked, they broke away from that organization and established a new union that is responsive to the wishes of rank and file. A reign of terror re-

sulted in which officials of the old union, the coal corporation, county and municipal authorities, and even the state
joined, clubbing, tear gassing, shooting, killing our people,
bombing our homes, making it impossible for us to assemble or to enjoy any of the rights to which the constitution
of this nation entitles its citizens. Therefore, in the face of
these intolerable conditions, we respectfully petition you.
Not only is our welfare at stake, but our faith in the ability
and willingness of government to protect and serve us is
menaced. Dare you fail us now?"

When the long and loud applause finally subsided,
Henry Horner figured it was his cue to nod his head, smile
broadly and give a friendly motion with his hand for the
women's representatives to come up to his office. When
he turned from the window, he was dismayed to note that
none of his staff seemed to be available, so he straightened
his jacket, adjusted his tie and reluctantly gave up his half-
smoked cigar to die a graceful death in the ashtray.

"Come in, ladies," Horner said when a small contin-
gent of women appeared in his doorway. "Welcome, and
so good to see you." With slightly trembling hands, he
reached for and raised his wooden humidor to offer a fine
Cuban to the women, but then realized what he was doing
and hastily moved it to a new location on the desk.

The four women who entered his office appeared cour-
teous but businesslike, a trait that Horner had often seen
in women but, despite sixteen years as a probate judge,
never quite grew accustomed. Mrs. Wieck introduced the
three other ladies. The governor, though, didn't remember to follow his usual habit of writing down the names
of the people he met—a fact he realized a moment later
when, with the exception of Agnes Wieck, he forgot all
their names.

"Now that was a mighty fine speech you gave on the

capitol lawn," he said to Mrs. Wieck. "I can assure you that I will personally do everything I can to help you fine ladies maintain your confidence in our great state."

"What we'd like, Governor," Mrs. Wieck said firmly, "is for you to assure that our men will maintain their constitutional right to assemble."

"Ladies, why can't you combine the two unions—or at least have a democratic vote to decide which union the men want?"

"We tried a vote, Governor," one of the other ladies said. "The UMW stole the ballots when they saw they were going to lose. Then John L. Lewis declared martial law. That's when we formed a new union that would abide by the interests of our miners."

"Well, then," Horner said, "what about the creation of a board of arbitration to decide on the issues of the dispute?"

"Governor." Mrs. Wieck gave Horner a look he had seen often on his wife's face when she was explaining something to their young son. "Lewis sold out to the coal company. It is our fundamental right to strike for the privilege to be represented by the Progressive Mine Workers of America."

Horner's mannerism quickly went into that of a judge-hearing-a-case-he-deeply-cared-about. He smiled, nodded his understanding, and waited patiently for Mrs. Wieck to finish explaining her case. After what seemed like a reasonable amount of time, he stood from his desk, lowered his head and began to pace. Years in the judicial system had taught him that folks appreciated long, thoughtful deliberations. As he knew they would, the ladies sat quietly, allowing him time to contemplate.

"May I ask you ladies one more question?" Horner said after an appropriate amount of time had elapsed. "I assume that each of your husbands are earning an income as leaders of the Progressive Union?"

"No, sir," the prettiest of the women in the room said. "Our husbands helped write the union bylaws, which stipulated they were not eligible to collect a salary when the majority of their membership are on strike, locked out or under suspension."

"Also, that there be term limits for officers," another of the ladies added. "We have faith in our government to help us bring about a peaceful and fair resolution to this conflict."

"I am not a prayerful man," Horner said as he moved closer to the exit, "but I am praying that you will keep that faith. For without that faith in government, the government cannot endure. When government goes, all is lost."

The ladies stood and took their cue as he knew they would. When the door was closed, Horner returned to his desk and removed a fresh cigar from the humidor. He was lighting it when his young aide knocked lightly and entered.

"Will there be any notes, Your Honor?"

"Not for the moment," Horner said, then added, "Phillip, wasn't your father a coal miner down in West Frankfort?"

"Still is," Phillip said.

"Which side is he on?"

"He's a hand-loader, so he's a Progressive, sir. He hates those machines. Says they make it hard to breathe and there's more chances of getting killed or hurt. He thinks the company should make six-hour work days so more men can have jobs."

"Huh? Work less for the same pay? That's the new American work ethic, I suppose." Horner slammed his hand down on his desk. "Damn it, son. Illinois is already the most corrupt state in the union. If Cermak dies, I'll have to deal with whoever those crooks in Chicago appoint to take over as mayor—probably that sleazy garbage collector, Patrick Nash. I've got Frank Netti running the mob while Capone's in prison, and the Shelton Gang running corruption throughout the entire downstate. If I don't get this state's economy going, there'll be hell to pay, and I don't have time to put up with a bunch of damned communists trying to shut down our coal mines."

The governor took a deep breath. "Make a notation, Phillip." Horner gave the boy a minute to retrieve his pen and paper, then, with his arms crossed on his chest, tilted his head back and said, "No deputy sheriff in the mining communities is to be hired or paid by anyone except the county. There will be peaceful picketing, free speech and free assembly allowed, but inflammatory agitation is a violation of the peace."

Phillip stopped writing and looked expectantly at the governor. After a long moment, Horner glanced up at the young man.

"That's all, Phillip." Horner turned back to his desk and began fiddling with one of the two-way radios. "You may go."

7

"In other words, Horner ain't gonna do a damned thing!" Vinnie shouted as loud as his weakened condition would allow.

Sam had been trying to keep the news of the governor's decision from her husband, but little Sid surprised her by telling his father what he'd heard at school.

"And to think there was a time when I couldn't wait for you to learn how to talk," Sam said to her son. "When was the last time you got a good bathin', young man?"

"Why just the other day, Ma. Don't you 'member?"

"Well, you smell like last Thursday to me."

"Yes, Mama."

A red-faced Sid hurried to get out of the house as he pondered how his ma could know by his smell that he had been avoiding a bath since Thursday.

"When were you gonna tell me?" Vinnie shouted. He rarely got angry at his wife.

While formidable in action, Sam was often slow in conversation, allowing silence to do her talking. She waited patiently for Vinnie to run his course of curse words. When he finally slowed, she gently guided him onto his back in the bed and pulled the covers up to his neck. He had perspiration on his forehead, but his body trembled. A moment later he fell asleep.

When she arose from the bunk and turned back to her

chores, she saw her father-in-law stood in the doorway.

"His mama couldn't have handled him any better," Antonio said.

"He'll sleep 'till mornin', I'd 'spect," Sam said. "Papa, I need to show you something."

* * * * * * *

Shorty Robert's filling station had become a tourist attraction since the bombing. People came from neighboring counties to walk through the still standing building with its bushes inside the walls. It was determined the only reason Sam survived was because she and Shorty had been in the office part of the building when the detonation occurred. No one could explain how the explosion had blown the building five feet into the air and then dropped it with little more damage than that the walls were at an awkward, obtuse angle.

Sam led her father-in-law into the building, which was now vacant of everything except a single, framed drawing that was still hanging on the wall and had somehow escaped damage. Antonio had been in the building several times since the attack, but it had been so full of debris he had never noticed the picture. Curious, he walked over and studied the drawing. It had clearly been done by a child, but had unusual detail and shading added by the artistically talented Shorty Roberts. It showed what appeared to be five adults and three children sitting at a dinner table inside a house. Above the house were three puffy clouds, a moon and several stars. Antonio gasped. Within the squiggles of one of the clouds he saw the faint, barely distinguishable outline of three faces looking downward—a woman and two boys.

"Who?" Antonio sputtered. "What?"

"Sid drew it with Shorty's help," Sam said. "It's Mama and her boys, looking down from heaven—and that's our family—and we are in this house, Papa."

* * * * * * *

The talk around town was that Antonio Vacca had lost his mind when he bought the two and a half acres that had belonged to Shorty Roberts. Most people thought the cost of cleaning up from the explosion was more than the property was worth. Still, nearly fifty men and women found time in the next few weeks to lend a hand, and Harley Eng brought in an architect from St. Louis to help preserve the existing building.

Several hundred people gathered the day a tower crane was brought in to assist in lifting the building in conjunction with several large jacks. Within a matter of hours, the walls were straightened. A big, curtain-draped sign was raised and attached above the door. The crowd cheered when Antonio Vacca pulled a string and unveiled a beautiful drawing in which a woman and two boys' faces were silhouetted against a night sky. Below were the words *Angeline's Place*.

* * * * * * *

Angie Eng was busy teaching on school days and helping at Angeline's Place evenings and weekends. She made every attempt to commit to tasks that required deep concentration. Mundane undertakings like grading simple arithmetic or pouring a cup of coffee allowed for too much opportunity to think about Corporal Michael O'Sullivan, the tall, handsome national guardsmen who misspelled words that even little Sid could get right.

Each day seemed to bring missed opportunities for a private moment with her Michael. Once, she saw him standing guard alone at the entry to the Hewittville mine, but before she could get within fifty yards, Lieutenant Sebuck and two officers exited the company office. Angie knew that regulations stipulated that a guardsmen caught fraternizing with a local, much less a Progressive, could be court-martialed.

Then one chilly morning in late April, she was adding a few coals to the school's pot-bellied stove when she heard the front door open and then close much more quietly than any grade-school student would have allowed. When she turned, her corporal was standing next to her. She momentarily felt awkward and a little dizzy to have her head tilted far back so she could look up into the eyes of the young giant. When he leaned forward to embrace her, though, the kiss that followed seemed as natural as if they had been practicing for years.

When they had finally satisfied their hunger, they just looked at each other. His eyes smiled honest and trusting. Angie loved this giant's rugged strength as well as the unbridled gentleness of his heart. She knew that the waiting for this moment had been well worth it.

* * * * * * *

Vinnie was sick of being sick. He felt terrible not being able to do his part for the Progressive cause. The fever came and went, but his strength didn't. The Progressives knew that after their revenge bombings following the murder of Shorty Roberts the company thugs would be looking for an opportunity to exact their own vengeance. Since the home of the local Progressive president, Jack Stanley, had already been bombed twice, they didn't think it would be targeted again. Still, his house was in a secluded area and surrounded by big trees, making it an easy mark. Posting a guard gave the Stanley family comfort, so Vinnie was quick to volunteer to be in a rotation taking turns as lookouts. The job amounted to little more than sitting on the porch and occasionally taking a trip around the outside of the big two-story home. Three guard dogs were also chained in various places around the building, so the odds of anyone getting close enough to plant another bomb was slim.

Sam had insisted that her husband be assigned the afternoon shift when it was warmer. Vinnie seemed to do well in the fresh air, and making the regular rounds was good exercise. After doing the sentry work for two weeks, he found he was getting strong enough to make the trip around the house without stopping to rest and without tiring too much. The man who relieved Vinnie and took the first night shift was Chuck Davin, a big, burly miner with arms as thick as a normal man's legs. The two formed the habit of making a round together and then enjoying a cigarette on the porch as Davin updated Vinnie on the latest news.

"The circuit judge issued an injunction against Sheriff Watson today," Davin told him one day during their visit.

"It's about time," Vinnie said. "Watson hasn't served a warrant against a company man in two months now. Does that mean they'll finally be able to bring charges against those Chicago thugs for the Dominic Calandro murder?"

"Hope so." Davin checked one of the two handguns he carried. "The sheriff's also been accused of letting the thugs beat up Earl Swanson."

Vinnie felt the blood rush to his face. He took a deep breath.

"You okay?" Davin asked. "Maybe you'd best head on home."

"I will in a minute." Vinnie was accustomed to developing a slight fever after the sun set. "What about the National Guard? Everyone knows that some of them were responsible for killing Josh Hardy and rolling his body into the South Fork River."

"No mention of that, but the judge did uphold the ordinance in Tovey that keeps our Women's Auxiliary from having their meetings."

This bad news made Vinnie feel faint. He flicked his cigarette aside and put his hand to his head.

"Come on." Davin stood and tucked his gun under his belt alongside the other one, then took Vinnie's shotgun from him. "I'll walk you to your car."

Vinnie didn't try to argue. By the time he reached his vehicle, he was feeling a little better. Sinking into the driver's seat, he shut the car door and accepted his shotgun through the open window.

"I'll see you tomorrow," Vinnie said.

Davin touched his cap and turned back toward the house. Just as Vinnie pushed the ignition, he heard the first of several shots. They came in such rapid succession he instinctively ducked down in the seat, snatched the gun back up, opened the car door, and dove out of the vehicle and onto the ground. He saw flashes of more gunfire coming from over a hundred yards away. Though he knew the shotgun wouldn't reach that distance, he fired both barrels. The shooting stopped and he saw two shadows running away.

"They shot my leg off, Vinnie!" Davin shouted.

Vinnie rolled over next to his friend. Jack Stanley and his wife ran out of the house. She quickly ripped a clothesline down from a pole and tied a tourniquet around the top of Davin's leg. Vinnie struggled to stand up and lean against his car as he watched, helpless to do anything.

"They shot my leg clean off, didn't they, Mrs. Stanley?" Davin repeated.

"No, Mr. Davin," Mrs. Stanley said. "Not clean off, but you are spouting a fair amount of blood."

It only took a few minutes for cars to arrive at the scene. Two Progressive miners immediately loaded Davin into a backseat and sped off toward the hospital.

"Did you see who did it?" someone asked Vinnie.

Before he could say he'd only seen shadows, Jack Stanley answered. "It was Archie Norton and George Lyman," He said. "Go tell the sheriff."

"To hell with that damned sheriff," a miner said. "We'll get those sons of bitches and lynch them ourselves."

Four men jumped into a car and sped away.

Vinnie wanted to go with them, but instead could only continue to lean against the car.

"I ain't good for nothin'," he said, then lowered his head onto his arm. "Nothin'."

* * * * * * *

It was Peg-Legged Kroll, the high school principal, who kept Chuck Davin's spirit up by expounding on the benefits of life with one leg.

"Without the distraction of excessive motion," Kroll told him, "one can sit on a porch swing and really appreciate the taste of whiskey and cigars."

The doctors had tried for three days to save the leg, though they knew that having been hit with six gunshots, it was a hopeless task. On the fourth morning, Davin had cheerfully offered up the limb to the sawbones.

"Get this appendage off me and bring me some whiskey and cigars," the tough coal miner told them.

Vinnie only felt slightly better when he heard how well

his friend was taking the loss of his leg, though he regretted that Archie Norton and George Lyman couldn't be found. Vinnie vowed to seek out the cowardly men when he was up and moving again. The need for revenge provided the incentive he needed to work harder at recovery.

The Vinnie Vacca of old was back.

8

Antonio had always had an interest in photography. Now that he was officially retired, he had plenty of time and found it was something he could enjoy with his grandchildren. Willie, Tony and Sid were often seen tagging around town in their grandfather's footsteps as they sought out interesting subjects for pictures. Having a keen sense of the value of history, Antonio saw every newly constructed building or automobile produced as an image worth preserving. Since Vinnie's house had a basement, Antonio built a dark room for developing pictures, as well as a wooden filing cabinet for organizing and preserving negatives.

While Willie and Tony enjoyed being in front of the camera, young Sid liked to set up interesting shots and help with the developing. When he and Grandpa discovered double exposure, they began creating comical photos, such as people standing behind giant loaves of bread or beside mushrooms that were six-feet tall. Soon the walls of Angeline's Place were filled with framed pictures that, along with the good food, brought in customers from all over central Illinois.

Since it was closed on Mondays, the family restaurant became a regular rendezvous place for the Vacca family and friends. Bullo usually enjoyed these occasions, but with the tensions that followed the shooting of Chuck Davin, he was increasingly less comfortable in the presence of Progressives, which, of course, defined everyone in his family except him.

Bullo was still plagued with guilt for the deaths of James Cheek and Henry Runnels. Everytime he allowed his thoughts to turn to that fateful day of the rock fall, he found new ways to blame himself. If he had only stood up to the mine boss and insisted on the hiring of more experienced men. If he had only sounded that roof himself instead of letting Highpockets do it. He took a deep breath. He was also frightened for his family, particularly hot-headed Vinnie, who thankfully was too sick to get himself into too much trouble.

Knowing that so many people in the community despised Bullo for staying with the United Mine Workers, he especially hated traveling to work every morning under the protection of the National Guard. He also had to constantly wonder if his own wife and sons respected him for what he was doing—if they understood that he truly did believe that, though John L. Lewis often acted like a dictator, the UMW leader was doing the right thing for the workers and the union.

It bothered him, too, that his wife Mary Kate seemed completely oblivious to the political strains that were plaguing the Vacca family. One Monday evening, the red-haired Irish woman hustled happily about the restaurant preparing a chili for the next day's customers. Since chili was her personal specialty, she was alone in the kitchen to get it seasoned just right while Antonio, Bullo, Vinnie and Sam sat at a long table visiting with Harley and Lena Eng, along with Ed and Agnes Wieck.

Bullo hated the Wiecks and wanted nothing to do with them. To him they were far-left lunatics who would ruin America with their crazy thoughts of socialism. Now he had to suffer through Agnes' insane opinions on women's rights.

"I do appreciate you men including us in these discussions," Agnes said. "I sometimes ask myself if it really is I, this Agnes Burns, who sits with women folk and joins in their gossip and trivial talk while the men folk sit in another room talking labor and politics. For most women, romance and adventure die when marriage is achieved. They go on to lead monotonous, mechanical lives, devoid of imagination."

Politeness dictated that Bullo refrain from comment, but he found it was such a struggle to not shake his head or roll his eyes he finally picked up his coffee cup and joined his wife in the kitchen. She was humming merrily as she tasted, then seasoned and tasted, and then seasoned again.

"Did you hear that woman?" Bullo whispered to his wife. "She uses her maiden name in referring to herself. That woman's against marriage and Christianity. What the hell is this world coming to?"

Mary Kate quit humming but continued her work. Tuesday being chili day, she was looking forward to the usual compliments from customers. It was the one day that was hers and hers alone.

"Taste this," Mary Kate said as she raised a wooden spoon to her husband's mouth.

Bullo took a sip. "My God, woman!" he said. "Don't you know the country is in a depression? We aren't going to make a profit on this place if you use that many ingredients." Bullo grabbed a bottle of water off the shelf and dumped it into the big cauldron.

"No, Bullo!" Mary Kate shouted and grabbed her husband's arm.

Bullo Vacca felt his brain and vision go completely dark and empty. But that didn't stop his free arm from backhanding his wife across the face. The sharp sound of the slap seemed to turn the lights back on in his head. He recognized that conversation in the dining room stopped immediately. In fact, everything in his world was frozen for just that instance. The astonished look on Mary Kate's face transformed to hurt and sadness, and then to anger.

Bullo tore his eyes from the blood trickling down his wife's mouth. He couldn't look at what he had done. He felt like he was dead. His spirit floating outside his body saw a monster of a man standing menacingly in front of the woman he loved. For a moment he studied the spice rack that he and Vinnie had built for the women. Then he saw the framed photo that Mary Kate and Sam had just that morning placed above the rack. Angeline Vacca standing in front of her garden, dressed for church, with an open umbrella over her shoulder. Bullo remembered his father taking the picture that past summer. His mother had not been in the mood to be photographed. The stern look on her face seemed made for this very moment. Her oldest son had just failed her.

Bullo followed Mary Kate into the dining area, his head and eyes lowered. He knew that Vinnie and Sam were ready to thrash him, a beating he would not refuse. Harley and Lena would, of course, try to hold them back. His father, though, just stood and looked at him with the same shock that had just been on Mary Kate's face a few moments before. Bullo was thankful the children were all at home in bed, enjoying the company of the Wieck's son, David Thoreau. For them to have witnessed this horror would have been unbearable.

Ed and Agnes, the feminists, rose from the table and saved the moment. When the couple gently each placed a hand on Bullo's shoulders, his first reaction was to resent their meddling and he shook them off with a childish twitch.

"You are all under a lot of pressure," Ed said, his voice calm and reassuring.

Seeing the glares from his family members as they comforted Mary Kate, Bullo allowed himself to be guided back into the kitchen. His eyes went immediately to the picture of his mother on the wall. When he looked at it this time, though, he thought he noticed a little twinkle of understanding in her eyes. Ed and Agnes Wieck seemed to share a similar empathy.

"The stress of this union war has brought down many a good man, Bullo," Ed said when Bullo's breathing slowed a little.

Bullo turned away from them. He placed the knuckles of his thumbs against his eyes for a moment. It felt soothing, as it did when he was down in the mine and the dust got bad.

"You don't know me," Bullo said when he lowered his hands and turned back toward them. "How do you know I'm not just a woman-beater?"

"Men who beat their women don't look as guilty as you did when you walked into that room," Agnes said. She pointed at the photo of Angeline Vacca. "That's your mama?"

Bullo nodded.

"I heard she was a good woman," Agnes said. "I wish I had known her."

"I doubt she'd have agreed with a lot of your notions," Bullo said.

"No, maybe not. But I'd 'spect that in these circumstances, she'd want me to share a few things with you."

Bullo looked at Agnes, though he could think of nothing she could say that he would want to hear.

"Trust your woman with your feelings and your problems, Bullo," Agnes said. "Don't ever go to bed at night carrying the weight of the world on your shoulders. You and Mary Kate are walking this Earth together." She looked hard at the picture, her eyes squinting a little. "I heard that ma of yours knocked a company thug out cold with one punch."

Bullo attempted a weak smile. "Yeah, he was no good."

"We could sure use more wives like her on the picket lines, couldn't we?" Agnes said.

"I heard you had a tragedy down in the mine a few weeks ago," Ed said.

Bullo looked away again and nodded.

"Son," Ed said, "was it your wife you confided your feelings to the night of that horrible accident?"

How does he know that? Bullo remembered that it was Vinnie he had wanted to talk to, but it was Sam whom he ultimately turned to. What was Ed getting at? Everyone knew it wasn't proper for a man to discuss work problems with his own wife.

"That bride of yours is part of all this, Bullo," Ed went on. "Everything that happens to you happens to her also. Maybe not in the same way, but if you get hurt in the mine, she and your boys get hurt too, don't they? If you lose your job and home, they lose their home too. Mary Kate has a right to know what it is you're dealing with, just as your ma had a right to stand in front of that picket line."

Agnes took Bullo's face in her hands and made him look at her just like his mother used to do. "Now you go talk to your best friend."

When she released his face, Bullo looked one more time at the photo of his mother. *Listen to your elders, young man,* Angeline had said to her boys countless times. *Weigh their advice before you make a decision.*

That night he and Mary Kate lay in bed facing each other, talking. Bullo shared with her his fears that she and the boys would not respect him for staying with the United Mine Workers. To his surprise, the mother of his children was able to not only articulate the UMW side better than was he, she also laid out the Progressive views in terms he had never heard before.

"I believe that in the long run," Mary Kate said, "the UMW will be proven right that the machines are inevitable. The Progressives, though, will forever change the way that Americans and unions view the company's manipulations. Eventually, company houses and stores will disappear. The question to be answered by socialism is, how much enablement can humans be provided before they begin to feel entitled and grow lazy? Greed is as common to capitalism as enablement and entitlement are to socialism. There has to be a medium ground. There must be an incentive for laborers to seek education, job skills and worker performance. There must also be a system that forces businesses to provide fair wages and working conditions for workers. Balancing this cannot be done purely through socialism or capitalism."

"So are you saying that a citizen must contribute to be part of society?"

"Yes!" Mary Kate said firmly. "If they want to be part of a society, then they cannot expect to receive handouts unless they have a disability. I believe in helping people get back on their feet if they are down on their luck, but I'll be damned if we should enable them to stay on their knees."

Bullo smiled at his mate's Irish temper. His brain was wheeling, though, as he tried to comprehend all his wife was saying. By the time they were through talking, the sun was rising outside their bedroom window. Mary Kate cuddled in her man's arms as the two, who were now more one than ever, watched the golden glow slowly spread across the eastern skies. Both knew that Bullo Vacca would never raise his hand to his wife again.

9

"Curse you, Peabody thugs!" Mother Jones shouted. She tossed Agnes Wieck, Sam Vacca and Lena Eng a tommy gun each. "You may be able to arrest our men folk, but you'll never stop the Women's Auxiliary."

The four women pulled the triggers of their weapons at the same time and began fanning them back and forth. A barrage of bullets made bloodless holes in the zoot suits of over two dozen gangsters. Most of the men fell immediately, but several waited until the smoke cleared before staggering forward into a sudden torrential downpour of rain.

One tough guy took longer to die than the others. He was wearing a fedora and had on a pair of crocodile shoes that matched perfectly the color of his striped, double-breasted suit. He appeared weaker with every labored step, but each limp hand stubbornly held a drooping thirty-eight caliber pistol. The gangster coughed several times, leaned forward in pain, then looked up and stared coldly at the three women, his eyelids struggling to stay open. He finally made his weakening legs carry him to the sidewalk's edge, where he crumpled into the street that was now a small flood of water rushing to seek the sewage gutter.

But he was not done yet. With a sudden surge of adrenalin he spun and threw both pistols, first right then left, through the big plate glass window beside him. Though full of invisible bullet holes, he rose, took a few steps, fell, got back up again for a few more steps, went into another coughing fit and fell again. He rose again, followed by a few more steps. Then he was down again and back up for one more step before dropping to his right knee. He looked at the women one last time. "I ain't so tough!" He fell face down, his head in the swirling water next to a gurgling drain.

"What did you say, Lena?" Harley Eng asked from the living room davenport. He lay his newspaper onto his lap.

Lena stopped rinsing the green beans and looked up from her reverie. She hadn't realized she had spoken aloud. "I was just thinking about that James Cagney movie last night." She poured the beans into the skillet. "Wasn't it good?"

"I suppose so." Harley set the paper on his lap and looked up at the ceiling. "Don't you think it was too violent, though? I heard a lot of people say it glorifies criminals."

"Well, he did die in the end," Lena said. "They'll never make a movie where the bad guy gets away."

"I suppose not." Harley turned to the sports section of the paper. "What time are you women leaving in the morning?"

"About six," Lena said.

"Well, be careful." Harley folded his paper so it would be easier to hold. "We don't want another Mulkeytown."

Harley was worried about her traveling down to West Frankfurt with a group from the Women's Auxiliary. Just seven months ago, Harley had been riding in a car with Antonio and Vinnie Vacca, followed by a caravan of hundreds of vehicles. The striking coal miners were on their way to Franklin County to get those colliers to join their strike, but they had been ambushed near Mulkeytown. Though no one had been killed, the violence had been intense. It was widely believed the UMW had sided with the coal companies to stop them from shutting down the mines. This mistrust had led to the formation of the Progressive Miners of America.

"I doubt we'll have any trouble," Lena said. "Besides, why would they bother a small group of women?"

* * * * * * *

Lena enjoyed the long drive to West Frankfort. Agnes Wieck's husband Ed drove. His wife sat between him and Lena in the front seat. Four women in the back chatted non-stop. That gave Lena plenty of time to learn from the woman who was being hailed as the Mother Jones of Illinois.

"If we need to stay the night, there's a farmer's home that will be very comfortable," Agnes told her.

Ed and Agnes worked on a shoestring budget with no real money coming from the Progressives for their efforts. They had both been in and out of work for years.

"How do you ever have time to take care of your home?" Lena asked.

"I don't." Agnes laughed and playfully poked Ed's leg when he nodded. "You should come out and see the place. It's like a cyclone went through."

"Ed," Lena said. "I think it's pretty nice that you support Agnes' work as a labor leader."

"The way I figure it," Ed said, "when a corporation hires a man, they also hire the services of his woman. She's there to keep her husband healthy and provide for his home and children on whatever wages he makes. If a man gets a pay cut, it is the woman who has to make cutbacks in food or clothing. If a man gets evicted, his wife and children are evicted too. That's why a woman should have some say in his pay and working conditions."

Lena had never heard a man talk in such a way. She admired the relationship of the Wieck couple. Her own husband Harley was a very strong and supportive man, but even he did not open up to her like Ed Wieck did to Agnes. It had taken years before Harley told her about his involvement at the Cherry Mine Disaster of 1909 and about his experiences during the war dealing with the Spanish Flu epidemic of 1918. Then when he lost his fortune in the big crash of '29, he had simply rose early the next day and went to work in the coal mine. While his cavalier attitude over that loss gained him the respect of many in the community, she wished he would've given her the opportunity to stand beside him during those tough times.

The hall in West Frankfort was packed that night. The women who spoke first were Agnes' trailblazers, as she liked to call them. First up was Katie De Rorre, a near-illiterate Italian immigrant who spoke from the heart about the need for the mining communities to act as a family and to chastise any Progressive who returned to the coal mine before their union was recognized.

"My man will be packing his own lunch box and sleeping alone if he dares bow down to King John and those UMW thugs!" Sister Katie said to rousing applause.

The next woman, Thyra Edwards, was a young, black woman who told how she and Katie had integrated their Progressive soup kitchen.

"'Come on in, all of you and sit down,' I'd say to Italians and Blacks alike. 'There's no such thing as white folks and colored folks here, we're all just folks.' And when some of them miners said it weren't proper for Whites to sit next to Blacks, Sister Katie dismissed that nonsense with a scoff, and one scoff from Katie is more effective than a hundred sneers from anyone else. Yes, ma'am, Sister Katie has a marvelous scoff indeed."

By the time Agnes Wieck stepped to the podium, the entire room was feeling the spirit of comradery. She opened with acknowledgements to the local auxiliary for inviting her as well as the previous speakers. When she placed a pair of reading glasses on, her somber attitude brought the room to a complete hush.

"I would like to read a letter that I received from the wife of one of your local miners:

> *"Four carloads of UMW thugs went to our Orient mine and beat my father nearly killing him. One fellow hit him in the face with a pair of metal knuckle guards, and they beat him and took him and drug him out in the yard saying they were going to take him off and kill him. They knocked him in the head with a gun. He was unconscious. They kicked him and kicked him, injuring his arm and kidneys, His arm is broke in the shoulder. They beat up more men there that same night in their own homes, and over thirty men in West Frankfurt. For God's sake, get ahold of Mrs. Wieck and tell her we need to hurry and get to Washington so we can do something. We slept in the garage last night and the thugs come and yelled and beat on the door of our house and flashed their lights in our bedroom. They shouted at my father that they were going to civilize the people here."*

Wieck set the letter on the podium and removed her reading glasses. She looked up at her audience. Lena recognized the effect that the moment of silence had on those listening. As was everyone in attendance, Lena was on the edge of her seat waiting for the next words.

"Civilize...us," Wieck finally said, the words a distant but clear reflection.

As if on cue, loud screams erupted and the hall was suddenly filled with dozens of club-wielding men. The men rushed through the chamber so fast, Lena never saw the baseball bat that knocked her to the floor. For several moments, she thought she had gone blind, but then realized the lights had been turned out. She saw only shadows of women trying to flee the room and big hulking men chasing them, bats swung menacingly over their heads, each swing bringing a swooshing sound followed by a sickening thud as they made contact with the women's heads and bodies. Screams and pleas for mercy echoed.

The assault ended as quickly as it had begun. The men exited, cruelly stepping on or kicking aside women lying in their path. The screams were replaced by moans and cries for help. The lights came on. Women lay in blood everywhere. Lena sat up, and when someone offered to help her to her feet, she declined.

"No," she said. "Help the others. I'll be okay."

She had blood on her face and clothes, but sensed it wasn't her own. Her cheekbone below her left eye was already swelling, and she longed to put something cold and wet on it. There were others in the room who were far worse. People still shouted, screamed and cried. One unconscious woman's forehead was smashed in. Another's jaw hung limply, her mouth gaping open. Men carried the most seriously injured out of the building and into ambulances. Others were simply laid out in backseats of cars and rushed to the hospital. By the time Agnes and Ed found Lena, her eye was swollen completely shut. They helped her to her feet and to a car waiting outside the building.

At the hospital, so many patients were being brought in Lena was placed in a chair in the hallway. An orderly was finally found who had time to do a quick inspection of her injury.

"If I were you," the orderly said to Agnes after getting Lena to answer a few questions, "I would take her home and let her get some rest. Come back in the morning and the doctors may want to lance that eye to get the blood out."

Katie De Rorre was standing beside Ed when Lena and Agnes came back into the busy foyer. Katie's pretty face was heavily bruised and her lower lip was stitched and swollen.

"Do you ladies feel up to another long car ride?" Agnes asked. In the bright light of the hallway, Lena could see that Agnes' forehead was bruised above an eyebrow. "I'd like to take a few of you who are able to travel back to Springfield to show our governor what good his lame edicts have done."

* * * * * * *

When word got out that Agnes Wieck and her four injured women were sitting just outside Henry Horner's office, all his legislative appointments for the day were cancelled. The governor was trapped in his office alone for three and a half hours that morning. He couldn't even go across the hallway to the restroom, so he relieved himself into the spittoon beside his desk. Luckily, no one saw him when he opened the second floor window and poured his pee into the grass below.

By lunchtime, Horner was starving and his mouth dry and sore from chain smoking cigars—something he hadn't done since his wife's eight-hour labor the day his son was born. Finally, with a scowl and an expletive, Horner put on his jacket, changed the scowl to a smile, and exited his purgatory. Agnes Wieck and the women were on him like the proverbial flies on shit. What few males were in the hallway quickly disappeared into the nearest doorways— at least a half dozen into the men's restroom.

"A few weeks ago you told us to have faith in our government," Agnes Wieck said as the women walked hastily alongside the governor. "That our civil liberties would be protected. Now I want you to take a good hard look at what that Franklin County sheriff's deputies and UMW gun-thugs did to my sisters."

"I'm sorry, ladies," Horner said as he continued at close to a run down the near empty hallway. "I do have a very important engagement I'm late for."

"You sure don't have no time to see the victims of your broken promise!" Wieck shouted, then coughed several times before continuing. "But we sure do have time to wait and compel you to see the price our sisters have paid for the Constitution your government has broken."

Agnes Wieck stumbled for a moment and coughed again. Horner made a break for it.

"The cloak of humanitarianism has now fallen from your shoulders, Governor!" Katie De Rorrer shouted after him. "You stand revealed as just another politician protecting the interests of the privileged few!"

"You need to seek recourse to the courts, ladies." Horner said over his shoulder. Having gained some distance away from them, he stopped walking and looked back at the four bruised and battered women as they struggled to hold a very sick-looking Agnes Wieck on her feet. "I cannot intervene except at the sheriff's request."

"'Tis your sheriff who beat our women!" Lena Eng shouted.

"We put you into office, Henry Horner," Katie De Rorrer screamed at the governor. "And now you would turn us out upon the icy streets of Springfield, even without mercy, let alone justice!"

Henry Horner appeared unruffled as he turned and, feigning a slow stroll, walked calmly around the corner at the end of the hallway, opened the doorway to the stairwell, and then ran down the steps two at a time.

10

Following the beating of the women in West Frankfort and the shooting off of Chuck Davin's leg, Vinnie took every occasion to talk up ways to wreak havoc on the UMW and Peabody Coal Company. It wasn't difficult for him to get support, since tensions in all the Christian County mining communities were now at their peak.

Fist fights occurred several times a day. They usually began when a group of men from one side found themselves outnumbering a group of men from another. The battles were vicious, but usually over before the National Guardsmen could be summoned—the Progressives knew the guardsmen would always take the side of the enemy. Gunfire became so common, most in the community had learned to judge the direction and how far away the shots were by the echo.

At night, miners on both sides as well as company men took turns guarding their communities by stationing armed sentries on roof tops. Most of the UMW and Peabody families lived in Taylorville or nearby Kincaid. Progressives learned to avoid these neighborhoods for fear they would have rocks thrown at them or even be shot at. The same went for any opponents walking in the mostly Italian Progressive communities.

Willie and Tony learned this the hard way. The two felt safer than most, being they were Italian on their father's side. Returning to their home in Hewittville one evening from the Taylorville Square, they found themselves suddenly bombarded with rocks coming from the widow's walk atop a home owned by a Progressive family named Ronchetti. The Vacca boys ran for cover behind a tree but a second brother appeared on the ground and continued the assault while carrying a bag full of rocks slung over his shoulder. Willie and Tony made a dash for it, all the while getting pummeled by heavy stones that, had they not feared for their lives, would have normally downed them. When they got to their backyard, they found young Sid lying on the back of their black pony as the little Shetland fed lazily on grass.

"Why, you're head's a bleedin', Willie!" Sid leapt from the pony. "I'd best fetch your Ma."

"No!" Willie said. "She won't let us go nowhere if she sees this. Bring me some wet warsh rags."

Sid ran to his own house while his cousins checked each other for injuries. When he returned with six dripping towels and a big chunk of ice from the icebox, Tony ripped a rag from his hand. Without so much as a thank you, he doctored his brother's scalp.

"Who done this to you?" Sid stood with clenched fists just as he had seen his father do when he got mad.

"'Twas your Progressive friends," Tony said, a little of his mother's Irish lilt in his voice. "The Ronchetti boys."

Sid didn't know what to say.

Willie remained silent and didn't contradict his brother. He and his young cousin usually got along pretty well. More often than not, they even took sides against Tony, a fact that often drove the middle Vacca child to go play by himself. This day made everything different. The coal mine war was upon them.

Sid pondered on the situation while the boys took

off their shirts to inspect and rub the many welts that were quickly turning purple on their arms and backs. He thought of the day the National Guard had destroyed their picket line in front of the mine gate by the school. Both Willie and Tony had taken part in the defense of the Progressive miners. He also remembered that Uncle Bullo had administered a good whooping to his sons that night when he found out they had sided with the enemy. Sid, on the other hand, had received a loving Dutch rub from his own Papa when he told him he had thrown snowballs and rocks at the guardsmen.

Sid didn't know what to do. He didn't want his Pa to be mad at him for going against a Progressive, but he couldn't stand by and see his own kin being abused either.

"I remember Grandma Vacca talking to our mamas one night when all these problems started," Sid said after some careful deliberation. "She said that our papas' hearts were being tore in half because they each chose the union that they thought would best help their families. Grandma told our mamas to make sure that no matter what happened, it was up to the women to always remind their menfolk that they are Vaccas first."

The older boys stared at their younger cousin.

"Now them Ronchetti boys ain't the smartest foxes in the henhouse," Sid said after a long pause, "but I ain't the tallest, neither, so I'll need your help."

* * * * * * *

As much as he loved and respected his father, Sid had learned what not to do in a fight by watching the war between the rival unions. He just couldn't understand why the Progressives and the UMW and Peabody kept taking turns getting revenge on each other.

Though Filberto and Libero had died many years before he was born, Sid had come to love hearing the stories about his uncles. It seemed almost every holiday someone would relate the tale of how the two youngest Vacca brothers had once moved the outhouse so Felina Harrison would fall in the shithole. And how Filberto had set an alarm clock so it went off just as Felina tried to steal it and make her escape.

Sid and his cousins would need similar cunning if they were to exact revenge from the much older and more vicious Ronchetti brothers. With that in mind, the three set up an elaborate plan—as well as contingencies in case things went wrong.

Most people thought of the widow's walk as a flat, gated place on a two- or three-story house where a recently widowed woman could watch what was going on in the neighborhood during her mourning period. Sid knew something else about widow's walks, though. They were usually built next to the chimney, both for ease of chimney repair and to allow the owner to drop sand down them in case the flue caught fire.

Sid received permission from Aunt Mary Kate for his two cousins to sleep over at his house. At a little after midnight, the young avengers donned the darkest clothes they could find, snuck out through the bedroom window, and then slid quietly down a drainpipe. It was a feat that had been well-rehearsed from previous adventures. All the supplies they needed were waiting for them in a big canvas bag under the crawlspace of a shed. Being it was a moonless night, the boys took the route along the railroad tracks toward the Ronchetti home. Willie carried the front of the bag by a strap with his two accomplices doing the same from the sides. They approached their target from the alley and, after opening the bag, each removed their required equipment and went about their assignments without a word.

Willie and Tony slung what they needed onto their backs attached by shoulder harnesses. Sid dragged an unopened bucket and the canvas bag around to the front of the house. He made sure he stayed close to shadows of the building and ducked low as he passed each window. When he reached the lattice that ran up to the widow's walk, he thought he heard the steady breathing of the Ronchetti boys above him. Hopefully, they were asleep. Sid placed a small handsaw in his mouth, and after climbing the lattice for about three feet, as quietly as he could, he cut the lattice just above his head until it was almost severed. He dropped soundlessly back to the ground and began spreading out the canvas directly beneath. Using a screwdriver, he removed the bucket lid and poured the contents onto the canvas.

In the meantime, Willie and Tony had climbed to the arched roof on the other side of the widow's walk. Like a medieval knight drawing a sword, Tony pulled a thin pole from the strap on his back. While his older brother held him upside down by his feet, he lowered himself to the long window that was used as an entry onto the widow's walk. This was the moment where the plan could go wrong. He had to use the stick to push the window shut without it waking the Ronchettis. He hesitated once when the window squeaked. One of the sleeping brothers snorted like a pig, then rolled over on his side. A moment later, the window was shut. Tony pulled the stick back up and jammed it firmly along the side of the window, effectively ensuring there would not be a simple escape from the widow's walk. He motioned for his brother to pull him back up—no easy feat for a twelve-year-old. By the time they were again sitting side by side on the slanted roof, both their faces were red, and despite the cool evening, were perspiring profusely.

They smiled and shook hands. It seemed that nothing could stop them now. Willie pulled a satchel around that he had carried on his back. He stood next to the smoldering chimney, waited for his brother to get a good start back down to the ground, and then dumped the contents into Santa's entryway. The black smoke began immediately, but Willie, fast as a squirrel, lowered himself down into the backyard. He and his brother were back in the alley before they heard the first screams from the Ronchetti brothers. Willie and Tony rushed around a neighboring house and got themselves in a position to enjoy the action.

That's when it all went wrong. They gasped as they saw their young cousin standing in the front yard, a stout, short-legged man holding him firmly by the arm. Sid and the man were looking up at the smoke and ash that was settling like a giant mushroom cloud all around the house. The cracks that were around some of the windows also began to spew smoke that was rapidly filling the inside of the house. Screams sounded from somewhere in the building. The Ronchetti brothers tried to open the window to get outside, but by the time they realized it was jammed shut, they were engulfed by the thick, black smoke. Coughing and gagging, they both lowered themselves down the lattice at the same time. They were almost to the ground when the lattice suddenly made a loud crack like a lightning strike, and the boys splashed onto the wet canvas. For a moment, they rolled around in the shallow, slippery pool trying to get on their feet. When they finally stood, they were both covered with a bright, pink stain that seemed to glow in the darkness.

The sentry holding the six-year-old took a step toward the wallowing boys. Like an angry dog, Sid bit the man's hand, and as the security guard screamed in pain, he tore loose and ran for it. One of the Ronchetti brothers started to give chase, but fell flat on his face. The other tripped over his fallen brother, joining him again in the muck. The security guard finished howling and began his chase just as Sid rounded the corner of the house.

Willie and Tony were on the opposite side, but they knew Sid would turn back their way if he beat the guard to the backyard. The brothers ran immediately the way they had come, and when they reached the area by the railroad tracks, they spotted the man running just behind their little cousin. They were too far away to help, but as they continued their sprint, they saw Sid reach out toward them with one hand as if he were begging them for help. Willie let out a little cry of frustration.

Then Sid reached toward a clothesline he was about to run beneath. In an instant and without slowing, he made a quick jump and pulled the line down. The next moment, the security guard's feet flew six feet into the air. His head and shoulders crashed hard to the ground.

Sid stopped and looked back at the man who lay motionless in the grass. "He ain't dead, is he?"

Willie and Tony each grabbed a hand from their cousin, led him quickly across the railroad tracks and deep into the woods.

Fifteen minutes later, they were safe back in Sid's bedroom.

"He ain't dead, is he?" Sid asked again.

"No, Sid." Willie said firmly. "I'm sure he's not dead. I saw a kid get clotheslined once and his legs flew higher in the air than that security guy's did. All he got was a little knocked out and a red line across his neck for a couple of years. Now quit worrying about him. I'm more concerned that he might've recognized you."

"Well, I sure didn't recognize him, and I'm pretty good at remembering faces." Sid grabbed a piece of half-chewed paraffin from his study desk and began rapidly chawing on it. "Why would he remember a little kid like me?"

"We gotta make you look different." Willie leaned forward, deep in thought.

"I could grow a beard," Sid said, his eyes brightening.

"Don't be stupid, Sid," Tony said. "That would take too long."

"Well, why are you so sure he'd remember me?" Sid asked.

"'Cause you got that blond hair like your ma," Tony said. "Nobody in town has hair the color of you and your ma."

"Oh, no!" Willie grabbed his hair with both hands. "What if a neighbor saw us? I've got black hair like Pa and Tony's got red hair like our ma."

"Why would people be looking at our hair?" Sid asked.

"'Cause we all have different colors," Tony said. "That's pretty noticeable."

"I wonder what makes people have different hair colors," Sid pondered, now sitting in the same thoughtful manner as Willie while he chewed gum.

"Would you just quit thinking about stuff like that for a minute?" Willie scolded. "We have to come up with a way to look different before morning."

"Well." Sid stopped chewing the gum. His cousins got silent when they saw the idea coming. "During the Great War, a lot of soldiers cut off their hair 'cause they was getting cooties when they was fightin' down in the trenches."

"I thought cooties was just something girls had," Tony said.

"He means head lice." Willie sat up on the bed and patted Sid on the back. "I think you have it, old boy. Go fetch your ma's scissors."

* * * * * * *

When Sam called the boys down for breakfast, she was prepared to scold them for running down the stairs and for having dirty hands and even for drinking milk out of the saucer. But they walked slowly down the stairs, sat quietly at the table, folded their napkins in their laps, and waited patiently for their food. When she noticed their heads she blinked twice and was at a loss for words. Since all three of the boys looked at her expectantly, she decided to completely ignore the patch-quilt look on their heads. Each of them had areas that had practically no hair and other areas that looked like tiny rugs of rabbit fur.

"Is your hair itchin', Ma?" Sid asked.

"Why, no," Sam said slowly. "Should it be?"

"No, Aunt Sam," Willie said. "We just thought you might want to cut it off like ours if you feel anything crawling around in it. Ours feels much better now."

11

Harley Eng had been so irate when Lena came back from West Frankfort with her eye blackened he actually loaded his shotgun and revolver and was heading out the door before his wife was able to talk sense into him. That was why, when he heard that Vinnie was instigating the Progressives to violence, he paid him a visit one pleasant afternoon in mid-May. The two reclined in lawn chairs beneath the tall oak trees that Antonio had planted back at the turn of the century.

"Everyone thought your pa was crazy for planting these slow-growing trees," Harley said. "I don't think folks still understand what a visionary Antonio Vacca really is."

"Visionary?" Vinnie asked.

"Sure enough. He and your mother planned this very moment long before you were even born. First they bought these five acres, planted those trees, then built themselves a house to live in. They raised four fine sons in that little home. Your pa sweated to make a living down in the dark and dusty coal mine, and your ma labored every day in that big garden of hers. They saved everything they could so they could build their boys a home on these five acres. Keeping the Vacca family together meant everything to your ma. Yes, sir, they tolerated the abuse of the coal company, but they also were successful at helping to make improvements in the wages and working conditions for all working men and women everywhere." Harley laughed. "By golly, they were a spunky team, your ma and pa. Did I ever tell you how they defied the company store by selling Angeline's produce from the garden?"

Vinnie nodded. He was tempted to ask for a retelling of the story, but sensing where the conversation was going, he remained quiet. He was reminded of similar discussions he'd had with his mother while he was growing up. Once in 1917, when he was but fifteen years old, she had discovered he was about to run away to fight the war in Europe. She never let on that she knew his plans, but through careful manipulations, she convinced him to go to work at the mine to help the family.

Now Harley Eng seemed to be maneuvering toward a similar agenda. However, Vinnie was not a naïve young man anymore and Harley Eng was not his mother. Still, Angeline Vacca's teachings were alive and well in her spirited son. *Respect your elders*, her voice echoed from somewhere in the young man's heart. As his mother had taught him, Vinnie turned his head and looked Mr. Eng in the eyes.

"Vinnie," Harley continued, "I don't know why the world can't change faster. All I know is that it is changing. It is improving. You have it better because your parents made it better, and you and Sam will make it better for Sid, and he for the next generation of Vaccas. But things are not going to improve if we Progressives seek revenge every time the UMW or Peabody bombs or shoots at one of us."

When Harley seemed finished talking, Vinnie finally let his eyes look up into the trees that were teeming with birds and squirrels. He weighed the advice carefully, as he knew his mother would expect. Harley Eng had been a millionaire before he lost his entire fortune in the crash of '29. Even before that, though, when he was still a successful capitalist, he had helped many people during and after the Cherry Mine fire of 1909 that killed 259 men and boys. In fact, the Engs had spent considerable time and money helping to bring survivors of that disaster to the Christian county mines. Harley was now a mine inspector and Lena was fast becoming a respected labor activist. Still, Vinnie and Sam had seen first-hand the poverty in the non-union mining communities of West Virginia. They had also witnessed the union successes that followed Sid Hatfield's gunfight victory over the coal companies' Baldwin-Felt detectives. Clearly, there were times when reciprocating violence could help sway the country to make improvements for laborers. But maybe Harley was right. Maybe for vengeance to work it had to clearly be an act of self-defense.

"I'll tell the boys to ease up for a while," Vinnie said. "I can't hold 'em back, though, if they have to fight to defend themselves."

"Fair enough," Harley said.

"We still don't know who it was that smoke-bombed the Ronchetti place," Vinnie said. "I suppose it's lucky that even most Progressives don't like the Ronchettis too much."

"Well, I hope whoever did it doesn't show the other UMW boys their methods," Harley said with a slight smile. "Most all the furniture and walls in Ronchettis' house was ruined, and they said the two boys' skin will be stained pink for at least another week."

Vinnie laughed. "Sounds like something my brother Filberto would have done."

* * * * * * *

The next two months saw a few minor successes for the PMA. Charges were dropped on two Progressives for the murder of James Hartman because it was discovered that all the State's witnesses worked for Peabody Coal Company and their stories conflicted. Antonio Vacca, the only person who actually saw the shooting, was not even questioned. Lawsuits were also brought against the sheriff and Peabody for several false imprisonments that had occurred since the mine war began. Then five sheriffs in coal mining counties, including Christian County, were issued temporary injunctions restraining them from interfering with the Progressive Miners of America.

Despite these gains, the mines continued to run under the protection of the National Guard. More strikebreakers were recruited from the low lands of southern Illinois. Since many of them were former members of the Shelton Gang and had no mining experience, they were often taken down to UMW workers' basements to be secretly trained in mining techniques.

Vinnie felt bad that he broke his promise to Harley once by joining two other Progressives in a fistfight. It had taken place in a back alley against three UMW men who were training miners. While in the end they did teach the scabs a lesson, Vinnie was embarrassed that, in his still weakened condition, he had been unable to hold his own and had to accept assistance to finish his opponent in the skirmish.

That humiliation and daily visits with one-legged Chuck Davin provided incentive for Vinnie to train harder. By the time his bruises from the fight disappeared, he was walking two miles every morning—and he went for days at a time without a fever.

"I'll knock your nose clean up in the sky!" Vinnie told George Michaels one day when he met him walking along the railroad tracks.

"Why you want to do that for, Vinnie?" Michaels was a

good head taller and quite a lot heavier. "I thought we was pards."

"'Cause you're a low-down, yellow-bellied, labor spy. That's why."

The expression on Michael's face changed from wonderment to anger. "I'm a good seventy pounds heavier than you, Vinnie Vacca."

"That's okay, 'cause I need the practice, and I aim to put speed burns all over your body." Vinnie took off his shirt, then blushed. "New shirt," he explained.

"Oh, well, it looks real nice, Vinnie." Michaels looked down at his own dirty work shirt. He started to undo the two buttons that kept his belly covered, but then thought otherwise.

For no other reason than politeness, Michaels waited patiently as Vinnie carefully folded his shirt and looked around for a place to lay it.

"Put it over on this here stump, Vinnie." Michaels gently took the shirt, placed it carefully on the stump and gave it a friendly pat. Turning back toward his adversary, Michaels led with a hard right to Vinnie's cheekbone.

The fight lasted a little over ten minutes. It ended with Michaels rolling around on the ground in a drunk-like stupor. Vinnie was sweaty and bloody and breathing hard, but he felt immensely satisfied as he put his new shirt back on and ran his fingers through his hair. He started to leave, but saw that Michaels had fallen out of consciousness in the middle of the railroad track. Though he suspected the big man would recover before the noon train arrived, Vinnie grabbed both the big man's boots and dragged him to a shady area beneath a weeping willow.

Two days later, George Michaels went back to work in the coal mines as a UMW man. He and Vinnie Vacca never spoke to one another again.

* * * * * * *

Dr. RJ Hiler had a tenuous understanding with Peabody Coal Company and the United Mine Workers that he be allowed to continue treating the Progressive miners' families during the conflict. With that perception in mind, RJ felt safe in delivering the first baby of a Progressive into the world in the early morning hours of June 16, 1933. It was only when he pulled the door shut and was leaving the miner's home that he experienced a sixth sense of doom that he had not felt since his days in 1914 Ludlow.

The Army-green, canvas-covered truck of the National Guard was a common sight at this hour of the morning as it picked up and delivered strikebreakers to the coal mines. The one roaring down the street toward him raised suspicion though, because it was in an Italian neighborhood that was one-hundred-percent Progressive. When the brakes squealed the truck to a stop in front of RJ's car, two guardsmen with bayonets on their rifles leapt from the back and came straight for the doctor.

"I'm Dr.—" A rifle barrel slammed into RJ's head. Dazed, he felt himself being dragged to the truck and thrown into the back with a half dozen Progressives. In unison, the captives shouted in protest at seeing the respected doctor treated so poorly.

"He was c-coming out of a Progressive house," Lieutenant Sebuck said with a laugh. "That's g-g-good enough for me."

RJ shook his head and felt the world slowly come back into focus. The truck roared on, stopping occasionally to pluck a Progressive off a porch or out of a garden. One poor fellow, who wasn't even a miner, was grabbed as he walked from his outhouse in a bathrobe.

By the time the truck was filled and on a highway out of town, RJ was treating cuts and stab wounds with whatever clean pieces of cloth could be salvaged from the confused men in the vehicle. Forty minutes later, the truck stopped on a country road and Sebuck ordered the captives to get out. Several of the men were badly injured and had to be helped to the ground. When they were finally all sitting along a ditch beside the dirt road, RJ counted twenty-two prisoners.

Four menacing-looking guardsmen trained their rifles on them as Sebuck paced in the road, a gleeful look in his eye.

"You men are d-d-done in these parts," Sebuck shouted, tobacco spittle oozing from the side of his mouth. "We'll s-shoot your head off if we see you back in Christian County."

The guardsmen loaded back up and the truck sped away, the spinning tires kicking dirt and dust on the nearest men.

* * * * * * *

From atop Williamsburg Hill, Joe Harrison saw the National Guard truck stop in the middle of the country road. He gasped when the soldiers unloaded human cargo and lined men along the ditch. Joe's breath came hard and his heart pounded. It was happening again. He looked down at the tombstones in front of him, then back up in time to see guardsmen raising rifles and pointing them at the men sitting along the ditch in the cold morning dew.

Thirty-five years before Joe had witnessed and taken part in a similar scene. In that case, over two-dozen Negro strikebreakers were brutally ambushed, murdered and buried right in the spot he was standing. The headstones at his feet belonged to three of the men responsible for the massacre, including that of Joe's friend, Art Cabassi, who, along with the others, had requested to be buried at the site. Joe understood why these men wanted to spend eternity there. He himself was filled with guilt because he was the one to pull the trigger and end the life of the last of those unsuspecting miners.

Now he watched as guardsmen climbed back into the truck and sped away from the scene. The Progressives shook their heads and relaxed their shoulders. A couple of them stood, but several were clearly wounded. These were the union miners Joe had turned his back on when he became a company man. They were the militants who couldn't be happy to just have a decent paying job. They thought they were smarter than the owners and operators. They wanted the federal government to take over the mines and let the workers run them so they could reap the full benefits of the produce. They felt entitled and were willing to kill innocent men who wouldn't join their union—strikebreakers who were themselves just trying to feed their own children.

Joe walked over to his automobile, got in and started it. He leaned his head on the steering wheel and shut his eyes. To the right the dirt road led down from the hill toward his new home in the village of Herrick. Left went back down the hill he had once traveled delivering those dead and dying Negro strikebreakers to the area he had just visited. Joe turned the steering wheel hard and slammed his foot down on the accelerator.

* * * * * *

"Maynard Ensley would have bled to death if Joe Harrison hadn't happened along when he did," RJ told Antonio and Harley later that evening as they sat at a table in Angeline's Place.

Sam, Mary Kate and Angie were cleaning up after a busy day, but listened to the doctor's story as they hustled about.

"Joe rushed me and the most seriously wounded to Pana in his car," RJ said. "We sent a truck back for the rest of the fellows. Two of them packed their bags and were on the afternoon train to St. Louis."

"What in the world was Joe doing up on Williamsburg Hill that early in the morning?" Harley looked at Antonio. "You don't suppose he was in on it and got cold feet, do you?"

Harley had never been as close to Joe as was Antonio. In fact, the two had several heated discussions over the years, with Joe most always sticking up for the coal company.

"No, Joe would never go along with hurting anyone," Antonio said firmly. "I've worked beside that man for years. He's saved my life as well as many other union men on more than one occasion. He was pretty close to Art Cabassi and, for some reason, those other fellows buried up on that hill. He knew them before he knew me. When they'd meet on the street they'd always make eye contact and nod at one another, but never with a smile."

Antonio looked at a photo above the booth at which they sat. He and Joe Harrison, shirts off and covered with coal dust, stood beside a boxcar. "It was as if those men had been in battle together."

12

It took Bullo over half an hour to set up the big Scott All-Wave Deluxe XV radio in Angeline's Place. Despite the economic depression, radio was the one entertainment that people across the country permitted themselves, and they were selling by the thousands. Antonio believed that having a radio would be good for business.

"But what if folks just sit and listen to the radio after they get their eatin' done?" Mary Kate asked.

"Then I'll show them the door," Antonio said with a swish of his hand. "Besides, we'll just play musical programs."

By the time Bullo was ready, the entire Vacca family had gathered in front of the radio, the adults in chairs and the boys sitting Indian-style on the wooden floor. Following several minutes of turning the dial, Bullo was able to bring in a station that had less static and fewer pops than the others. They heard two country boys talking about their first experience seeing an elephant.

"It's Lum and Abner!" Willie shouted. "I heard this show over at Tommy's house."

Mary Kate shushed her son.

> *"I was just looking at that elephant a while ago, Lum, I believe he's deformed."*
> *"Deformed?"*

"Yes, sir. Now just look at him there. He looks like he ain't big enough for himself, don't he?"

"Ain't big enough for hisself? What're you talkin' about?"

"Well, his skin don't fit him very good. It's a way yonder too big for him."

"Oh, well, he just ain't growed into it yet. He ain't more than half growed, you know."

"What do they do? Just give them a skin that's big enough for a growed elephant and then just let them grow into it?"

"I don't know, Abner. This is my first experience with an elephant. They just ain't built for style—they run more for comfort."

"Well, there ain't much shape to 'em, I'll tell you that. Now, just look at them legs. They just go straight up and down. Looks like his legs run down to the ground and stopped all of a sudden, like he's bogged down in the mud or something, don't it?"

The three Vacca boys rolled on the floor laughing, and for the first time in weeks, even Vinnie and Bullo looked at each other and shared a smile.

The radio worked just the way Antonio predicted. Business was better than ever. Saturday nights when the Grand Ole Opry played, table and chairs were moved aside to allow for a dance floor. Vinnie and Sam swung with the best of them while Antonio watched, occasionally glancing fondly at the photograph of his beloved Angeline that hung over his favorite booth.

* * * * * *

Agnes Burns Wieck was bedridden for almost two

months after the assault on the Women's Auxiliary and her hallway meeting with Governor Horner. She suffered from exhaustion with severe headaches and laryngitis that was so bad she had to cancel several speaking engagements.

Lena went to visit her in Spillertown twice during her illness. Then in late summer, after Agnes had been back on the speaking circuit for a few weeks, she surprised Lena with a telephone call. At the urging of the American Civil Liberties Union, UMW President John L. Lewis had agreed to meet with Progressive representatives as long as the meeting would not be open to the public or media. Agnes wanted Lena to attend as a representative of Christian County.

"I saw John L. Lewis speak in Taylorville in about 1914 when he was just starting to become a union organizer," Lena told the Wieck's a few days later as Ed drove to the meeting. "At that time he spoke very highly of Mother Jones, but years later the two became bitter enemies. I don't know what he's like now."

"Well, now he's sort of squat and wears his hair long," Ed said, "and he talks without moving his mouth. He walks up and down the floor and pours forth a torrent of eloquence. People go to see him and come away as if they'd had a dose of hop. He never had that effect on me, but he does on a lot of people. Add a habit of arrogance, a tendency to sarcasm, a voice that rises to thunder and drops to a whisper, a practiced theatricality, and, when he's pleased, a practiced courtesy and deference."

Ed's description of John L. Lewis seemed comical, but Lena had to suppress a laugh when later that day she actually met the man. He did indeed talk without moving his lips. Perhaps it was the cigar clenched firmly between his teeth, but Lena imagined he would have made a wonderful ventriloquist.

Rabbi Ferdinand M. Isserman, chairman of the American Civil Liberties Union, presided as mediator. PMA President Claude Percy joined Agnes and Lena at the table across from Lewis, UMW President for Illinois John Walker, and a lawyer named Douglas Eubanks. Of the three men, it was the obese Eubanks who made Lena uncomfortable. The lawyer was well-known throughout downstate Illinois as an attorney for the Shelton gang. He had successfully defended the Sheltons for the murder of Caesar Cagle in 1922, and then for the attempted Kincaid Bank robbery later that year.

After the Rabbi explained the reason for the meeting, he asked the United Mine Workers to begin. Lewis stood and, pacing like a caged lion, preached for nearly two hours explaining his case as to why the actions of the Progressives were illegal and must be dealt with severely. He finished his oration with a comparison.

"Because the Progressives are trying to steal my union's contract with the coal companies," Lewis claimed, "they have no right to picket or hold meetings. They have left their father's home and now there is no mercy for them. If the thirteen original colonies would have been defeated and King George triumphed, history would tell us that our revolutionary forefathers were traitors who had to be smashed. Possibly you and I would believe that story. If the Progressive Union would have been successful, they would have been the heroes of tomorrow. But they have failed in their plans and therefore must pay the consequences."

Lewis sat down and received a satisfied nod from Walker and Eubanks.

Now Agnes Burns Wieck rose to her full five feet and began her barrage. "First of all, Mr. Lewis, it is not *your* union contract—it is the miners' contract. You are in power only because the workers put you there, and now the colliers in Illinois don't want you there anymore. They voted you out. But you, Mr. Lewis, stole the ballots and assumed dictatorial power. You are the one responsible for the violence and the plight of our people. We recently had a miner's wife dying beside her newborn baby in the strike-torn village of Kincaid. As she lay on her lingering deathbed from lack of food, her last words cursed you, John L. Lewis."

Lewis leapt back to his feet, fists clenched and started around the table toward Wieck. "I won't stand for this!"

Rabbi Isserman stood and stepped in front of him. "Sit down, John."

"That is a total lie!" Lewis shouted. "There are no Progressives anywhere in Illinois dying from starvation. That is completely absurd!"

"Let the Illinois miners have a fair and honest election under the supervision of the ACLU," Agnes said.

"I'll remind you, Mrs. Wieck, that the United Mine Workers are a national organization," Lewis said. "If we are to have a vote, it must include workers everywhere, and I think you know what that means."

"You bet I do," Agnes said, her jaw set. "Since you're in cahoots with the coal companies in the other states, it means you'll have those workers fired if they don't vote for you."

"Your own people are getting sick and tired of your socialist ideas, Mrs. Wieck!" Lewis shouted back at her, then settled into a quieter voice. "Maybe it's time for your Progressives to understand that without your damned reds running things, they could get a much better deal."

* * * * * * *

"We need to do something about that woman," Douglas Eubanks said later that evening. He, his brother Stephen Eubanks, and mine boss Bill Stork were lounging in their hotel suite in front of a table full of food, cigars and alcohol.

"I have some acquaintances who could waste the bitch," Stephen said. "Or they could just make her disappear from the face of the earth."

"That would only make her a martyr," Bill Stork said. "Her supporters are already calling her another Mother Jones. Besides, John L. has been against using violence ever since those scab killings down in Herrin, Illinois, back in twenty-two. He and the UMW took a pretty big hit for that little indiscretion."

"I agree," Douglas said. "We need to discredit her. What Progressives do we have on our payroll?"

"Huh!" Stephen laughed. "What Progressives we don't have, we can buy for the right price. How about that pretty Eng lady? She would look real good in a new car and wardrobe."

"Not likely," Stork said. "Her husband would have survived the crash in twenty-nine if he hadn't spent so much helping the coal miners. They are both do-gooder communists from way back. No, we need to use some of the higher-up Progressives who have already taken money."

"It shouldn't be that difficult," Stephen said. "The southern Illinois miners are the more radical, socialist types. With all that fascist shit happening in Europe right now, it won't be hard to play up the communist angle to get rid of people like Wieck."

"Commies are anarchists who like to use terrorism to get what they want," Stork said. "The public won't like the Progressives much if shit starts getting blown up."

"Violence is your department, Stephen," Douglas said. "Bill, you work the influence angle and get things stirred up against radicals like Wieck. Now, pour me another shot of that good brandy."

* * * * * * *

"They are trying to push Agnes out of the Women's Auxiliary." Lena was so angry tears filled her eyes. It was only a month since the confrontation with Lewis, but the ideological civil war within the PMA was already in full swing. "They just can't do that. Agnes founded the auxiliary."

"It's not just her, Lena," Harley said. "The Progressives are not going to be able to gain national sympathy if they are run by communists, socialists and anarchists. They're also pushing aside men like Jack Battuello and Gerry Allard. They're all just too radical."

"I don't think they're too radical."

"Well, look at this, Lena. At the Women's Auxiliary Convention last year, Agnes said the following." Harley put his reading glasses low on his nose and quoted from a magazine. "'I was a good teacher. I didn't know any better. I taught my students the Pledge of Allegiance to the Flag of the United States...And then one morning I read in the paper of the battle at Ludlow where women and children were shot by soldiers and burned to death. Liberty and justice for all! Think of it! I vowed I would never again teach children to say the Pledge of Allegiance to the flag.'"

Harley lowered the magazine. "That is not only radical, it is also dead wrong."

"How is it wrong, Harley?"

"The Pledge of Allegiance is not a contract, Lena. It is an ideal that no one can deny is a good one. We need to teach our children that the Pledge says very clearly 'for which it stands,' meaning the flag only stands 'for liberty and justice for all.' It is still up to us to make that ideal come true. Until a better system comes along, it is the responsibility of Americans to elect representatives who will fight to preserve that liberty."

"I don't think Agnes was complaining about the ideals in the Pledge," Lena argued. "She was saying that she doesn't want our children indoctrinated to where they will blindly follow the government. She wants to teach them to hate militarism and war." Pacifism + anti militarism

"Then she doesn't understand that having a military doesn't mean you have to use it. It is naïve to believe there isn't evil in the world. Not being able to defend yourself guarantees that you will be attacked. I do agree with her, though, that we should always fight for the civil rights of our people. I would be fine with Agnes teaching our children about what happened at Ludlow and how, in that situation, there were people in our government who abused their power. But to not teach our children about the freedoms we as a nation are trying to achieve—what so many men and women have gave their lives to create—freedoms such as no other nation in the history of our planet has ever come close to achieving. No, my dear. That is not educating."

Lena sat quietly for a few moments. "I still think radicals have a lot of good ideas. Maybe the world just isn't ready yet and what Agnes told me was right." Lena pulled the end of her apron up and wiped tears from her face. "Sometimes leaders just get too far ahead of their army."

* * * * * * *

Horatio Sebuck was born to be a Navy man like his father before him. Unfortunately, his grandfather had rushed him when young Horatio was but three years old by throwing his grandson into the lake and expecting him to swim, as had all his grandchildren previously. While that experience could have been the death of him, Horatio would always believe it was the moment he actually came alive. At least, it was the first and oldest memory he had, pulling himself along the bottom of the lake by the rocks and weeds that sometimes grow ten feet beneath the surface. Whether someone saved him or he somehow floated to the surface, Horatio didn't remember. He did remember though, to avoid deep waters, thus bringing about the first generation of foot soldier in an otherwise seafaring family. He also never overcame a stuttering problem that more often resembled a drowning man than it did a speech impediment. But the one naval trait Horatio Sebuck never did overcome was the belief that women could never be anything besides housewives or those wanton ladies who stood on port docks waiting for ships to arrive.

"Why can't you answer?' Sebuck asked, placing his hand on the flat of the woman's stomach. When she didn't push him away, he added. "What would it t-t-take—"

He had cornered Kieran Phelan's wife in the dark alleyway as she returned from the outhouse. One of his favorite parts of enforcing the curfew law was harassing people who thought a trip to the outhouse was legal. Of course, it *was* legal, but it still provided opportunities to snatch up citizens and either drop them off in the country or take advantage of young beauties such as the one standing before him. The woman's husband was at that moment passed out drunk on the front porch.

"If I told you," Felina interrupted, in almost a breathy whisper, "you wouldn't be able to handle me."

"Hell, baby," Sebuck said. "There ain't nothing I ain't seen nor done."

"Would you cut a man's throat for me?"

"Yes," Sebuck said, still smiling. He had met several

street women who talked like this.

"Would you watch as I licked blood from his mouth?" she added.

Sebuck struggled to hold his facial muscles in the shape of a smile. His mind told him to run, but the beautiful woman reached up, pulled his face down to her and licked him from his neck to his ear. He found himself gasping and almost shouting, "Y-y-yes, yes!"

"Would you be able to wait until his body went cold and his manhood limp inside me?" Felina expertly undid the Lieutenant's britches and let them fall around his knees. "And then would you remain bone-ified if I was still breathing hard and unsatisfied?"

Felina's laugh was shrill as she watched the fat Lieutenant struggle to pull his pants up as he ran away from her. She wondered how he would fix his fly since she had popped the buttons off when she ripped his trousers open.

She had always loved power—at least one kind of power. The power that decided life and death. Nothing excited her more. Gangster movies were popular and her husband loved going to them. Felina though thought they were too fake. People got shot but the movies never showed blood or the gray matter of the brains splashed like vomit all over the person's clothes and the wall. Movies were just never able to capture the true excitement of watching a person's death shutter or the rattle of their final breath as life drained from their body. Felina often thought she would make a good director for a film. She could show them what death really looked like, especially if the movies ever became colorized instead of that dull black and white stuff.

When she came back around to the front of her house, she was dismayed to see her parents standing over and looking down at their passed-out-drunk son-in-law. Kieran had somehow managed to roll out of his chair and fall belly-down onto the porch. Big, black ants crawled across his face.

"What do you two want?" Felina said coldly.

"Well, that's a fine how-ya-do for your mother!" Myrna Harrison said. "You always did think your shit don't stink."

Joe Harrison stepped between the two and held his hands up, palms out. "It was my idea to stop by," he said. "I was asked to talk to your husband, but that's obviously not going to happen tonight."

"Why are you still with this scum, anyway?" Myrna asked.

"I would have run off with Charlie Birger if the little Jew bastard hadn't gone and got hisself hung." Felina lifted her foot and crushed an ant crawling across her husband's forehead, then turned to her father. "Now, what the hell do you want with him?"

"I came to tell Kieran that he's gonna get killed, and maybe you, too, if he doesn't stop helping the coal company recruit scabs."

"What do you care?" Felina said, nostril's flaring. "You haven't done nothin' for us since we got married. We want to open a tavern. Why don't you give us money? That's what other parents do."

"Because you and this deadbeat would go spend it on booze and gambling," Myrna said. "Take me home, Joe. I'm getting such a headache."

She walked toward the car, but her husband continued to stand, looking at Felina.

"What the hell are you looking at?" Felina asked, then added, "Daddy?"

"The only reason I can even look at you," Joe said, "is because I'm not your father. If you want to know who your father is, you'll have to ask your mother."

The man named Joe Harrison turned and walked away from Felina, vowing to never see her again.

13

Bullo knew that the election of three United Mine Workers to the Kincaid Village Board would cause a lot of friction. When it was announced there would be a parade that evening to celebrate the victories, he went out to the toolshed to clean and load his handgun. After thirty minutes, he was satisfied the weapon was in good working order, so he tucked the pistol behind his back and beneath his belt, then let his shirt hang out over it. When he entered the house, Mary Kate was in the kitchen cleaning and the boys were shooting marbles in their bedroom.

"Honey," he said to Mary Kate, then took a deep breath. "I'm going to go over to the Brass Rail and have a couple of beers with the boys. I won't be too late."

"Okay, darlin'," Mary Kate said over her shoulder. "Have a good time."

Bullo felt a little guilty not telling his wife about the parade, but he rationalized that he had told her the truth. He did indeed intend to have a beer at the Brass Rail in Kincaid. His ability to share troubles with his wife had improved tremendously since his bad behavior at the restaurant that night. Still, discussing problems in the workplace was one thing, but putting his wife's life in danger was another matter. Besides, he didn't really think things would get out of hand. The Progressives had experienced worse losses than a small town election. Nevertheless, this would be the first time he would be carrying a weapon since his mother's death. He hesitated at the door. The gun felt uncomfortable pressing against the small of his back, and he considered returning it to the gun case. The moment of indecision passed.

He walked out of the house just as Vinnie was leaving his own home next door. The two brothers both hesitated at the same time and looked at each other. For some reason, it crossed Bullo's mind that the eye contact between them was probably similar to the look that occurred between brothers across Union and Confederate lines during the American Civil War. The elder brother tried to lighten the tense moment with a slight nod of the head, but Vinnie's only response was an angry glare. The two turned away from each other, walked down their respective porch steps, across their lawns, got in their automobiles, slammed their car doors, started their engines and drove off in the same direction toward the village of Kincaid. Flo Ziegfield could not have synchronized the brother's movements any better.

When they reached a country road, Vinnie turned left toward the village of Langleyville, which was a mostly Italian-Progressive community. Undoubtedly, he intended to join up with a group of his friends there and they would then caravan to Kincaid. A confrontation between the rival unions seemed increasingly inevitable. As Bullo turned onto the hard road toward Kincaid, he thought about the hateful look Vinnie had given him. He was definitely the Vinnie of old—a defiant rebel ready to take on the world with a scowl on his face, hair long and unruly, with even his shirttail hanging loose around his—

Bullo almost stopped his vehicle in the middle of the road. Yet, he didn't know why the sudden revelation was a surprise to him. Vinnie was often well-armed when he went places. In fact, so was Sam, and it wasn't uncommon for the couple to park their car along a creek bed or river bottom and take target practice. Still, in just a matter of a few hours the two brothers might be pointing deadly weapons at each other—an unsettling thought to Bullo. That thought was made even worse by the realization he was certainly more disturbed by the thought than Vinnie. Bullo almost turned the car onto the next country road so he could circle back home. But he didn't.

* * * * * * *

Each seat at Scruby's Tavern in Langleyville held a miner who was a veteran from the rapidly disappearing hand-loading days. They were hardened men. Every one of them had survived countless near-death experiences in the mines, their lives often being saved by one or more of the men sitting in the smoke-filled room. Vinnie would have been happy to have any one of them beside him in a foxhole. In fact, he was sitting at a booth across from brothers Lambert and Forrest Hardin. They were the miners he and his father had been trapped in a mine with back in '22.

It was Vinnie's wife who had received most of the credit for that rescue. Sam had squeezed herself through a dark, narrow hole for thirty feet and then stumbled blindly through various passages searching for the trapped miners. Bullo, though, was the one who found a way to keep the cutting machine cool so it could dig faster into an adjacent chamber. When he and his rescue team made it through they found Sam. She saved them precious moments by directing them to the areas in the mine she had not already searched. They found the four men walled up in a chamber where deadly gases were just about to suffocate them.

Vinnie was not one to socialize much, and neither were

the Hardin brothers. Lambert and Forrest sat solemnly, contemplating their coffee mugs and cigarettes. Vinnie sat likewise, holding a cigarette in one hand and his other wrapped around an untouched shot glass of whiskey. Most of the other men in the room talked loudly, passing jugs full of homebrew and thumping their chests in anticipation of the conflict to come.

Vinnie had taken part in two gun battles during the West Virginia coal mine wars, and he was reluctant to be in another. Those had only been long-range fights with rifles, the shooters on both sides more intent on scaring than killing. He had been witness to the gunfight at Matewan that left nine men dead, and was also present a year later at the assassination of the hero of that gunfight, Sid Hatfield. In both instances, the devastation caused by the victims' gunshot wounds was a memory he would never forget.

That evening he had seen Bullo walk into his toolshed carrying his handgun. Vinnie knew his brother was giving it a long overdue cleaning. Sam was meticulous about keeping guns in good working order, a habit the mountain girl had developed from using hunting rifles that had been assembled before the Civil War. She was never afraid to chastise her brother-in-law for neglecting his weapons and even went so far as to pull one out of Bullo's gun rack on occasions and sit at the kitchen table cleaning and checking the mechanisms. Mary Kate usually cringed when her sister-in-law did this. She didn't care much for guns, but had learned to tolerate them since the rest of the Vacca's viewed them as little more than common household utensils.

Thinking of this made Vinnie depressed. He liked Mary Kate, Willie and Tony, and hated the idea of facing off with Bullo if a conflict developed. He felt something was wrong with him because he had never in his life really understood the word *love*. Loyalty, responsibility, honor—those were words he understood.

As he rolled the shot glass around between his fingers, he tried to remember if he had ever told anyone he loved them. Maybe he had said it during his wedding vows. He couldn't remember, though, because the Justice of the Peace had been hurrying through the service so he could get to court, and Vinnie had been trying to remember if he had tied the mule that brought him and Sam into town securely to the hitching post.

Vinnie looked across the table at the faces of the Hardin brothers. Those two had made the decision to wall themselves up in that chamber with Vinnie and his father and take the chance on a slow and ghastly death. They had done it for one reason—to give young Vinnie a chance to live. The brothers were both retired now and had forgone their retirement pensions with the United Mine Workers because Vinnie had asked them too. Regardless of what word described Vinnie's feelings toward his family, he felt the cause of the Progressives was where his loyalty must lie. If the new union was victorious over the UMW and the coal companies, it would help tens of thousands of colliers all across the country.

"Bullo's a fool to stay with the United Mine Workers," Vinnie muttered.

"Yes, that's true," Forrest said without looking up from his cup of coffee and cigarette, "but he sure is a good man with a cutting machine."

* * * * * * *

When Peabody Coal Company superintendent Bill Stork called Dr. RJ Hiler and ordered him and Nurse

Giovanna to attend the UMW parade in Kincaid, the doctor lied and told Stork he could go but his nurse was out of town. Hiler was not about to allow Giovanna to be put into a dangerous situation. The parade was bound to cause a fistfight at the least and a gun battle at the worst. He was still haunted by the death of his beloved wife Carmela at the 1914 Ludlow, Colorado, massacre. Besides that, Nurse Giovanna was still in mourning over the death of her spouse, who had been one of the fifty-four miners killed in last Christmas Eve's Moweaqua Coal Mine disaster.

With a variety of possible catastrophic scenarios on his mind, Hiler loaded his car with every kind of medical supply and equipment he anticipated needing. As he drove the seven miles from Taylorville to Kincaid, he wondered why the coal company wasn't having the National Guard monitor the celebration. Or were they hoping the Progressives would instigate a confrontation?

That possibility seemed even more probable when he neared Kincaid and passed several National Guard trucks heading away from the village. The doctor parked his automobile in front of the Sears and Roebuck mail order catalogue building. He followed a small group of women and elderly men through the establishment, up the stairs, and into a prime viewing point on the roof.

He had no sooner found a comfortable place to stand than he heard the squeal of a police car siren coming from the south. The county sheriff's car led the way, followed by the grand marshal of the parade, a ninety-five year old miner named Jesse Hubbard riding in a pit car pulled by a mule. Behind him came a bandwagon with four high school students in uniforms, three local housewives playing flutes, and one out-of-breath elderly gentleman trying to a keep up on a rusty trombone. Hiler speculated that in the mostly Italian-Progressive community there was probably a shortage of students with UMW and coal company parents—which made him wonder how in the world three UMW men had gotten elected to the Kincaid Village Board.

Next in line were the three board members sitting in wooden chairs, each carried by burly coal miners whose sleeves were rolled up to their shoulders to show off powerful biceps and forearms. Behind them came the United Mine Workers banner, followed by about a hundred mostly stumbling-drunk colliers. Many of them carried torches, and, across their shoulders, pickaxes and shovels, reminding Hiler of the mob in the recently-released movie *Frankenstein*, who chased after the monster near the end of the film. Many of the miners shouted profane cheers, while a small group of others tried to rally the more sober men into a chorus of "Union Forever."

Then the moment arrived that everyone feared. From his vantage point on the roof, Doc Hiler saw the much anticipated Progressive contingency emerge from the darkness of the trees shadowing the nearby high school lawn. They fanned out quickly, making their numbers seem greater than they actually were. Hiler estimated there to be less than fifty, but UMW witnesses would later tell the grand jury there were over two hundred. Though they were not in the street and showed no signs of wanting to stop the festivity, the men behind the UMW banner halted immediately and stared menacingly at the Progressives.

Then all hell broke loose.

* * * * * * *

RJ Hiler was the last witness called to testify before the jury that was considering first degree charges against two Progressive miners for the murder of newly-elected village board member Frank Angenendt. By the time Hiler took the stand, no one really cared what the good doctor had to say. Everyone knew no guilty verdict was going to be returned because at least half the members on the jury were allies of the Progressive Mine Workers. Vinnie Vacca, though, wanted to hear the doctor's version of what happened that night. As the testimony began, Vinnie took a seat next to Cuthbert Hardin in the front row of the courtroom.

The judge presiding over the proceedings was the Honorable Rupert T. Harding. Old Judge Harding had always run a loose court. Truth be known, he enjoyed the drama of trial watchers being incited to such a state of emotion they would shout out or even attack the witness stand. Harding sported a fine handlebar mustache that he liked to stroke—and sometimes even wax—during court proceedings.

His bailiff for the past twenty years was a big, burly man named Wilber Noffke. Though having the mind of a child, Wilber had a punch that could bring down an ox, a feat he had once achieved as a teenager at a county fair when a docile steer called Luke made the mistake of strolling up behind Wilber and licking the powerful young man's buttocks. When Judge Harding heard about the deed, he had immediately recruited the normally passive youngster to oversee his courtroom. It took His Honor several months to convince his new bailiff that knocking an unruly court spectator in the head was lawful and, in fact, less objectionable than laying out an impolite oxen.

Now, though, the temperament of the audience in the courtroom the past several days had taken a toll on Wilber's nerves. He didn't really understand why people who had always been friends and neighbors were wanting to fight each other. The judge had on several occasions tried to explain something about rival unions, but Wilber couldn't seem to wrap his mind around the concept that any man would pick an organization of workers over his own kin.

Now Wilber didn't know which side of the courtroom to stand on. The seating in the chamber reminded him of a wedding in that the UMW members all sat on the bride's side and the Progressives on the groom's side.

When Doc Hiler took the witness stand, Wilber's hands shook a little as he held the Bible for the doctor to be sworn in. Surprisingly, he had not yet needed to cold-cock anyone in the gallery during the proceedings. Dwight Damdam would have been the first, had he not tripped during his attempt to flee the witness stand. Damdam was being asked some embarrassing questions concerning his relationship with a barmaid at the Brass Rail when he saw his wife enter the courtroom. He was making a mad dash toward the jury room door when he fell face down on a step and knocked out his two front teeth. To add insult to injury, Judge Harding ordered him to finish answering the questions. Most felt his hard fall might account for his lost eye teeth, but the cauliflower ears he sported for the next week were generally attributed to a more domestic issue.

"Where were you when the UMW parade began?" Defense attorney Leal Reese asked Doc Hiler.

"I was watching from on top of the Sears and Roebuck catalogue building."

"Describe to us what you saw."

"When the UMW group came past me, Kieran Phelan was in the lead. I heard him shout at the men to get ready for some action. It wasn't sixty seconds later the Progressive boys stepped out of the shadows and from behind trees."

"How many were there, Doctor?"

"No more than fifty, I'd say."

"Did any of the Progressives display a weapon of any

kind?"

"I saw none until they were fired upon."

Judge Harding let the murmurs of discontent from the UMW side of the courtroom subside. He wiped his big, handle-bar moustache with the back of his hand and leaned forward. "Continue, Mr. Reese."

"How far were the Progressives from the UMW men?" Reese asked.

"They were spread out, but I'd say the nearest ones were about fifty yards away."

"What happened next, Doctor?"

"I heard a single gunshot, and when I looked back, I saw Kieran Phelan fall flat on his stomach. He held a smoking gun in one hand. He crawled underneath a near-by truck, where he lay cradling his head with his arms until the shooting stopped. After that, so many things happened so fast I—"

"Are you going to let that old sawbones talk about you like that?" Felina shouted at her husband.

The entire courtroom hushed as everyone turned toward the couple sitting in the third row. Kieran Phelan's face was red as he glanced at his wife, then at Wilber Noffke's formidable bare forearms. Phelan put a hand on the back of the seat in front of him and pulled himself into a half-standing position.

"That's," Phelan began in a voice much too low and shrill to sound angry, "that's a, a damned lie."

The Progressive side of the courtroom erupted in loud and long laughter. Phelan covered his ears and glared at the Progressives. When he caught sight of Vinnie Vacca, he balled his fists and launched himself across the room. Like the poor oxen at the county fair twenty years before, Kieran Phelan never saw anything except a fist as large as a hambone, followed by a bright light and then darkness.

The room grew instantly silent again. Felina Phelan jumped from her seat and stormed from the courtroom, pushing aside spectators standing in front of the doorway. All eyes turned expectantly to Judge Harding, who calmly rose from behind his bench, walked around and looked down at Phelan.

"Kieran Phelan," the judge said, holding his gavel over the unconscious man's head, "I fine you twenty-five dollars for sleeping in my courtroom. Bailiff, remove this man."

Even the UMW men cheered as Wilber hefted Phelan completely off the ground by the back of his suspenders and, without any visible strain, carried him to the rear of the courtroom and out the double doors. When the bailiff returned a moment later, men on both sides of the aisle gave the gentle giant pats on the back.

"Read back the last words the doctor said before being so rudely interrupted," the judge said to the court reporter, and the gallery hushed immediately.

"After that, so many things happened so fast I—" the reporter said.

"Go on, Doctor." The judge nodded toward him.

"Well, I was about to say that from my vantage point, I saw several things happen at once. The nearest Progressives pulled guns and began firing back. Men on both sides ran for cover, even as they reached for their weapons. I'd say that most of the seven men who were shot were hit in those first sixty seconds."

"How long did the shooting last, Doctor?" Reese asked.

"No more than three minutes, I'd think. I'd say fifty or sixty shots were fired."

"And what brought an end to the shooting?"

Doc Hiler looked toward the Progressive side at Vinnie Vacca and then at Bullo Vacca sitting on the UMW side.

"Forrest Hardin was lying in the middle of the street,

bleeding badly. When the shooting slowed a little, Vinnie Vacca walked out from behind a tree, dropped his gun, and walked toward Hardin. There were three or four shots taken at him, but they all missed. Then Bullo Vacca rose from behind a car and walked toward his brother. The Vacca boys both reached Hardin at the same time and knelt beside him. There were no more shots fired after that, and I rushed down from the building to begin treating the wounded."

"Tell us about that, Doctor."

"All seven men were brought to the sidewalk. I instructed some of the wives to treat the least serious with pressure to the wounds. Forrest Hardin and Frank Angenendt were in the worst shape. I treated them the best I could, and when the first ambulance arrived, rode to the hospital with them." Doctor Hiler paused and looked at Cuthbert Hardin sitting next to Vinnie. "Hardin died two days later, and we lost Angenendt eight days after that."

"And did you see who shot Angenendt?"

"No, sir," the doctor said firmly. "And with all the gunfire going on in those brief moments, I'm not sure anyone except maybe the shooter would know who got him."

14

Vinnie hated himself. He knew there was no one except himself to blame for Forrest Hardin's death. The brothers had only joined the Progressives because Vinnie asked them to. Though they were retired, Cuthbert and Forrest had given up their standing with the UMW and had endured criticism from their friends as well as their own wives. Now Forrest had made the ultimate sacrifice.

The fact that Bullo had bravely followed his brother to Hardin's side made the situation even more confusing. Why didn't Bullo just act like the low-life scab he was? Why did he keep looking at him with that stupid reassuring smile every time they were together? If not for his father and the memory of his sainted mother, Vinnie would sell out and take Sam and Sid back to West Virginia.

As he dwelled on this most recent loss, Vinnie became more and more withdrawn. He wanted to just take his gun and move up into the mountains—alone. So many people had lost their lives in a futile effort to make things better for working men everywhere. In his guilt-ridden mind, he found a way to blame his own poor performances for every one of the deaths. Forrest Hardin was only the most recent. Vinnie convinced himself that if he hadn't been so self-absorbed on his wedding day back in '21, he might have realized the three men standing on the steps of the courthouse were there to assassinate Sid Hatfield and Ed Chambers.

Then there was his own mother and James Hartman, who had both been killed while Vinnie was asleep with a fever. A fever that he could have avoided if he hadn't been so careless handling the animals he shot. Even the loss of Chuck Davin's leg was because the big miner was babying Vinnie by escorting him to his automobile.

The fact that no charges were brought against anyone for any of these crimes irked Vinnie to the point he thought he might be going insane. In the weeks after the trial, he took his frustration out on everyone, including Sam. Then one day little Sid left the pasture gate open, and the pony and two heifers spent the night foundering themselves in the grain bin. The next morning, Vinnie used a belt to give his son a harder butt-licking than he intended. The event would have probably gone unnoticed, except Sid had to see Doc Hiler the next day for a toe that had become infected a few days after his pony stepped on it. After supper that night, RJ came knocking on the door.

"Vinnie, how have you been feeling?" RJ asked when Sam left the room to make coffee for their guest.

"I haven't had a fever in weeks," Vinnie said.

"That's good." The doctor's practiced eyes studied Vinnie as if trying to detect symptoms of a hidden malady.

Vinnie squirmed a little and looked toward the fireplace.

"By the way," the doctor said, "let little Sid's toenail come off on its own. No need to give the boy extra pain by pulling it off prematurely."

Vinnie nodded.

"That boy can sure handle pain though, can't he?" RJ said.

Vinnie nodded.

"Why those welts on his butt didn't even seem to faze him," RJ said. "No, sir, I wouldn't worry too much about that toe, but you might want to put a little ointment on his backside a couple of times a day."

Vinnie lowered his head and nodded before wiping his eyes with the back of a hand.

Doc Hiler remained quiet for several minutes.

"You know," RJ finally said, "I had some jerk venison yesterday that our boys brought up from down Missouri way. It was so full of buckshot I damned near chipped a tooth. I think you need to get back down there for a few days and show those youngsters how to get a clean kill."

Vinnie realized the doctor was prescribing a vacation. *Why can't people just say things right out?* Vinnie thought as he watched Sam bring the doctor a cup of steaming coffee. *Don't they understand that I get even more upset when they try to manipulate me? Doc is doing it just like Harley Eng did a few weeks ago, and they both did it just like . . . just like . . . Ma always did.*

The next morning, Vinnie told Sam he was going to join other Progressives in Missouri, hunting and fishing to help supply the picketers. By noon, as he was motoring over the rolling green hills of eastern Missouri, he felt an almost instant relaxation of the muscles in his back and shoulders. He began whistling, and when he found a hunting area he was familiar with, he drove down a long, almost indistinguishable pathway to a secluded glen where a little brook gurgled quietly into a small pond. Quickly but methodically he set up a pup tent and organized his camping equipment. At last satisfied that everything was in order, he took out his miner's lunch bucket from behind the back seat of the car. That morning when Little Sid had found out his father was going hunting, he asked if he could pack his dad's lunch. Vinnie smiled when he opened the bucket and found a large chunk of ham, a slice of cheese, a boiled egg, a big golden apple and a black licorice stick—Sid's favorite school lunch.

After eating, he locked up most of his guns and other valuables in the trunk of the car and walked south. Three miles later, he strolled quietly up to an old wooden line shack the Progressive boys had been using as a base camp since the previous fall. Four of the older teenagers sat on milk cans around a tree stump playing cards, while two younger boys stood nearby playing a stretch version of mumbley-peg with pocket knives. Several coon and bird dogs slept soundly in the shade of the cabin. For a moment, Vinnie considered firing a shot in the air, but then decided it might set a bad example. Instead, he followed standard frontiersman procedure and hailed the camp that he was coming in. The boys whooped with delight when they saw their mentor and friend.

"Vinnie Vacca!" yelled Miles Perkins, the tallest and oldest of the boys.

"Well, I'll be danged," said Johnny James. "Ol' Dan'l Boone is back."

The poker players jumped to their feet and ran over to shake hands—though not so excited that they forgot to palm their cards as they greeted him. One of the boys playing stretch flicked his knife to the ground, accidently sticking it on the side of his friend's boot—a feat that went unnoticed during the excitement.

"Vinnie, Vinnie, Vinnie!" A tall, hefty woman with gray hair tied in an unorganized bun ran out of the cabin. "Where's my little girl Sam? Didn't your bride come with ya?"

"No, Lottie," Vinnie said as the big woman gave him a tight bear hug. "She had to stay home and help Mary Kate with the canning."

"Well, what you doing in these parts, Vinnie?" Miles asked.

"Doc Hiler said you boys been feeding our Progressives too much buck shot," Vinnie said truthfully. Then, feeling clever, he added, "He's getting tired of treating colliers for stomach ailments."

"Oh, my God, Lester," Miles said. "I told you not to use that shotgun on that buck. Now you've gone and poisoned our union men."

"Well, now, Vinnie," Lester stammered. He took his Coke-bottle-thick glasses off and cleaned them with the end of his dirty shirt. "You see, Vinnie, this is the way it was. I was a huntin' one day for pheasant with my shotgun, and this here deer just jumped right out of them there thickets. My rifle was back at the camp because Lottie had fixed flapjacks for breakfast and—"

"Oh, for goodness' sake!" Lottie shouted. "Just get straight to the point, Lester. We don't need to hear what you had for breakfast."

"Well, I was fixin' to get to the point, Lottie, don't ya see?" Lester's face turned red and he crossed his arms.

"Oh, don't feel bad, Lester," Miles said. "Lottie probably wouldn't have got along very well with Jesus either. Christ would've started telling one of them long parallels about some old man and his two sons, and she'd have screamed at Him to hush up and get to the point."

Vinnie laughed and gave Lester a friendly slap on the back. He recalled that the boy was color blind, as well as near-sighted. "That's okay, Les. We'll put you in charge of rodent hunting. I'll show you how to bark squirrels to save the meat."

The remainder of the afternoon was spent drinking, eating Lottie's good venison stew, and then sitting around the campfire telling tall tales and boldfaced lies. About an hour before sunset, Vinnie announced he was going to return to his camp. No one questioned his solitude. When he and Sam hunted with them before Vinnie's illness, the married couple had always set up camp away from the single men. Before leaving, though, he did promise to join the boys the next morning.

"I'll walk a ways with you, Vinnie," Miles said. "So's I can show you a few traps you can check tomorrow on your way in."

Vinnie predicted that Miles had something he wanted to discuss in private. The lanky youngster stopped after half a mile, sat on the mossy trunk of a fallen tree, and, unlike his friend Lester, got right to the point.

"Vinnie, did you come down here looking for George Lyman and Archie Norton?"

"Why would you say that?" Vinnie was taken somewhat aback by mention of the men who had shot off Chuck Davin's leg.

"A lawman named Schrader has been seen in these parts lately," Miles said. "Rumor is that Lyman and Norton are running with the Shelton gang and maybe using some of the caves down this way to hide in."

Vinnie took a few moments to think about this possibility. There were many hidden caves in Missouri, and people were constantly discovering new entrances behind rocks or stands of bushes. He had seen a few of the caverns and remembered that some of them had chambers large enough that locals sometimes held hoedowns in them.

"Maybe Lyman and Norton are with the Sheltons, but I doubt they'd be hiding in caves," Vinnie said. "Those Sheltons are bold. They live right out in the open and enjoy being seen. No, sir, I'd 'spect those gangsters won't be venturing further south than St. Louis."

"I'd 'spect you're right, Vinnie, but someone oughta tell that police officer. Those law boys of his has been scaring off the bigger game, and sometimes they get bored and just shoot 'em for sport. I sure do hate to see critters kilt and not used for eatin'."

For the next two weeks, Vinnie worked with the hunting party shooting and trapping game while the two younger boys set trotlines and noodled for catfish. Skinning the animals and cleaning fish was Lottie's job, although all the boys helped her when she got behind. Every few days, an ice truck would arrive to load and carry the valuable food to Progressives who were picketing throughout Illinois.

Vinnie always took time to talk to the driver about the latest on the strike and to read the days-old newspapers he brought. Almost every visit brought news of more bombings, shootings and fistfights. It had gotten so bad, several businesses throughout the mining communities in Illinois were closing their doors for a time rather than have their establishments destroyed during fights between the Progressives and the UMW and coal company thugs.

Then one morning during his third week, Vinnie got word that Archie Norton had been seen in Belleville, Illinois. The ice truck driver told him three members of the Shelton gang were being held in the county jail on vagrancy charges. Blackie Armes, William Bad-Eye Smith, and a young hothead named James Hickey were scheduled to appear before the Justice of the Peace that afternoon. Because they were all three suspects in various bank robberies, the hearing was drawing quite a lot of attention.

Vinnie didn't hesitate. Two hours later, he was running up the St. Clair County Courthouse steps. He stepped into the courtroom just as the hearing for the three men began. Since all the seats were filled, he stood with several reporters along the back wall and quickly scanned the faces, anxiously looking for Archie Norton. Then, disappointed and feeling a bit of a fool that his impulsive trip was in vain, he turned his attention to the proceedings.

The first witness was Officer Joe Schrader. Vinnie had read a lot about Schrader lately. The lawman was fast becoming a legend in the law enforcement field. He was credited with more arrests in the St. Louis area than any other policeman. When the St. Clair County Banker's Association paid him an exorbitant amount to moonlight for them as a private detective, Schrader displayed an aptitude for anticipating when and where robberies would take place. He claimed his personal acquaintance with the Shelton brothers gave him insight into their minds, but most suspected that he had an informant within the gang.

"These here boys are a plight on our society!" Schrader told the justice in a booming voice.

The three men being accused all glared at the lawman, but the one who had been introduced as James Hickey suddenly gripped the end of the table in front of him with both hands. His fingers turned white and his face a bloody red.

"Running them out of the county is too good for this scum!" Schrader shouted, his eyes now on Hickey alone. "They need to be locked up and the key thrown into the deep waters of the muddy Mississippi River."

"You son-of-a-bitch!" James Hickey screamed at Schrader. "If I get out of here, I'll kill you! I'm warning you, you son-of-a-bitch! I'll kill you! I swear I will! "

Blackie Armes, a dark-skinned man in a black suit, viciously grabbed Hickey around the neck and pulled him back down in his seat.

"Hickey, you damned fool, shut up!" Armes shouted. "You're signing your death warrant!" Armes turned to Sheriff Munie, who was casually sitting in the front row, his arms and legs crossed.

"Sheriff, you're square, but keep that Schrader off us," Blackie Armes said, white showing all around the pupils of his eyes. "He'll kill us!"

Munie just leaned farther back in his chair and smiled. Vinnie looked to the witness stand. Schrader lit a big stogie, never taking his eyes off James Hickey.

* * * * * * *

"I'm looking for Archie Norton," Vinnie told Schrader and Munie. After the hearing, he had followed them through the courthouse to the sheriff's office. "I heard he was running with those three that just got kicked out of the county."

"You know what Norton looks like?" Schrader asked.

"Sure do. He was a UMW thug up in Christian County. My name's Vinnie Vacca."

"You Sam Vacca's husband?" Schrader asked. "The woman who shot it out with the Sheltons during the Kincaid bank robbery?"

"The same," Vinnie said. He'd grown used to being the husband of the famous Sam Vacca.

"You're a lucky man," Schrader said.

"There's a lot of folks complained to that fact," Vinnie said.

Schrader stepped back and eyed Vinnie as if studying a horse for purchase. After a long moment of contemplation, he looked at Sheriff Munie, who gave a shrug.

"Well," Schrader said slowly, "you might be useful if you can identify Norton. He's wanted for several robberies. You got a gun?"

Vinnie pulled his M1911 from behind his back.

"Nice piece," Schrader said. "Any good with it?"

"Not as good as my wife."

Schrader smiled to Munie. "I like this fella. Well, Mr. Vacca, I'm gonna give you a crash course on how to deal with crime. Five words. Shoot first and talk later. That's all you need to know. Shelton and company don't have the intestinal fortitude to stomach their own medicine."

"You expecting to run into Carl Shelton too?" Vinnie asked.

"Oh, hell, no!" Schrader said. "Big Carl's a teetotaler. He only goes on one job in a hundred. He leaves it to his henchmen to do the dirty work. Besides, now that I'm after these three, I'd 'spect he won't want nothin' to do with them."

* * * * * * *

The roadside tavern was set far enough back off the hard road only the locals frequented it. Carl Shelton sat at a table watching Douglas Eubanks stuff his face with cookies as he counted a big pile of money. Two of Sheltons' men stood behind him, smoking cigarettes and drinking whiskey. Their pin-striped pants were held mid-belly by colorful suspenders against white, long-sleeved shirts. Both were glaring at the three men standing across the table from Shelton.

Blackie Armes and Bad-Eye Smith kept their heads down as if they were children waiting for the school principal to decide on consequences. Holding their hats in front of them, they both fidgeted with the brims while Armes related the story of the court hearing. James Hickey, though, shifted his weight from one foot to the other like a fighter before a boxing match.

"Any man who can arrest you with a smile on his face can shoot you with a smile on his face," Carl said when Armes finished talking. "You boys stay away from my joints. I don't want you getting any blood on my floor when Schrader kills you."

"Come on, Blackie," Hickey said, his face frozen in a perpetual sneer. "We don't need this two-bit gangster. Let's go back to Signal Hill. We'll form our own gang."

"Shut up, Hickey!" Armes said. "Just shut up!"

When the three men left the room, Big Carl extracted a piece of paper and a short pencil from his shirt pocket, scribbled a quick note on it, and handed it to Douglas Eubanks. The lawyer looked at who the note was addressed to, took his white straw hat from the hat rack, and exited the building.

* * * * * * *

Riding in the back of the police car made Vinnie feel like a child. Schrader had smoked cigars non-stop throughout the day, but now as he drove along the darkened street, he clenched an unlit one between his teeth. Sheriff Munie sat next to him in the front passenger seat, but never said a word. Instead, he concentrated on unloading and loading the two forty-four caliber revolvers that he finally tucked into holsters on either side of his vest.

Vinnie had heard much squawking coming from the big radio attached to the dashboard, but could make out nothing the person on the other end was saying. Despite all the static, Schrader seemed to understand. He finally spoke into the microphone. "Signal Hill, check. Over and out."

That was when Munie began working on getting his weapons ready. Vinnie had no doubt his own pistol was primed for action, but his queasy stomach made him think maybe he wasn't. He had killed a man once by smashing a bottle of chlorophyll into the temple of his head. That had occurred during the gunfight in Matewan, but it had been a purely defensive reaction and happened so fast he hadn't had much time to think about it.

Shoot first and talk later. Schrader's words had seemed so simple when Vinnie first heard them, but now he imagined complicated scenarios. What if an innocent person stood in his line of fire? Or what if civilians were behind his target and a miss could possibly hit one of them? Sam had told him that during her short shootout with the Sheltons, she recognized the sound of several ricochets, at least one of which may have been responsible for one of the wounds the Shelton boys received. The possibility of an errant bullet made a gunfight seem pretty chancy.

When Schrader stopped the car in an alleyway and turned the engine off, Vinnie was tempted to ask some questions about battle protocol. But when he started to speak, Schrader turned toward him and held a finger to his lips. The officers slowly and quietly opened their car doors and got out. Fearing he couldn't be as quiet, Vinnie thought about squeezing through the open window, but decided he would look foolish. He finally opened the back door on the driver's side and was able to follow the two lawmen without making too much noise.

The neighborhood was alive with the sound of barking dogs, but none seemed to be directed toward them. An occasional cat shrieked and the yards were filled with the sound of crickets and bull frogs. Though it was now well after midnight, lights were still on in several of the homes they passed. After about five minutes, they came to a two-story house on the hill. The musty smell of leaves burned earlier that day still hung in the damp air.

Schrader quietly gave a sweeping hand signal to Munie. The sheriff pulled both guns out and pointed them toward the sky. As he disappeared around the side of the house, Schrader raised himself up on his toes and peered into a window next to the back door. He then stepped past the entrance and held up three fingers to Vinnie.

Vinnie found himself overthinking again. He didn't know if that meant three men were in the room or that the lawman planned on entering the building in three seconds. There was no time to ponder the question, because a moment later, Schrader pulled out his gun, kicked the door wide open, and rushed into the building. Before Vinnie could get to his own pistol tucked inside the back of his belt, gunshots rang out. Vinnie was rammed by someone exiting through the open door. The collision knocked him several steps back, but he recovered immediately. He had somehow been able to hang onto his weapon—which was now pointed directly into the pig-like face of Archie Norton.

The little man froze like a statue, his eyes crossed as he peered at the end of Vinnie's gun, which was only inches from his nose. Norton's hands sprung up in defeat, allowing Vinnie to see his left hand held a pair of tens along with an ace, king and queen. Vinnie was shocked that in that moment of crisis, the first thing his brain considered was whether the gangster planned to go for more tens or draw on the inside straight.

A second series of gunshots came from inside the house, and Norton took a step backward. His eyes moved from the gun pointed toward his head to Vinnie's face. *Shoot first and talk later,* Vinnie thought. *But he has no weapon.* Norton read the hesitancy on his face. A second later the thug responsible for shooting Chuck Davin's leg off ran around the side of a carriage house and out of sight.

* * * * * *

155

Though a gun was found firmly grasped in his bloody hand, James Hickey never got a shot off. Two other men had tried to escape through the front door, but were arrested by Sheriff Munie. They were charged with plotting a kidnapping. Schrader didn't criticize Vinnie much for his failure to apprehend Archie Norton. He seemed satisfied with the night's work and showed no signs of worry when it was pointed out that though Hickey died instantly with the first shot to his heart, he had somehow been able to pick up his pistol with a bloody hand.

Vinnie wrote out an affidavit and was able to truthfully state he had been outside the building the entire time and never saw any actual shooting. He had no doubt, though, that Schrader's philosophy of shoot first and talk later had been the sole reason for the raid's success.

15

It seemed the big oak trees were crying golden tears. Bullo sat alone on his front porch, watching leaves pile up on his lawn, drinking his early morning coffee, and dreading Thanksgiving. From within the house, for the third time, came Mary Kate's shrill Irish voice ordering Willie and Tony out of bed. In Bullo's present mood, the words were a ghostly echo of his sainted mother, who had often used a similar Italian wake-up call on her own four sons. The recollection depressed him. Here, at last, was the first Thanksgiving any of his family had ever known without Angeline Vacca. Bullo wondered if his father would offer up a prayer for their Libero, who had died the day after Thanksgiving in 1918. And then in another two weeks, the family would be mourning Filberto's death day from that same horrible year and from the same deadly Spanish Flu. *Deathday,* Bullo thought. *Is it even a word?* Yes, in the Vacca family, there would be more deathdays than birthdays between Thanksgiving and his mother's murderday on January 3.

Bullo set his cup on a wicker stand beside his chair. He took a small bag from his shirt pocket and, with trembling hands, attempted to roll a smoke. Little flakes of tobacco splashed away from the paper like rain water from a puddle. He cupped his hands to catch those little leaves that had become so much more precious since the stock market crash of twenty-nine. Then he felt soft hands around his own. Before she had become a Vacca, Mary Kate Danaher had learned to roll cigarettes for her father William, who had become an invalid after an accident in the coal mine. He'd passed on the very day their little Willie was born.

After licking the paper and sealing the tobacco, Mary Kate kissed her husband on the mouth. Content that she had dispatched him as much love as possible, she replaced her lips with the cigarette, struck a match on the side of the chair, and held it up for him. Bullo took a long draw and, with a nod of gratitude, offered his wife his first closed-mouth smile of the morning.

Their moment was broken by the sound of an automobile turning onto their street. Vinnie was back from his hunting trip. His brother's sudden return sparked an unexpected memory of the last time the two brothers had hugged. It had been the day Libero died. Bullo had delivered the news as Vinnie walked home from a day of fishing. They had stood in the middle of the dirt road, holding one another and crying for several long minutes. Then, after Filberto passed on December 9th, Vinnie became more angry and withdrawn. He took to sidestepping any physical contact more affectionate than an occasional handshake, his mother's embrace being the only adoration he was unable to avoid.

Now seeing his brother returning home and with his own head so full of sad reminiscences, emotions flooded Bullo's heart. He stood as his last living sibling pulled his flivver into the dirt driveway between their houses. When Vinnie opened his car door and stepped out, Bullo stood before him, looking at him with eyes that pleaded for comfort, understanding, peace.

Vinnie turned away, but before he could step toward the trunk of his car, Bullo grabbed him in a tight embrace and buried his head against his brother's shoulder.

"What happened?" Vinnie asked. "Did someone die?"

He started to raise a hand from his side, but put it back down when Bullo said, "No, nothing bad happened. I'm just glad you're home."

Vinnie pushed his brother away. "Scab!" He hurried inside his own house.

Mary Kate stood on the porch watching, her hand over her mouth. When her husband returned to his own home, she gently placed her arm around his waist. Bullo gave her a kiss on the cheek, stood straight and went inside to hug his sons.

* * * * * * *

For the sake of his father and the holiday memories the three Vacca children would one day have, Vinnie sat quietly across the Thanksgiving table from his brother. The next morning, he even stood between Sam and Sid while his father asked the family to join hands in a circle as he offered up a tearful and almost incoherent prayer for Libero. To no one's surprise, it was Mary Kate who stepped in when Grandpa Vacca's voice failed to bring about a suitable amen.

"Our Heavenly Father," Mary Kate said in a confident voice, "thank you for the gift of Libero in this life. The treasure of his soul is entrusted to you, O Lord, until we are with him forever in the joy of your Kingdom. We are comforted to know that you stand beside him, along with his brother Filberto and mother Angeline, and that you will fill our hearts with strength in these troubled Earthly days. Help us, Lord, to appreciate and enjoy the beauty and comfort and love of the Vacca family, and when we become entwined in the desolation of our journey to be with you, remind us of our true homeland in Heaven. In Jesus' name, amen."

In the two weeks leading up to the anniversary of Filberto's passing, Vinnie stayed busy organizing picketers around the mines. The National Guard, though, tolerated little more than the Progressives screaming insults and throwing rocks at the trucks as they ushered strikebreakers in and out of the mines each day. Then on December 8, Miles Perkins arrived unexpectedly at the Tovey mine, pulled Vinnie aside from the other picketers, and surprised him by announcing that George Lyman was in town.

"That son-of-a-bitch that shot Deaver's leg off is in the back room of the Brass Rail Beer Parlor right this minute," Miles whispered to Vinnie, "getting drunk with a bunch of Chicago thugs,"

"Is Archie Norton with him?" Vinnie asked.

"No, they say that little squirt headed for Chicago after Schrader kilt James Hickey. The crazy thing is that the Brass Rail is filled with Progressives. They don't know anyone is in the back room. Bob Daugherty sent his workers on home. He's scared to death there will be trouble and his place will get shot up." Miles shook his head. "It ain't good, Vinnie. I fear somebody's gonna die tonight."

Vinnie hadn't forgotten his promise to Harley Eng to try to keep the Progressives out of undo bloodshed. Revenge against George Lyman, however, was another matter. Ever since his failure to stop Archie Norton, Vinnie had convinced himself his hesitation would never happen again. The words *shoot first and talk later* were ingrained in his brain. The only trouble was, the National Guard had done such a thorough job disarming the Progressives, he was at that moment unarmed. In recent weeks it had become a common practice for guardsmen and sheriff deputies to search and then beat anyone they found carrying firearms. He assumed that any of the Progressives who were getting drunk at the Brass Rail were also unarmed. But George Lyman and the Chicago thugs would not be without weaponry. Of that he was confident. Being a leader and responsible for the success of the strike as well as the lives of the men, Vinnie was once again torn between responsibility and his own desire for revenge.

To avoid suspicion from the other picketers, he excused himself on the grounds that he was needed at home. Since fewer people would recognize Miles' pickup truck, he rode with him into Kincaid. Unfortunately, Miles didn't know the Vacca clan normally avoided passing by the house in Tovey where Angeline Vacca had been killed. Vinnie couldn't avert his eyes in time to see the porch where his mother had been standing when a stray bullet from the mine yard ended her life. A black wreath still hung on the porch—a sign of what he must do.

It only took a few minutes for them to reach the Brass Rail. As Miles parked next to another pickup truck, Vinnie noted there were few vehicles. Then he spotted Joe Harrison's Ford. The last thing he wanted was for his father's best friend to get caught between the two sides. Joe was a pacifist and hated guns. In fact, his disdain for violence was the reason he'd given up his well-paid position as a company man. The murder of Angeline Vacca had changed Joe Harrison's life as much as it had the members of the Vacca family.

When he and Miles entered the tavern, he saw Joe and Bullo standing at the checkout counter talking to Bob Daugherty. A large bag on the register between them was labeled "Daugherty's Italian Beef." Vinnie hoped they would take their food and leave, but the dozen or so Progressives drinking and talking loudly were his first order of business. He glanced at the closed door to the back room, then turned and faced the men in the tavern.

"See if you can get their attention," Vinnie told Miles.

The tall, slender teen immediately put his fingers to his lips and gave a loud, shrill whistle that brought every eye in the place toward them.

"I need you boys to go down to the Tovey mine," Vinnie announced when everyone grew quiet.

"There gonna be trouble, Vinnie?" one of the men asked, a smile on his round face.

"Maybe so," Vinnie said. "We just want to make sure we don't get outmanned."

The Progressives quickly swallowed the remainder of their drinks and headed for the door.

"Thanks, Vinnie," Bob Daugherty said quietly after the last of the men had exited the building.

Vinnie avoided his brother's eyes and followed Miles outside. A few vehicles were already leaving, but standing beside a pickup truck were six men arguing over who was sober enough to drive to the mine.

"They can all ride in the back of my truck," Miles said and started toward the men.

"Look at the cowards run!" a voice said from the tavern door behind Vinnie.

Before Vinnie could turn all the way around, one of the drunk Progressives reach inside his jacket and pull out a revolver. Then came the volley of gunfire.

* * * * * * *

When Bullo had seen his brother and Miles Perkins enter the tavern, he knew something was up. Vinnie Vacca had never had the ability to hide his emotions from people who knew him best, and no one knew him better than his brother. Vinnie's fists were clenched, but his face showed a worry that Bullo had rarely seen.

After Miles whistled and Vinnie's announcement emptied the tavern, Bullo heard voices coming from the back room. A moment later, five men opened the door and came out, pistols in hand. They went straight for the front door. Bullo and Joe followed them, and when the first shots were fired, they launched themselves onto the backs of the hired gunmen. Two of the inebriated thugs dropped their weapons. Joe picked up one of the revolvers and aimed it at them. Those two staggered to their feet and immediately put their hands in the air. In the meantime, two of the others ran around the side of the building and down an alley. Bullo recognized the remaining man as George Lyman. Lyman jumped into an automobile and, with his tires spitting dirt and dust, wheeled out of the parking lot.

"Get him, Vinnie," Miles yelled as he lay on the ground holding a bleeding leg.

Vinnie jumped in Miles' truck and was immediately in hot pursuit.

Bob Daugherty came out of the tavern holding a shotgun.

"Watch these two," Joe said and quickly traded the pistol for the shotgun. "Let's go!"

Bullo jumped in Joe's Ford, and they were in the wake of the other vehicle's dust before it had time to settle.

* * * * * * *

Vinnie kept an eye on the distant taillights, certain they belonged to Lyman's Oldsmobile. The body of Miles' little truck wasn't much to look at, but the new V-8 engine was the best in the county. Vinnie was gradually creeping up on his adversary, but he had to make certain that Lyman didn't suddenly exit the road and turn off his lights. Luckily, the cornfields were harvested, making visibility to the side roads unobstructed.

Vinnie didn't have any idea what he was going to do without a gun. Maybe he would tail Lyman to wherever he stopped, then go borrow a weapon from someone nearby. He just wanted to catch the son-of-a-bitch and tear him apart for what he'd done to Chuck Davin.

He shifted his pickup truck into third as he left the dirt road for the much wider hard road. The speedometer climbed. Forty, fifty, sixty. Finally, at seventy miles per hour, he let his foot relax. He had to concentrate intensely on the flat, narrow expanse of highway in front of him.

As the high speed chase caused Vinnie's adrenalin to rise, so did his anger. Chuck Davin represented everything good the Progressives stood for. He was a gentle man who simply wanted to do an honest day's work for a fair day's wages. No one deserved the crippled life Lyman and Norton had left him. More than anything else, though, Chuck Davin had guts like Vinnie had never before seen.

Vinnie swore as a vehicle's taillights turned onto the road in front of him. He switched his right foot to the brake pedal and began to slow his machine. The heavier Olds would be no match for the speed of the pickup truck, but obstacles like this one could cause him to lose sight of Lyman's car. Vinnie revved the motor again as he recognized the taillights as belonging to an old farm truck. He swung around the slow moving vehicle and buried his accelerator to the floor. As he passed, he saw an old man and his wife out of the corner of his eye. They were both wearing straw hats and peered through ghostly eyes at the dark highway in front of them.Back at the tavern, Vinnie had turned in time to see his brother and Joe Harrison leap onto the hired gunmen. That bold move had doubtless saved a second round of gunshots at the Progressives.

But what about his brother's position with the coal company? Might he lose his job for helping? *But why should I care?* Vinnie thought. *He's still a scab!*

Before he could reflect on it further, he saw the Olds. The big, bright taillights hovered omnipotent in front of him. Vinnie was struck with the realization of the size difference between the vehicles. Though the Olds was larger, Miles' pickup truck might be the best weapon Vinnie would have. When the rear of the car loomed dangerously close, Vinnie tapped his brake and spun the steering wheel counter-clockwise to get in the other lane. But he was too late. The front edge of his truck slammed against the rear of the Olds. Both drivers compensated for the action by adjusting their speeds. Lyman increased, then pumped his brakes. After releasing his foot from the brake, Vinnie touched the accelerator and shot into the left lane alongside Lyman.

For the first time since before Davin had been shot, Vinnie caught a glance of Lyman. The silver-haired man glared hatefully over his dash at the torn front fender on the truck racing alongside him. Dark wrinkles lined Lyman's hard face. A faint glow of recognition showed in the man's face. The gangster raised a revolver with his right hand.

Vinnie went against his natural instinct to hit the brake. Instead, he ducked forward and pushed hard on the accelerator. The bullet buzzed just behind the back of his head.

Lyman rammed the side of his car into the pickup truck.

The screeching of metal tearing and grinding made Vinnie clench his teeth. He couldn't turn his head, though. He had to watch the road and somehow escape the repeated beating by the big car. The left wheels of the pickup truck hit the grass. A mailbox and then a road sign bounced off the hood and put a long crack in the windshield. Realizing they were coming up on an area he was familiar with, Vinnie devised a desperate plan. He turned his wheels hard to the right, catching Lyman off guard, and pushed his way back onto the highway.

The friction of hot rubber against the hard road brought smoke from beneath the two vehicles, and they once again raced side by side. Vinnie dared a glance at his speedometer. Sixty miles an hour—just the right speed to try his idea.

As a boarded field-entry came up on the right side of the road, Vinnie pulled the steering wheel down hard to the right with both hands. Once again, the two vehicles met. This time, sparks flew as the bare metal rubbed back and forth in a sickening, grinding squeal.

Lyman pulled hard left on his own steering wheel, but there was nothing to stop his momentum. Skidding in the grass on the opposite side of the road, Lyman overcompensated to his right and then back to his left again. For a moment, he swerved uncontrollably from one lane to the other.

Vinnie had braked hard, turned behind Lyman into an empty field and gunned his engine to catch the Olds at the intersection. The pickup truck raced at an angle on a collision course with the careening car.

"This is it, scumbag!" Vinnie yelled.

The pickup truck struck the culvert hard and went airborne. When it landed, it slammed into the rear of Lyman's car. The Olds spun sideways, then crashed in a shallow ditch.

Vinnie wasn't as lucky. The truck flipped three times and rolled into a telephone pole. In those terrifying seconds, he thought about his mother, Filberto and Libero.

* * * * * * *

Joe Harrison's jawline was like granite and his eyes blazed with determination. From the moment they set out from the tavern after Lyman and Vinnie, Bullo had never known his father's best friend to look so formidable. He'd always thought of him as old. Sometimes Joe was a little stiff when he walked and didn't always get up from a chair easily if he'd been sitting for very long. But the way he spun his Ford out of the parking lot and into action was nothing short of masterful.

The pickup truck Vinnie drove spat out enough exhaust fumes that Bullo thought they could follow it by smell alone if they had to. They seemed to be catching Vinnie— until they hit the hard road. Then, Joe fell a little farther behind when an old farmer in a pickup truck chose to hog the middle of the road rather than let them pass. When his horn didn't persuade the man to move, Joe gave the rear end of the truck a firm tap with his front bumper. That persuaded the old gent to get over, but as they shot past, the angry farmer tossed his straw hat at them, bouncing it off the windshield.

A few miles later, Bullo saw Miles' pickup truck upside down alongside a telephone pole. Lyman's car sat sideways in the ditch, its driver's side badly damaged.

Bullo sucked in his breath.

George Lyman, revolver in hand, walked from his car toward the overturned pickup truck. Joe floored the accelerator.

Lyman turned toward Joe's Ford, then ran and dove behind Vinnie's truck just as Joe spun the steering wheel and skidded the car to a stop twenty yards away.

Lyman fired two rounds into the front windshield.

Joe dove down behind the dashboard. Bullo, though, was already out of the car and running as fast as he could to where Vinnie lay on his side with his back against a tree.

"No," Vinnie yelled. "Get away!"

Lyman fired at Bullo. His shot kicked up dirt at Bullo's feet. The older Vacca dove on top of his brother and covered him with his own body. He looked over his shoulder.

Lyman moved toward them, reloading as he came.

Vinnie pushed weakly, trying in vain to get out from under his protective sibling. Bullo pulled his injured brother's head down and covered it as best he could.

"Die," Lyman said. "Die, you sons of a—"

Lyman's head exploded. A pussy, grey matter rained for several seconds on the two men huddled beneath the tree. When it stopped, Lyman's nearly headless body collapsed at the brothers' feet.

Bullo cleared his eyes of Lyman's bodily fluids. Joe Harrison, looking like a statue, was still pointing a smoking shotgun at the spot where the gangster had been standing just a moment before.

Bullo spun back toward Vinnie.

"I'm okay, Bullo," Vinnie said. "Just get off me."

Bullo jumped to his feet and hurried over to his friend.

Joe dropped to his knees and vomited.

The pickup truck they had passed a few minutes earlier chugged to a stop behind the Olds. An elderly man in Farmer Johns and a huge woman wearing a dirty, white apron with a crocheted chicken on the front strolled down the road toward them. The man carried a shotgun and the woman a meat cleaver.

Bullo hurried to meet them before they could see the dead body.

"Looks like you ran someone else off the road, huh?" the old man said, peering around the Olds toward the dark shadows behind it. "What you doin' in these parts, boy?"

"Just passing through," Bullo said as calmly as he could.

"Satanists!" the woman shouted in a voice so loud they could have heard her from a hundred yards away.

She had a look of such hate and anger, Bullo thought that she might be a little possessed herself.

"Eunice gets a bit excited," the husband said. "We had some trouble with a satanic cult about twenty years ago. There's been similar trouble lately and she thinks they're at it again."

"Well," Eunice shouted, "this time there was nothing left of them cows but a butt hole! Twenty years ago, they left the cow and took the damned butt hole!"

"That's all that was left?" Bullo asked.

"And a pool of blood you could swim in." the woman said as she walked around behind Bullo to inspect the overturned pickup.

"Erwin?" Joe walked up and stood beside Bullo.

"Do I know you, mister?" the man asked.

"I'm Joe Harrison, Erwin," Joe said. When the man didn't reply, he added. "I was there on Williamsburg Hill."

Bullo didn't know why, but the man lowered his shotgun.

"Who's that fella lying over there with his head blowed off?" Eunice asked.

"George Lyman," Joe said.

"The hired gunman?" Eunice asked.

Joe nodded.

"What's you gonna do with him?" Erwin said.

"I figured I'd load him in the trunk of my car and take him to where the others are buried," Joe said. "Soon as he bleeds out, that is."

Eunice walked over to the body, grabbed it by the coat, and lifted it almost clean off the ground. "Looks pretty bled out to me," she said. "Did ya see where the head went?"

"I'd 'spect," Vinnie said, causing the old woman to

jump when he slowly rose from the shadows, "it mostly splattered up into the trees."

"You fixin' to bury this fella too?" she asked, raising her meat cleaver toward Vinnie. "He may not be quite dead enough."

"He's my brother," Bullo said.

"Erwin," Joe said, "could you get rid of the Olds?"

"Well, yes, I could dump it in the Sangamon, I suppose," Erwin said. "I got some feed bags in the back of my truck you could wrap Lyman's body in. But why not just dump him with the car?"

"No," Joe said. "The hill is the right place."

Erwin shared an understanding nod with Joe and went to his truck to retrieve the feed bags.

Later, when they were on their way back to town with Vinnie lying in the backseat and Lyman tightly wrapped up in the trunk, Bullo asked, "What happened on Williamsburg Hill, Uncle Joe?"

Joe didn't turn his head nor change the bland expression on his face. "Nothing that concerns you, son," he said. "No, sir, nothing that concerns you."

16

When Vinnie awoke the next morning, he found himself back in the bunk bed of his father's house. RJ Hiler was hovering over him and touching his face, although Vinnie couldn't feel the doctor's hand. When he tried to speak, pain pierced his lower jaw.

"I wouldn't try to talk for a while if I were you," RJ said. "Your face is black, blue and puffy as a chipmunk."

"Nothing broken, but you sure ain't gonna be no pretty boy for a few days," Bullo said from the doorway.

"He's still purty to me." Sam entered the room, carrying a big chunk of ice blanketed in a towel. "Now you men get out so I can take care of my man."

RJ followed Bullo, who didn't stop in the living room but instead walked out onto the porch and sat in a wicker chair next to one that held his father.

"Vinnie doesn't know that Dominic Hunter was killed in the shootout," Bullo said quietly to the doctor.

"We were afraid he'd go after the two thugs that got away last night," Antonio added, "so we only told him that five of our boys got shot and were recovering nicely."

"No doubt he would have been hard to keep down if he'd known about Dominic." RJ took a seat in the porch swing, lit a cigarette, and then added, "You don't need to worry about the sheriff. He's busy investigating over three dozen bombings, fifteen murders and just as many disappearances. Since all the victims of the Brass Rail gunfight are Progressives, I'm sure he'll place it in the bottom of his files."

The three sat quietly for a few minutes and watched a distant thunder cloud roll slowly in from the west. The sound of a low squeak came from the porch top as RJ began a slow swing.

"Miles Perkins was pretty upset about his truck," Antonio said, breaking the silence, "but when the Progressives told him they'd replace it, he seemed pacified."

"What about the disappearance of George Lyman?" Bullo said in almost a whisper.

"Hell, that son-of-a-bitch didn't even warrant a report," RJ said. "And the good news is that since the gangsters are all from Chicago, they have no idea who jumped them when the shooting started. Looks like you and Joe are off the hook."

Antonio looked more relieved than his eldest son. "I'd still like to get Vinnie away from here for a while."

"Wait a minute." RJ put his feet flat and brought the swing and its squeak to a sudden halt. "I have a friend down in Shelbyville who just left for Texas. He and his family will be gone for a couple of months. Why don't we send Vinnie, Sam and Sid down there for a few weeks? At least until his face heals up."

"Wouldn't that look a little suspicious if he disappears right after the gunfight?" Bullo asked.

"We just tell people that they went back down to Missouri to help with the hunting again," RJ said. "Everyone knows that Vinnie and Sam are the ones who run that whole shebang."

Antonio was suddenly out of his chair and heading inside.

"Where you going, Papa?" Bullo asked.

"To tell Sam to pack her bags," Antonio said. "I'll not be losing anyone else in this family."

* * * * * *

With Vinnie's family gone and Bullo working, Antonio had too much free time on his hands. Even photography was no fun with Sid out of town and Willie and Tony in school. So when Joe Siglar showed up at his house one day and asked Antonio to serve as a special policeman for the village of Bulpitt, Antonio jumped at the opportunity.

The coal mining villages of Kincaid, Bulpitt, Jeiseyville and Tovey could have easily been considered a single town, since little more than streets divided them.

Antonio enjoyed passing the time with Joe Siglar. The two often just sat in front of the hardware store whittling and talking old times. Siglar had worked the mines almost as long as Antonio, and had been quick to join the Progressives when the mine trouble began.

"Did you know that Bulpitt was called Hog Waller until the big frog infestation of 1875?" Siglar asked Antonio one night as they walked the neighborhoods checking locks on businesses.

"I'd heard something about that."

"This place still has more frogs than anyplace I've ever seen," Siglar said.

"Yes, and they're too small for eating," Antonio said. "Come to think of it, I thought 1875 was the big year for the locust."

"It was." Siglar paused to spit some tobacco on a slug sliming its way across the hard road. "My grandpa said they thought the world was coming to an end that year. I remember he told a story about a Chinaman who ate fried locusts." He laughed. "Yee doggie! That Asian must have been in hog heaven that year!"

Antonio had never met anyone who didn't like Joe Siglar, including United Mine Workers and company men. That was why, when the mine trouble began and he joined the Progressives, the townsfolk made him a Special Police Officer. Many fights were averted by the presence of the amiable constable, with his ability to find humor in the darkest of situations.

"Hey, you boys!" Siglar yelled at two young boys standing near a woodpile smoking a pipe. "You git on in your house before I tell your ma you're stealing your pa's tobacco."

"We ain't stealing Pa's tobacco, Mister Siglar, I swear we ain't," the bigger boy, who was about ten, said. "We found this pipe in the garbage and we filled it with dried leaves. You can take a draw on it if you don't believe us."

The boy walked over and held the pipe out to the police officer to inspect. "Please don't tell our ma, Mister Siglar."

Siglar sniffed the pipe. Antonio noticed an ornery look come over the policeman's face.

"You boys like tobaccy?"

"Sure do," the younger boy said, then hesitated. "Well, we think we do, but we ain't really had a good opportunity yet."

Siglar held out a square of chewing tobacco. The boys' eyes lit up and they each tore off a small piece.

"No, youngsters," Siglar said as he ripped off two big plugs and handed one to each child. "Big as you boys are, you'll need a man-sized chaw."

The boys tossed the tobacco into their mouths and began chewing vigorously. For a moment, they reminded Antonio of a coon dog chewing on a hambone. Then the older boy's throat gave a little swallow. He stopped chewing and his face turned red, then scarlet, then green. It didn't go down as easily for the younger boy, who gagged, spit, and then vomited.

The boys made enough noise that a light came on in the house. They used their fingers to finish cleaning their mouths before the window could open all the way. Both boys were standing at attention when their mother leaned out and shouted. "What's going on out here?"

"Just caught your young'uns playing around in the outhouse, Ethel," Siglar said.

"Outhouse?" Ethel shouted. "What you two doin' in the outhouse when you got a perfectly fine pot right there in your bedroom?"

"By the smell," Siglar said. "I'd say they did you a favor by going outside, Ethel."

"Well, they know there's an ordinance against children being out after dark!" the mother shouted. "Did you whip 'em for me, Joe?"

"Sure did, Ethel. I gave 'em both what fer."

"Then send them on inside," the mother said, "and I'll give 'em double what you did."

"Oh, Ethel, I wouldn't do that if I were you," Siglar said. "I whooped 'em good enough they may have trouble sitting in school tomorrow."

"All right. Thank you, officer," she said. "I'll be sending you and yours these boys share of apple pie I'm fixin' to make tomorrow. Goodnight, Joe."

"Night, Ethel."

"Thanks, Mister Siglar," the older boy whispered.

"Why are you thanking him?" his brother said as went back to hacking and spitting. "I'd rather he woulda beat us than feed us that poison."

As the boys hurried inside, the two policemen continued down the street.

"I thought you were a nicer person than that, Joe," Antonio said with an elbow nudge.

"Well, those two boys will be forgetting about tobacco for a while, don't you know?"

It was well after two in the morning when the police officers passed by the Hyde Park Beer Parlor. Five men stood in the parking lot smoking and talking. Antonio recognized them as Progressive miners who had come up from Marion to help out with the picketing. They were a hard lot, as many of those from southern Illinois were. Williamson County was where the Herrin massacre had left nineteen strikebreakers dead back in '22. It was also heavily populated with Ku Klux Klan members, as well as gangsters from the Shelton gang.

Just as Siglar opened the tavern door to go in and tell the proprietor it was closing time, an inebriated man staggered out the entrance and almost fell into the police officer.

"Ocifer Joseph," the man said. "I'm so glad you're here. I require your s-s-services, Ocifer Joe, ol' buddy, ol' pal."

"Why, Hugh O'Donnell, you old drunk." Siglar said as he tried to lean the man against the hitching post. "I haven't seen you this sober since your still blew up. What's the occasion?"

"Y-you're being facetious, are you not, Joseph, ol' buddy, ol' pal?" O'Donnell asked. "Escort me to my abode before these Progressive rascals have their way with me. I'll not have my remains found floating down the South Fork this cold night."

"You know that Antonio and I are Progressives, don't you, Mister O'Donnell?"

"Y-yes, but you ain't the b-b-bad kinda Progressive."

"What's the bad kind of Progressive, Mister O'Donnell?"

"You know what I mean, the red kind. Th-those b-bullshevist c-commies."

"Okay, Mr. O'Donnell," Siglar said. "We'll take you home. Antonio, why don't you fetch the Ford? I don't want to have to carry him if he passes out."

O'Donnell was hanging out the back window of the Model A five minutes later when they pulled up in front of his house. During the short trip, Antonio had taken a good grip on the back of the man's suspenders to keep him from falling out. He and Siglar found it was easier to pull the drunk the rest of the way out through the window rather than shove him back inside so they would be able to open the car door. They almost had O'Donnell to his porch when the man suddenly lurched out of their grip and stumbled around to the side of his house.

"Just look at them bullet holes in the side of my house." O'Donnell pointed. He grabbed Siglar's arm and pulled him toward the building.

"Why Hugh, there ain't many houses in Christian County that don't have bullet holes in 'em somewhere," Siglar said. "Just thank your lucky stars they didn't blow up your outhouse like they did others, or you'd be walkin' over to ol' Jonesy's to do your business."

"What's all this racket out here?" Howard Jones shouted as he appeared on the lawn wearing a white night robe and black galoshes. "And what's this I hear about my outhouse?"

"Ya-Your outbuilding is in-intact, Mr. J-Jones," O'Donnell said. "Not a bullet hole in her, unlike my house. Ain't that right, Ocifer Siglar?"

Howard Jones and O'Donnell had been mining partners and neighbors for over twenty years. Both had stayed with the United Mine Workers when the trouble began. Everyone respected the much older Jones for being somewhat a father figure to the often irresponsible O'Donnell.

"Why, Hugh O'Donnell!" Mrs. O'Donnell ran from her house. "Have you had a snoot-full again?"

O'Donnell staggered toward her, held up one finger, started to say something, but then froze.

"He'll be fine as soon as I get him to bed," Siglar said.

"Better to just leave him on the porch swing, Joe," Mr. Jones said. "He'll just puke all over his house if you take him inside."

"You may take care of my husband down in the mine, Mister Jones, but I'll take care of him in my home."

"Antonio, why don't you take the car and make sure the other taverns have closed up?" Siglar said. "I'll be along directly, soon as I get O'Donnell tucked away for the night."

Antonio nodded, tipped his hat to Mrs. O'Donnell, and got into the Ford. As he leaned forward to push the ignition, he saw a shadow move behind a nearby carriage house. Before he could give it a second look, the Ford backfired and sputtered to a stop. He adjusted the choke, and on the third try got the flivver going.

He had only driven a block down the street when he heard over a dozen gunshots explode through the night air in less than five seconds. Antonio slammed on the brakes, pushed off the ignition, and was rolling out of the car even before the vehicle had sputtered itself quiet. He ducked around the side of the Ford. Three men ran down the far end of the block, jumped into a car, and screeched away from the scene.

Mrs. O'Donnell's screams were so terrifying, Antonio almost turned to run away. He didn't want to know what had caused the woman to make such a horrible sound. His legs felt like lead weights as he forced them to take one miserable step at a time back toward O'Donnell's house. The sight before him was eerily familiar, and for the third time in his life he understood what the word *surreal* meant. When his beloved Angeline had been shot, he had rushed to her side before the dreamlike state had absorbed him. Then when his neighbor was killed, he had stumbled across the snow in time to hear the death rattle as James Hartman's soul left his body.

Now he saw Hugh O'Donnell swaying in a drunken stupor over the fallen Howard Jones and Joe Siglar. Mrs. O'Donnell hid her face in her husband's shoulder while holding him on his feet. Antonio ran toward the scene, but the harder he ran, the farther away they seemed and the heavier his legs felt. He could have gotten there more quickly if he had driven the car, and for a moment, he considered going back for it. When he finally knelt between the two fallen men, he was relieved they were both breathing steadily. Howard Jones lay on his side facing Siglar. Five separate blood stains spread out on the back of his white robe.

"Don't blame O'Donnell," Jones said weakly. "He had nothing to do with this." His eyelids went shut but he continued breathing.

Antonio left his side and moved toward Siglar.

"I'm okay, Antonio," Siglar said. "I think they missed me."

"Lay still, Joe," Antonio said. "You've got some blood coming out of you somewhere."

"Help me up then, bud," Siglar said. "I'll be in real trouble if my wife finds stains on this jacket."

Antonio put a hand under his friend's back, but Siglar made no effort to move.

"Well, I'll be damned if I can't even sit up," Siglar said with a laugh.

Antonio looked over his shoulder. About twenty men had gathered in the yard. On one side stood over a dozen Progressive miners. On the other side were eight who were either company men or United Mine Workers.

"The ambulance is clear over in Morrisonville, Antonio," one of the UMW men said. "You want to take them to the hospital in my sedan?"

"No!" one of the Progressives shouted. "We'll take care of our own. We don't need you scabs interfering."

Antonio jumped to his feet and stepped between the two groups of men. The palm he had placed under Siglar's shoulder was wet and sticky. He held his bloody hand between the two factions. "Enough!" he shouted. Then he lowered his voice and raised his head. "There's been enough blood spilled in this county to last all of us a lifetime. Every man who has lived in this area for more than two years knows and respects these two men. One is a Progressive and the other is a United Mine Worker. The only ones who would dare shoot either one of these fine men would be hired thugs who were brought in here to do the dirty work that family, friends and neighbors would never do to one another. It's time for men of honor on both sides to stand up to these criminals and stop the violence."

For a moment, Antonio thought the two sides hadn't heard a word he'd said. They looked at one another hard, every man in a combatant stance. Then a few from both unions unclenched their fists and turned their heads toward the two fallen men. One UMW man walked toward Siglar and Jones, and several from both sides joined him. A big sedan arrived, and both of the wounded were gently placed in the back. Only after the vehicle pulled away did Antonio squat and begin wiping his bloody hand in the wet morning dew.

* * * * * * *

"I should have made you go into hiding with Vinnie,"

RJ told Antonio as they climbed the little hill in the Oak Hill Cemetery to the spot Joe Siglar was being laid to rest. "You're not going to keep your mouth shut, are you, my friend?"

"Nope," Antonio said quietly.

"Then would you at least control those damned hands of yours when you talk?" RJ pleaded. "Waving them around makes people think you're a lunatic sometimes."

The thousands of people who were silently gathered around the flag-drapped coffin parted, allowing the good doctor and Antonio Vacca to approach the graveside. RJ gave his condolences to the widow and moved on to shake the hands of the four young children.

Mrs. Siglar spotted Antonio. Placing her arms gently around his shoulders, she pulled him into a tight and heartfelt hug. "My Joe so enjoyed your company, Antonio," Mrs. Siglar whispered in his ear. "He talked about you every day."

When she finally released him and stepped back, Antonio struggled to speak his words of condolence. "Folks came from all over when my sainted Angeline passed," Antonio said. "Many of them didn't even know her. I remember that a lot of those who are here today couldn't get to my wife's funeral because the governor had the guard block the roads and even fly airplanes over the funeral to intimidate us. But they're here today, by golly. Men and women who haven't spoke to one another in a long time are here because Joe Siglar was a good and honest man who treated everyone fair, even if he didn't agree with them."

Antonio's hands went into the air but he remembered what the doctor had said and brought them back down into his pockets. He leaned forward and searched the hushed crowd with his eyes. To his left stood hundreds of the Progressive Miners of America, and to his right, dozens of UMW and company men, including his son Bullo. Most everyone was looking down at the ground.

"This is how many of us stood that night after the shooting," Antonio said, "And then we stood this way the other day when Howard Jones was laid to rest, and now here we are again—afraid to even look at one another."

Several from both sides glanced up. Those that did displayed misty eyes.

"My friends, we can find a more peaceful way . . . ." Antonio voice cracked and he fought to hold back his own tears as he took his hands from his pocket and held them palms upward toward the four Siglar children. "Our children. Please think about what all this is doing . . . ."

Mrs. Siglar stepped forward as Antonio's voice faded and gave him another long hug. Then RJ Hiler took his friend's arm and led him slowly back down the hill. The crowd parted once more. This time however, when they came back together, they stood as one.

17

Brewster Hill road sloped sharply down into the Kaskaskia River Valley. The hard road was narrow, with barely enough room along the edge for a pedestrian to walk
without sliding off into the deep ditches on either side. Giant elms saluted the automobiles that rushed to and from
the sleepy little town of Shelbyville. The long branches of
those trees created an archway above the highway, giving
the entire three-mile drive through the valley a hollow,
eerie effect. This was especially haunting in December,
when the leafless limbs resembled skeletons. Because the
highway was straight with few intersecting roads, drivers
often raced through the valley at perilous speeds. Those
who hurried did not notice the big white house that lay
hidden in the middle of the valley behind a long row of
hedge bushes.

In a second floor bedroom of that house, a cool breeze
coming through the slightly open window hummed a
ghostly lullaby. The breeze caressed Sid Vacca's forehead
with its gentle kiss of morning air, causing a thin blanket
to billow softly around him.

The room appeared almost as any other boy's would. A
football lay on the dresser, and a dartboard with hundreds
of tiny holes in the wall behind it was suspended from the
ceiling by a kite string. A clumsily-built wooden bookshelf
leaned precariously against the foot of the bed. Near the

window lay a cane fishing pole and a forty-five pound, fully strung bow alongside a quiver full of arrows.

As little Sid slept, his mind was not on the boyish pursuits for which his room was so well-prepared. Instead, the recurring nightmare he'd experienced for weeks haunted him once again.

In these dreams his body was floating above the ground—being pulled very slowly into a tunnel that was gradually growing darker and darker until all trace of natural light disappeared. In that moment all happiness was gone. In fact, he couldn't even remember what the word *happy* meant or if he had ever known anything but the limitless sadness that now filled his entire being.

He was conscious of two selves. One was the sleeping body that lay immobile in the bed, heart pounding, eyelids flickering in mild convulsion, terrified by what was about to happen next. The other was the Dream Sid Vacca, who seemed more real, more vulnerable, and completely convinced that if he died in the dream, he would also die in real life. Despair was overtaking his very soul. His torso arched backwards, his hands reached upward and his mouth opened wide in a silent, horrified scream.

Then, strangely, different shades of blackness began to move, although not quickly. They swooped in, out, around and even through his body. The shadows were icy cold and smelled so bad Sid wanted to vomit. He fought hard to prevent his soul from being pulled into the shadows and becoming one with them. The effort took so much out of him he began to tire. Just as he felt he was ready to give up, something appeared in the far distance. It was a tiny light no bigger than a pinhole.

The Dream Sid tried to run toward the light, but when he pushed with his legs, his hands were forced to the ground. He stopped himself from falling by putting his fingertips in front of him. Suddenly, he was near weightless and ran on all fours like the apes he saw in the zoo. As he moved toward the pinhole of light, two downy white clouds came from within it and grew larger and larger until they hovered in front of him. Behind the clouds, a face materialized. The sleeping Sid clenched his toes beneath his quilt as the face became known in the image of one he loved.

His mouth called to her. "Grandma!"

Sid lurched yearningly towards his grandma as the clouds transformed into arms, open and inviting. He recalled that once a thing called happiness existed, but, for now, he only felt terror, sadness, and despair. Then, the image began to sway back and forth in little Sid's mind faster and faster until all he could distinguish were the arms which remained still, their bare skin now slowly turning gray and crusty and lifeless.

"Stop, stop!" he shouted. "Please, God, make it stop!"

As the nightmare was slowly replaced with reality, Sid awoke completely. He sat up in bed. Looking out the window at the brightness of the morning, he tried to forget the dream by focusing on the nearby Chinese elm. A gray squirrel sat up on its back legs on a thick branch, its cheeks puffed with part of the little chestnut it held in its paws.

"Did you enjoy the show?" Sid whispered. Then, trying to remove the uncomfortable dream from his mind, he added, "I hope you get a nut soaked in castor oil."

As if he understood the little boy's curse, the animal threw the nut away from its mouth and scampered nimbly to the opposite side of the tree.

Sid took his time getting dressed. Five minutes later he headed downstairs for breakfast.

"The Engs are coming for a visit this morning," his mother announced as she scampered about the kitchen cleaning.

"Angie, too?" Sid asked.

"Yes," his mother said, "and Margaret."

"Can I run into town and get a couple of those good oranges for Miss Eng?" Sid asked. He reached into his trouser pocket and when he pulled it out held up an open palm that contained two pennies. "I have money."

"Okay, but don't cross that bridge if any cars are coming."

Sid ran out of the house. Despite his mother's warning, he stopped a moment in the middle of the massive steel bridge to watch the fishermen, who, thirty feet below, relaxed patiently on the banks, nibbling on a few crackers or bits of cornbread for their breakfast. He waited five minutes until a truck crossed that was heavy enough to make the bridge bounce and rumble. Then he clung to a rail with both hands and giggled when he felt the happy little tremor in his stomach.

Moving on, his thoughts turned to Grandma Vacca again. For fear they would make fun of him, Sid hadn't told anyone the idea of death haunting him almost every night. His trepidation was made worse because of the stories he'd been told about a death that had taken place in the Kaskaskia River Valley just that past summer. A widow, having just given birth to her second child, apparently became disillusioned with life. She had given up trying to feed and support the children. She left a note saying they were better off in an orphanage. According to the fishermen who saw the woman die, she walked to the center of the bridge one hot summer night, took off her shoes, and fell back first into the rapidly moving water. An undertow did the rest.

Sid shuddered a little as he crossed the threshold of the bridge. He imagined he was walking right above where the woman's body had been found. Trying to shake off the morbid thought, he broke into a run. It seemed that death was everywhere since Granma Vacca died. First, it had been his good neighbor Mr. Hartman. Then Shorty Roberts, who had been Sid's good friend. Now, yesterday's newspaper had brought word that Mr. Siglar had been murdered. Sid remembered him as the nice man who often sat on sidewalk benches telling children stories as he whittled little bamboo flutes for them.

Not wanting anyone to see the tears streaking his cheeks, Sid left the highway and took a shortcut through the wooded valley. After a quarter mile, he stopped and sat in the grass. Below him, the current flowed gently between the banks of the muddy river. Frogs croaked, birds chirped, and two gray squirrels raced nimbly along the branches of a tree. A fish head broke the surface of the water, then its gills and body emerged. Finally, at the apex of its leap, the tail gave a sharp twist and the huge bass was suddenly parallel to the water. As the fish fell back into its silent domain, tiny ripples formed in the shape of the animal's body and swiftly moved away from the center, growing farther and farther apart until they finally were no more. A water snake made its way along the shoreline to its nest, only to find its eggs broken in pieces, eaten by another predator. A few yards away, a little blue gill lay on its side in the mud, one cold, glassy eye staring up at him. Sid felt like crying again. He sat with his chin on one of his knees.

Angie Eng came toward him along the shore from downriver.

"Sid Vacca! I saw you running away from the highway," Angie said as she sat in the yellow grass alongside him. "What? Did you spot my Papa's car and decide you didn't want to see me?"

"Oh, gosh, no, Angie—I mean, Miss Eng."

"So are you enjoying your little get-away with your parents?"

"Oh, yes, ma'am. I like livin' here. Seems a lot quieter than back home. Except for a few hunters, I ain't heard many gunshots and never a bomb like we had two or three times a month back in Taylorville."

Sid and Angie sat quietly for a few minutes enjoying the morning.

Sid stole a glance at his teacher, then lowered his eyes. "Why does everything have to die, Miss Eng?"

"Do you think everything dies, Sid?"

"Well, sure. Everything has a beginning and an end."

"Will there be an end to the love and the life lessons that your Grandma taught you?"

Sid thought for a moment. "When I die, I guess they'll be gone."

"Won't you pass them to your children?"

"Yes. Sure, I will."

"And do you think they'll pass them to their children, and on and on?"

"I hope so."

"Well, then that's something that will never die, Sid," Angie said. "You see, your ma and pa have worked their entire lives so that your world will be a little better than theirs, just as Grandma and Grandpa Vacca made things better. Those accomplishments and the love they pass on to you are the things that will never die, as long as we keep them in our hearts."

Sid looked at the dead fish. "So what will that fish pass on?"

"Has it nothing to pass on?"

"I guess it'll make good eaten for those other critters."

"And won't that make them stronger?" Angie took Sid's hand. "You see, Sid, everything fits together. Just because

188

this life ends doesn't mean it didn't make a difference."

Sid laid his head against his teacher's shoulder, and she cradled him in her arms.

"When I have kids," Sid said. "I'm going to share with them what you just taught me. That way a piece of you will live forever, won't it, Angie?"

"You bet it will," Angie said. "Now, let's go home."

18

Michael O'Sullivan thought himself very clever. His National Guard unit was one of those given furlough for Christmas vacation. When his division boarded the train at the Taylorville station, he simply walked back through two passenger cars and exited on the opposite side before the train left the depot. Fifteen minutes later, he was in the Vacca family backyard with Angie Eng cuddled comfortably in his arms.

"You must not leave this property until your unit returns in two weeks," Angie scolded him after she had satisfied herself with kisses.

"I know," Michael said. "Antonio made that very clear. I just wish his sons were taller. I don't know how I'll get any sleep in those little beds."

Christmas at the Vaccas' was a crowded affair. Luckily, the little kitchen in Antonio's house had a large archway opening into the living room, creating just enough room for the five adult Vaccas, three Engs and Michael O'Sullivan, who was so tall he had to duck when walking through the doorways. Margaret Eng chose to play with Willie and Tony in Antonio's bedroom, but little Sid didn't want to let the big soldier get out of his sight, so he sat Indian style on the couch between his father and Uncle Bullo. Antonio and Harley enjoyed the rocking chairs and, when she wasn't helping the women in the kitchen, Angie found room on the loveseat with her beau.

Mary Kate and Sam had gone all out to decorate for the holidays. They preserved most of the traditions Angeline Vacca had always loved, but they also added some of their own. In an effort to bring cheer to Antonio, the walls were adorned with the grandchildren's drawings of snowmen, Santa, and his reindeer. The fireplace mantle was unchanged from the previous year, except for additional candles for those who had died in 1933. The center candle was pink and much larger than all the others, since it was for Grandma Vacca.

Michael O'Sullivan seemed to enjoy himself, yet, when the wine was brought out after dinner, the soldier announced he was not a drinker.

"An Irish Catholic who doesn't drink?" Antonio bellowed. "Why, I never heard such nonsense. You'll drink a toast with us, won't you?"

O'Sullivan nodded, and Antonio filled glasses for his guests. Everyone stood.

"To Angeline Vacca!" Antonio said. He tried to say more but couldn't.

By the time they had toasted all the deceased family and friends they could recall, O'Sullivan was swaying. When everyone returned to their seats, the big soldier dropped so hard into the loveseat it made a sad, creaking sound.

Vinnie was quieter than the others. Despite all the two had recently been through together, he still wasn't comfortable being in the same room with Bullo. The reason had nothing to do with his big brother's being a scab, but rather because an argument was always just a few badly chosen words away. Vinnie knew his own verbal limitations. Just about anything he said would almost certainly be poorly constructed. Everyone agreed that the murders of Joe Siglar and Howard Jones had caused the natives of

Christian County to wake up and realize what the mine war was doing to their community. Both sides began to use different tactics. The conversation in the room turned quickly to that subject.

"Roosevelt's National Recovery Act guarantees workers the right to choose the union they want," Antonio said. "The mine companies are going to have to reinstate Progressives or be in violation."

"Peabody Coal has already rejected that idea," Harley Eng said. "PMA attorneys are seeking an injunction in federal court that will restrain coal companies from operating mines until Progressives are given work."

"How can Peabody think they can get away with that?" Antonio asked.

"The Recovery Act has no teeth," Harley said.

"What does that mean?" Vinnie asked.

"It means our government has a check and balance system," Bullo said, "and until that legislation wins a challenge in the courts, Peabody can do whatever the hell they want."

"The good news is that other parts of the act will create jobs that will get our boys back to work," Harley said. "Some Progressives are already signing up with the Civil Works Administration to expand the city water system in Stonington."

"And quite a few fellows have gone to work for the Civilian Conservation Corps," Vinnie added. "They get paid thirty dollars a month, but they have to send most of it home to their families."

"What do you city folk think about all this, Michael?" Bullo asked.

"Well—" O'Sullivan emptied still another glass of wine, and with half-closed eyes said, "Since you asked me, I'll tell you that some of it is pretty stupid. The fellas who wrote the Recovery Act wanted to relocate poor people from the cities and give each family a farm to live on."

"How is that stupid?" Angie asked.

"Well, they sure don't understand city folk," O'Sullivan said. "The poor people I know can live off the street, but you ask them to do a day's work and they'll just laugh at you."

"So you don't believe in socialism?" Bullo asked. "I'm glad to have someone in this house who agrees with me."

"I can't believe that socialists can be so naïve about human nature," O'Sullivan said with slightly slurred words. "How can they possibly think that humans will continue to get an education or get a job if they can make a living without going to school or learning a trade?"

"Do you think everyone should contribute to society equally?" Angie asked.

"No, but I think deadbeats shouldn't expect society to feed them if they screw up their free public education and don't try to develop job skills."

Angie rubbed the back of her neck, then glanced over at Sam, who was busy tidying up the kitchen. Everyone in the room except Michael knew that Sam, with less than a third grade education, couldn't read or write very well. When her mother died, she'd been forced to stay home and take care of her baby twin sisters.

"Not everyone has the same opportunity to learn job skills or get good schooling, Michael," Angie said, her voice sweet but firm. She stood, walked over to the fireplace, and stared for a moment at Angeline's big, pink candle.

"Why, Angie," O'Sullivan said, his eyes half-shut, "where would any of us be if we didn't have an education?"

"How do you spell school, Michael?" Angie said quickly, without turning toward the soldier.

O'Sullivan laughed, but when no one else did, he swallowed hard and said, "Okay, teacher. Its s-k-o-o-l, school."

Little Sid was the only one who laughed. "That's funny, Miss Eng. The Corporal's pretending like he can't spell." He stood at attention and recited, "School, s-c-h-o-o-l, school."

O'Sullivan's face turned red. Angie continued to stare at the candle. Everyone else in the room found their eyes glued to anything besides the National Guardsman, who not only couldn't handle his liquor but couldn't spell, either. A moment later, Corporal Michael O'Sullivan rose from his seat, went to the bedroom, grabbed his duffle bag and walked quickly through the kitchen and out the back door.

* * * * * *

The tavern was filled with United Mine Workers from southern Illinois. They were called *swampies* by Progressives, and most of them had come to Christian County without their wives and children. They were there not just to mine the coal, but to fight whoever tried to stop them from working. The men thought the half dozen women in the room were there solely for their entertainment and pleasure. Little did the miners know the women were as hard a lot as they were and took home more money each night than even the best of the men made in a week.

The doors to the backrooms—as well as the beds in them—were like the squeaking sound of cash registers to Kieran Phelan, the owner of the tavern. He was mopping blood off the dance floor when Corporal O'Sullivan opened the door and walked in. Conversations stopped and every head turned toward the tall, muscular man. They stared at him for a long moment before turning back to their circle of friends to make sneering comments about either his height or, if they recognized him as such, as a National Guardsmen.

Phelan was one of those who did recognize the corporal despite his being out of uniform. It was hard to miss someone his size, although it was the young man's good looks that gave Phelan the most concern. Felina was at that moment on all fours shooting craps with a group of men, one of whom was standing behind her laughing and making obscene gestures at her well-defined buttocks. Crass men like that didn't worry Phelan, for he knew his wife's tastes well. The handsome young soldier whose silhouette almost completely shrouded the entire doorway was a different matter. Phelan sighed and, resigning himself to the inevitable, began mixing the Mickey Finn.

True to her form, Felina sensed immediately the wane in the adoration of her admirers, and when she rolled snake eyes twice in a row, she turned to see what could possibly be more interesting than her own magnificence. The sight of the man in the doorway made her clutch her chest and gasp. She had frequently seen the handsome soldier around town and spent many happy moments imagining what she would do to that body if she ever got it alone in her boudoir. Her only question was which of her two passions she would indulge first. Sex then murder, or murder then sex.

* * * * * * *

Lena was tougher on her daughter than were Mary Kate and Sam. Angie was following O'Sullivan when he stormed out of the house through the kitchen door. She weakly cried out his name, though she knew he was too drunk to hear it.

Her mother immediately began chastising her for embarrassing a guest. "I thought I taught you better than that," Lena scolded. "That poor soldier's never drank before, and now our men have got him so drunk he'll probably get himself arrested—or worse."

"Maybe he went to the church," Angie said hopefully.

"Angie, he's been drinking—and he's a man," Mary Kate said. "In his mood, the only thing he'll be praying for is another drink. He'll be going to a pub, he will."

"The corporal would know better than to go to a Progressive tavern," Sam said. "Big as he is, everyone in town knows him. The closest drinking hole would be Phelan's Tavern down on Oak Street."

Angie saw the look of horror as the other women looked at one another. "What?" she asked.

"If that's where he went, then we need to get him out of there," Sam said. "Fast!"

"Why?" Angie put a hand to her chest.

"Felina Phelan," Mary Kate said in almost a whisper.

* * * * * * *

Felina lay in the bed next to the unconscious giant. She was completely nude, as was Michael O'Sullivan. Her husband watched from the next room, where a wayward bullet had recently created the perfect spy hole. His voyeurism was fine with her. If she didn't get satisfaction from the giant, she may have some use for Phelan, pathetic as he was.

She had just finished shaving and putting lotion on the man's chest. It was now clean and smooth, allowing maximum exposure to each of O'Sullivan's massive muscles. With one bare, white leg draped over both of O'Sullivan's, she began breathing heavily as she made a shallow incision with a straight razor. Recent experience had taught her that basting a man's torso with blood made for a more intense—as well as rapid—conclusion to her pleasure.

She started at the bottom of his neck and ran the blade in a straight line through the valley that lay between the two big mounds of muscle on his chest. From the wake of skin that she expertly opened came little creeks of blood zigzagging their way from the cut. When the razor arrived at the little pulsating bulge of a hill that was created by the man's heartbeat, she deepened the incision. Fascination filled her face. The blood ran darker and thicker here.

Satisfied, Felina laid the blade on the pillow next to O'Sullivan's neck. She allowed the sharp side of the razor to rest on the jugular vein that was pulsing in rapid synchronization to her own heavy breathing. Using both her hands, she smeared and painted his chest with his own blood, and then, swinging her leg completely over, she sat up on top of him.

That was when she heard the gunshot.

* * * * * * *

Most of the patrons of Phelan's Tavern left immediately when O'Sullivan arrived and Felina and her husband drugged and then half-carried him into one of the backrooms. The only ones who stayed were the men who were unaware they might need an alibi later when the young giant came up missing. Those four were shooting pool when Lena, Angie and Mary Kate followed Sam into the establishment.

"We're looking for a man about six and a half foot tall with shoulders as wide as this doorway," Sam said to the men. "You seen him?"

"What you pretty gals want a fella like that," the thinnest and dirtiest of the men asked, "when there's four fine-looking gentlemen right here prepared to satisfy your every need?"

"All we want is to know if you've seen him," Sam said without flinching or taking her eyes from the man.

"Well, I just don't think I'm gonna tell you," the thin man said, "and soon as I finish this pool shot, my friends and me are fixin' to give you ladies a special Christmas present."

"Eight ball," Sam said.

"What?" the thin man asked.

Sam pulled a small pistol from her handbag and aimed it at the man's stomach. His eyes grew wide.

"Corner pocket," Sam answered. She lowered the gun several inches and fired. The bullet caromed the eight ball into the man's stomach with such velocity he fell forward onto the table, gasping for air.

"Now, do you other fellas want to tell us if he was in here?" Sam said as she aimed the weapon at the men, "or do you want to see another trick shot?"

All three men quickly pointed to the door that went to the backrooms. Angie was the first one through it. The other women followed down the short hall, where Angie threw open the first door to find Kieran Phelan staring at her, his pants down to his knees. Sam led the way to the next door, and when she flung that one open, Felina grabbed up a straight edge razor and held it to Michael O'Sullivan's throat.

"You make that cut and it will be the last thing you ever do," Sam said, her gun leveled at Felina's head.

Felina gave a laugh as loud and shrill as an alley cat, all the while grinding her crotch hard and fast against the unconscious man's bloody stomach. The moment Felina tossed her head back in obvious ecstasy, Angie Eng threw herself forward, knocking the razor aside with one hand and punching the woman hard in the face with the other.

It took both her mother and Mary Kate to pull Angie off Felina, who continued to laugh uncontrollably even as the young school marm pummeled her viciously.

Kieran Phelan ran into the room and threw a blanket over his naked wife.

"Get away from her!" he shouted as Felina pulled her legs up to her chest and cuddled her knees in her arms. "Can't you see she's a sick woman?"

"She's sick?" Mary Kate said with hands on hips. "And you with your pants down, peeping through a spy hole the whole time."

Sam disappeared back into the bar and emerged a moment later, leading two of the pool players at gunpoint. Angie was wrapping a blanket around O'Sullivan.

"These are cut to shreds," Mary Kate announced as she picked up the soldier's clothes from the floor.

"Bring 'em," Sam said, then waved her gun at the two miners. "You two, carry him to our car."

The two miners struggled to lift the dead weight of the unconscious giant, but finally found a firm grip and followed Angie out of the room. Lena walked behind.

"What do you want me to do with these two?" Sam asked Mary Kate, aiming her pistol at the Phelans. "Can I shoot 'em?"

Kieran Phelan's eyes showed white all around. "Don't shoot me, please," he whispered as he moved quickly away from his wife, who, still in the fetal position, rocked herself back and forth. "It was her that done this. She's got the devil in her, I tell you."

"No, don't shoot them," Mary Kate said. "They're too pathetic. Shooting them would be doing them a favor. They'll be gettin' their comeuppance soon enough when they meet their maker."

The two women followed the others out of the room.

* * * * * * *

The next morning when O'Sullivan opened his eyes, the ceiling of the bedroom was spinning so violently he was certain he was in the middle of a tornado. When he turned onto his side, he felt dizzy and off balance and almost rolled onto the wooden floor. The sight of a chamber pot swaying back and forth below him caused him to gag. Then came the taste of bile rising in his throat, followed immediately by extreme convulsions in his stomach. The big soldier was suddenly on his knees hugging the big, white pot, everything in his stomach coming out through his mouth and nose all at once.

In the kitchen, Antonio, Harley, Bullo and Vinnie sat quietly reading the newspaper.

"Oh, good," Antonio said without raising his eyes or lowering the paper, "sounds like the corporal is up."

Vinnie glanced at the clock on the wall. "Well, I'll be!" he said. "If I drank as much as he did, I sure wouldn't be awake at seven o'clock."

"Soldiers are accustomed to rising early," Harley said as he studied the business section of the paper.

Bullo set his own sports section down. He rose and prepared a mixture of tomato juice, raw eggs, soy sauce and a half dozen other ingredients into a glass. When he was finished, he set the drink down on the table and returned to his reading.

Ten minutes later, O'Sullivan stumbled into the kitchen. He held open his night shirt and looked at the bandages that ran down the center of his bare chest. "What happened to me?"

"Starting to hurt, I'll bet." Antonio said. "I'm sure the mickey Finn Phelan gave you was pretty powerful to make you sleep through the slashing his wife gave you."

"Sit down, son," Harley said, "and we'll tell you when you recover a bit."

O'Sullivan sat at the remaining chair. Antonio cringed at the moan the chair made, but pointed at the concoction Bullo had placed on the table. "Drink."

O'Sullivan's stomach made a sound similar to the one made by the chair. He started to decline, but he decided he was already in enough trouble, so he'd better just follow orders. Holding his nose, he downed the mixture that tasted as bad as it smelled.

"Oh, I'm in so much trouble with Angie," he said when he finished it. "Why didn't I just keep my mouth shut?"

"How much do you remember?" Vinnie moved the stinky, empty glass off the table and tossed it into a sink full of water.

"I remember everything until I walked into the tavern." O'Sullivan lowered his head and rested it on the table where the drink had just been.

"Then you're remembering too much," Harley said.

"What do you mean?" O'Sullivan raised his head and looked at the smiling men.

"What we are about to share with you," Vinnie said, "is never to be repeated except among those fellow males you can trust. Agreed?"

"Of course," O'Sullivan said, "but what is it?"

"It is the entire reason men go to taverns after a fight with their women," Antonio said. "We husbands call it 'selective memory'."

* * * * * * *

"What happened last night?" O'Sullivan asked when he and Angie were alone in the living room later that afternoon. "The last thing I remember was standing around toasting people who had died."

Angie struggled to think of an answer. All day she had been thinking about what she was going to say to Michael, but amnesia was a variable she hadn't prepared for. The unexpected ailment caused her to change tactics.

"Um," Angie said, "I think you may have had a little too much to drink and you went for a walk to clear your head."

O'Sullivan took Angie in his arms and kissed her. "I want you to tell those Italians that they are never to give me wine again. Promise?"

Angie buried her head on her man's chest. "Promise!"

Later she went over to Mary Kate's house to help the women prepare for supper.

"Did you two apologize to one another?" Lena asked.

"There was nothing to apologize for," Angie said. "He didn't remember any of it."

"Sounds like a good case of 'selective memory'," Mary Kate said.

Lena and Sam smiled and looked away.

"What?" Angie asked.

"Never mind, dear," Lena said. "All it means is that your man loves you but can't admit that he made a mistake and that you are right."

19

Bullo was thrilled. The Progressives were divided, and so were his family and their friends. For once it didn't matter that he had stayed with the United Mine Workers, and few were paying attention to him. He enjoyed a cigarette in the living room of his father's house while Vinnie, Sam and Lena sat at the kitchen table arguing with Antonio and Harley. Angie was at the sink washing dishes with Mary Kate and trying to decide which side she was on.

"Those miners at Superior Mine in Wilsonville," Lena argued, "have stated they are ready and willing to share their work with miners who are laid off from mines that have mechanized. The company said no to the idea because they don't want hand-loaders."

"Yes, I agree we should picket to get the company to go along with job sharing," Harley said, "but that does not give the workers the right to completely take over the mine company's property."

"I agree with Harley," Antonio said. "We must respect the property rights of the owner. He paid for his land just as I have paid for mine, and I sure as hell wouldn't allow anyone to come on my land and stay for days at a time."

"Daddy," Angie interrupted, "where did they get the idea for a stay-down strike?"

"A few months ago," Harley said, "General Motors workers in Flint, Michigan, successfully used a sit-down strike to shut down automobile production and eventually force recognition of their union."

"Traditionally," Vinnie interjected, "we always strike outside a company. When we do that, we have to stop scabs from getting into the plant to make our strike successful. If we decide to do a stay-down strike at Wilsonville, we will physically take over the inside of the coal mine and keep management and scabs out."

"Then why are the Progressive leaders against the idea?" Angie asked.

"Because they are in the middle of a fight right now to get the PMA recognized by the American Federation of Labor," Antonio said. "Bad publicity could destroy that opportunity."

"The more radical Progressives see this as an opportunity to force socialism," Bullo said loudly from his rocking chair. "They want to flex their muscles and force the coal companies to accept job sharing wherever the machines replace the hand-loading coal miner. They don't recognize that the coal companies have rights, too."

"What about *human* rights?" Vinnie asked, the vein in his forehead pulsing. "Don't the workers who contributed sweat, blood and lives to improve that mine have rights?"

"Yes," Antonio said as he clapped the palms of his hands in front of him, "but union leadership must be the ones to authorize it, and right now is not the right time for a stay-down strike."

"Papa," Vinnie said, "did you confer with the union president when you told your workers to throw the water out of their dinner buckets and wildcat strike?"

Antonio opened his mouth to speak, but no words came out. He had been a strong union leader who often led the war for workers' rights by standing in front of the coal miners, opening his dinner bucket and pouring the drinking water on the ground. The meaning was clear. Throw out your water, men—we won't need drinking water because we're all going home until the coal company listens to us.

"*But*," Antonio said, lowering his head as well as his voice, "wildcat strikes didn't put my family in danger. Things are different now. I don't want to lose any more family."

Sam walked over and placed a hand on her father-in-law's arm. "I won't go to Williamsville if you don't want me to, Papa."

Vinnie shook his head but kept quiet.

"The stay-down strike has already begun," Lena said, tossing her coffee tin into the sink, "and I plan to help the Women's Auxiliary take care of those five hundred miners that are down there fighting for their rights."

* * * * * * *

On their way to Williamsville, Harley and Lena Eng stopped at the Miner's Cemetery in Mt. Olive. The two knelt side-by-side and said a prayer for the United Mine Workers who had been killed at the Virden massacre of 1898. They then stepped back and held hands as they did the same for Mother Jones.

"She was the greatest lady I ever met," Lena said after they had crossed themselves. "I want to honor her by doing what I can to make the lives of working men and women better."

"You will, Lena," Harley said, "and you already have. I'm very proud of you."

"You didn't have to come with me, you know," Lena said. "I respect your right to disagree with the stay-down strike."

"We are in this together, fair lady." Harley kissed his

wife. "I wish Angeline could be with us."

"Oh, but she is, my husband." Lena put her arm around his. "She is with us always."

* * * * * * *

The cage dropped three-hundred-twenty feet to the bottom of the coal mine. Harley had told Lena about his first experience on the lift, so his wife had a firm grip on the center bar when it began its rapid descent. Two other women who were carrying cases containing musical instruments were less prepared and immediately clutched the men next to them. The cage conductor knew to take it easy on the ladies, so the drop was more comfortable than the ones normally given the experienced miners.

When they reached the dimly-lit bottom, Jack Battuello, the leader of the strike, led them to the left, where Harley was assigned a pit car to sleep in at night. Lena insisted on taking a moment to unpack her husband's sleeping bag and extra set of clothes and make the little sleeping area as comfortable as she could. When she had finished, they continued the tour.

"Over here we have a hose line for showers," Battuello said, pointing to an area just past the sleeping chamber. "Each man gets a few minutes of water every other day to clean up."

They circled back past the cage again. A group of musicians were setting up instruments on a small wooden stage in the main entry.

"Our entertainment for tonight," Battuello explained. "Tomorrow evening we will have a group of local actors put on a play. During the day, we will have labor speakers and whatever other activities we can come up with to entertain the men."

"How long do you think the stay-down strike will last?" Lena asked.

"We are prepared to remain as long as necessary," Battuello said. "Hopefully no more than a month, though."

"Do you think the men can handle being confined that long?" Lena asked.

Battuello pointed to a commissary to the right where a large contingency of men were already dining on food that had been sent down by the Women's Auxiliary. Across the entry to Lena's left she saw tables set up with men playing cards. In the next open chamber, men pitched horseshoes.

"I think most men will be content," Battuello said. "Some of them have said they're looking forward to getting away from their wives for a while." His face reddened. "Sorry, Mrs. Eng, it's just a standing joke men say to keep their spirits up."

"No offense taken, Mr. Battuello," Lena said with a smile. "I'm quite certain the wives have their own version of the joke."

Following the brief tour, Harley escorted Lena back to the cage.

"You know you could take the sloped walkway back to the surface, if you'd prefer," Harley told her.

"What, and miss the entire experience of what it is like to be a coal miner?" Lena kissed her husband and stepped into the cage. Before the lift began its ascent, she added, "I'll see you in a few weeks, cave man."

When she was gone, Harley returned to the commissary, poured himself a cup of coffee, and sat at a table next to Battuello and several other men.

"Glad to have a mine safety inspector and rescue team member with us," Battuello said. "There aren't many from your ranks willing to stand beside the Progressives."

"Well," Harley said, "none of them are married to

someone like Lena. She believes strongly in improving conditions in the mines."

"We need more like her," Battuello said, then lowered his voice. "Harley, we need to work hard to keep an eye on the men."

"Are you afraid the company may try something?" Harley said.

"Possibly. But I'm more concerned that if a few men get frustrated and leave, then others will follow. We must do everything we can to keep morale high."

For the first couple of days, Harley thought morale was high indeed. There were lots of good-natured shenanigans, the miners often acting like boys on a camping trip. Then on the fourth day, a couple of fights broke out. Harley recognized tension in the men as well as himself. The nights were becoming almost unbearably uncomfortable in the hard pit cars. When the miners woke up on day five, there was a lot of grumbling and several men complained to an older miner nicknamed Icicle that his snoring kept them awake.

"The vibration of your snores are gonna bring down that top," a young miner told Icicle as they walked to the main hallway for roll call.Icicle had received his nickname because of the preponderance of his long, pointy nose. "That schnozzle of yours is gonna get us all kilt," another minor agreed.

Icicle's demeanor was melting fast. Roll call was a time when a miner with something to say would often stand and give a speech while the men were counted. A memory of something a close friend had once told him brought Harley to his feet and compelled him to walk on slightly quivering legs to the front of the room. He stood on the wooden platform where visiting bands and actors had performed for them each evening.

"We've certainly heard some mighty fine speeches here this week," he said, "but last night as I rolled around in my pit car trying to sleep, I remembered a story a friend of mine once shared with me. So, I thought I might take a try at telling you about a man named RJ Hiler." Harley spoke slowly, and his quiet voice caused the miners to lean forward so they could hear. "In 1914, RJ and his wife Carmela traveled to a place called Ludlow, Colorado, to help about twelve hundred colliers with their strike. Now, I know that all you fellas have heard about Ludlow, but you most likely never heard this story. The Hilers had to sleep in a small pit dug beneath their tent. At night, in an attempt to keep strikers awake, the National Guard would fire several shots every five minutes or so into a few of the tents in the camp. Every morning, Carmela and the other women would search their tents for bullet holes and stitch them up if they found any.

"Well, as you know, on April twentieth, the National Guard began shooting colliers and burning those tents. Two dozen men, women and children died that day, including Carmela Hiler." Harley hesitated to let the story sink in. "Now as I lay there last night, my hands and feet going numb from the cold and being unable to find a comfortable position, I thought about those men, women and children at Ludlow who slept in those little holes every night while bullets tore through their tents trying to find their flesh. Well, boys, I don't know about you, but I think I can endure quite a lot more suffering than what I've had these past few nights if it means our children and grandchildren will have better wages, working conditions and job security than what we've had."

Harley was humbled by the rousing applause, and though he didn't see any miners apologizing to Icicle, he had a sense that they did catch the message in his words.

While he was certain the miners were hardy enough to endure the physical discomfort of their situation, Harley wondered if many were lonely. For Harley, being away from Lena for such a long time was the most difficult aspect of the strike. It was the longest he had been separated from his wife since his return from the Great War in 1918. Before he could ponder the problem further, he heard Jack Battuello's shouts echoing through the caverns.

"We took a head count and came up one man short," Battuello said. "Each section needs to send out search parties immediately. Look under the rocks and coal cars to see if we have anyone hurt or, hopefully, asleep. Send men into adjacent chambers, but stay together in large groups in case the coal company is at the bottom of this."

Men scattered. The search went on for four hours, and when men began returning to the main foyer at noon, Battuello was nearly in a state of panic.

"I don't want to lose a man, no matter what the circumstance," Battuello told his lieutenants when they gathered at a commissary table. "It would especially hurt our cause if any man abandons the strike."

"Someone's coming!" a man yelled. "I see a little ol' dim light coming from the airshaft direction."

Everyone turned in the direction of the sloped main entryway.

"It's Dominic Bollestra!" someone shouted.

Battuello ran over to Bollestra, grabbed him by the shoulders, and shook him hard. "Goddamn you son-of-a-bitch!" Battuello shouted, "where in the hell have you been for the last four or five hours?"

"What kind of a son-of-a-bitchin' union have you got here?" Bollestra yelled and jerked away from Battuello's firm grip. "I sent a note up to my wife to meet me in the airshaft and make love. And now you say the union says I can't make love? Well, by God, I sit down here for five days and do my part! Hell, I never complain, and I sure as hell ain't no scab! But now you tell me I can't make love with my wife? What the hell kind of a union do you got here?"

There was a long moment of dead silence except for the familiar humming coming from the motor room. Then Jack Battuello began to laugh. It was a deep belly laugh, and it was immediately followed by over five-hundred men laughing and slapping one another's backs. When it subsided, Battuello raised his hands and everyone grew quiet and listened.

"Well hell, son," Battuello said, "I'm just sorry that I didn't made such an arrangement with *my* wife."

* * * * * * *

The following four days were uneventful. The five-hundred-forty miners settled into a ritual of meals, motivational speeches, horseshoes, and card games, followed by guest entertainment in the evenings. The ninth day ended with a highly entertaining bluegrass band from Missouri. When the musicians were finished and as the miners stood to head to their pit cars to be serenaded by Icicle's snores, Jack Battuello walked to the podium and asked everyone to sit back down. As they settled into their seats, John Fisher, president of the Gillespie local Progressive Miners of America, stepped forward.

"We are justified in saying that our stay-down strike has accomplished its primary purpose," Fisher said to the suddenly hush audience. "It has dramatically promoted national attention to the fact that miners are paying the cost of mechanization in terms of less work, less pay and fewer jobs. Our immediate strike is merely a rehearsal of a greater struggle that looms in the coal industry on the issue of mechanization and consequent effects on the lives of the people who depend on mining. Unless greater social and economic reforms are enacted to give the miners a greater share of the benefits of mechanization, labor action will manifest itself with greater intensity and on a broader scale. Our stay-down strike now terminates, but the struggle to meet mechanization goes on, and we call upon the miners of America to join us in this demand for the six-hour day as the first step to meet the problem. Therefore, after nine days of arduous service marked by unsurpassed loyalty and fortitude, I hereby release you fine men to return to your loving families."

Harley thought that the sporadic cheers that followed the announcement was a mixture of confusion, disappointment and elation.

"Like kissing your damned sister!" Battuello said as the men scattered to gather their belongings. "We didn't win anything. National attention? Hell, the *company* won! They still won't accept job sharing."

"We can't let it just end like this," Harley said.

"What can we do about it?" Battuello said.

"Well," Harley said, "I seem to remember hearing that the Notre Dame football coach, Knute Rockne, had ways to bring his teams together whenever they lost a football game. I think I know a way to show the public that we are all in solidarity despite not getting what we wanted. I'm just not sure how big, burly coal miners will take to the idea."

* * * * * * *

Though it was ten o'clock at night, the Williamsville mine yard was filled with journalists from as far away as Chicago and St. Louis, as well as hundreds of family members of the striking men who were down in the mine. As usual, newspaper men milled around, asking questions of the wives. It had been that way until well after midnight for nine long days. "What is that sound?" someone shouted. The crowd grew hush as they strained to hear the synchronized shuffling coming from the sloped entrance. Like a train approaching a railroad station, the sound grew louder and louder. The miners were five abreast as they emerged from the dark walkway. Their duffle bags hung from their backs so, in a style similar to Rockne's Notre Dame football players, they were free to hold the hands of the men next to them. Their faces were so intense no one in the crowd said a word for several seconds.

"Is the strike over?" One of the journalists finally shouted. "Did the company agree to your demands?"

None of the striking miners spoke until the final man emerged from the walkway. They then broke ranks, and some searched the suddenly noisy crowd for loved ones. One pesky newspaperman ran from miner to miner, begging for someone to give him a quote, but the men ignored him.

"Do you have anything to say about the strike?" the little man holding a pen and notepad asked Harley Eng.

"Solidarity." Harley said. When he saw Lena running toward him, he pulled his duffle bag from around his shoulder.

"Can't you give me at least one complete sentence that I can print?" the journalists pleaded. Harley resisted the urge to punch the annoying man in the face.

Lena suddenly had her arms around Harley. She took her husband's face in her hands and kissed him hard on the mouth. Then she turned toward the journalist and offered the man the complete sentence he asked for.

"Solidarity forever!" she said, then turned toward Harley. "Let's go home, darling."

20

The next morning when the Eng's came outside carrying cups of coffee, they were shocked to find Antonio sitting on their porch. Lena immediately handed her cup to the Italian and, without a word, went back inside to get herself another.

"Did you come here to find out what happened in Williamsville?" Harley asked as he took a seat in a wicker chair.

"No," Antonio said, shaking his head. "I bring bad news. A grand jury just indicted thirty-six of our boys on racketeering charges."

Harley's mouth was still open when Lena returned to the porch.

"What is it?" Lena asked, seeing the shock on her husband's face.

"Trial will begin next week for thirty-six of our Progressives," Antonio repeated for her benefit. "They are being charged for railroad bombings, racketeering and conspiracy to obstruct the mails."

"Antonio," Lena said, "everyone knows that the UMW and the coal companies are the only ones who benefited from all these shootings and bombings. They committed most of those crimes themselves so the governor would send in the National Guard to keep the mines open."

"You know that no jury is going to find them guilty,"

Harley added.

"They are bringing in a special prosecutor and judge," Antonio said, "and they're stacking the jury with their own people. It doesn't look good. I fear that if we lose this case, it will be the end of the Progressives."

* * * * * * *

On the first day of trial, Vinnie had trouble finding a parking spot near the Sangamon County Courthouse in Springfield. After finally squeezing his car between two poles, he walked the three blocks to the building. When he turned onto Ninth Street, he saw dozens of men on each side of the road dressed in their Sunday best. The ones he recognized as Progressive miners were being pushed with rifle barrels by the lawmen.

"No loitering!" one of the officers shouted.

"What about those guys?" a Progressive yelled, pointing angrily across the street.

"Well, they be witnesses for the prosecution," the U.S. Marshal replied. "They was most likely subpoenaed to be here."

"Witnesses? Hell!" the Progressive said. "Half of them were with the PMA a month ago."

"Those turncoats took the four-hundred-dollar bribe that Lewis's men offered them!" another coal miner shouted. "Hell, I beat the shit out of the dirty scumbag that offered me blood money to betray my brothers."

Vinnie crossed the street and was immediately stopped by two officers.

"I'm a representative for the Progressive Miners of America." Vinnie held out papers. After the documents were examined, he was searched thoroughly by two police officers before being escorted into the courthouse.

The halls were filled with journalists who were scurrying among the visitors, demanding to know who he was and why he was there.

"Are you a company or union man?" a pudgy reporter asked Vinnie as a flash from a camera went off next to him.

"Union man."

"Which union?"

"The only union," Vinnie said. "The Progressive Miners of America."

He was searched again, then ushered into the courtroom and placed behind the defendants. The thirty-six accused, as young as twenty and as old as sixty, wore suits and sat quietly. Under any other circumstances, they might have been taken as church elders waiting for a Sunday service to begin. They hailed from counties all across the central and southern coal fields of Illinois. The one Vinnie knew best, Ray Tombazzi, turned and gave Vinnie a confident smile.

Compared to the hallway, the courtroom was reverent, with only whispers among those present. Upon court order, armed U.S. Marshals were stationed along the walls. The space for onlookers was at a premium, with less than one hundred seats available and no standing permitted.

"Steve Mason," the handsome, well-dressed young man next to Vinnie whispered as he extended a hand.

"Vinnie Vacca. You a miner?"

"No, a lawyer. But I have a keen interest in the Progressives, since my pa and brother are miners."

The bailiff stood. "All rise. The Court of Sangamon County is now in session, the Honorable Judge Charles Briggle presiding."

Everyone remained standing until the judge entered and took his seat. He was a distinguished-looking man in his early sixties with gray hair receding to the middle of his head.

"Please be seated," Briggle said. "Bailiff, call the day's calendar."

"Your Honor, today's case is the State of Illinois versus the Progressive Miners of America."

"Are the attorneys ready?"

"Yes, Your Honor."

"The prosecution may begin."

"May it please the court and gentlemen of the jury, my name is Douglas Eubanks," Eubanks began in an affluent drawl, "counsel for the prosecution in this action."

For the next hour, Vinnie watched and listened as Eubanks had each of the defendants stand as he identified them by name. That followed a thirty-minute summation of the charges, followed by Eubanks walking over and standing directly in front of the jurors as he addressed them.

"The state will prove beyond a reasonable doubt that these thirty-six defendants used Progressive relief funds, which were financed by union check-off dues, to buy dynamite, batteries and other bombing paraphernalia. The violence was intended to intimidate mine and railroad officials as part of a campaign of terrorism against firms handling UMW-mined coal. The indictments also charge conspiracy to obstruct mails and interfere with interstate commerce."

When he was finished, Arthur M. Fitzgerald of Springfield, a defense specialist, took his turn and gave what Vinnie thought was a surprisingly honest argument for why the defendants were innocent.

"The defense will prove," Fitzgerald said, "that the United Mine Workers and the coal companies used tactical bombing they knew would be blamed on the PMA and would force Governor Horner to send in the National Guard to protect the coal mines. Think about it. The PMA would have nothing to gain from such bombings. In fact, such terrorist tactics would only serve to turn the public against them. Any violence that would cause the National Guard to protect the coal mines would only hurt their cause. The mines could not open without the protection of the Guard, because there were thousands of picketers surrounding them."

The first witness called for the prosecution was a man Vinnie had seen around the mine yards for years.

"I was an undercover man for Peabody Coal Company," Edward Marshall of Taylorville testified in a monotone voice that Vinnie thought sounded rehearsed and memorized. "I was there when the PMA leaders told us we might have to shoot ourselves out of the labor controversy down in Coulterville. Then they stored two boxes of dynamite out on my farm. Progressive President Jack Stanley offered me one-hundred-fifty dollars to take the dynamite and destroy the airshaft at the Woodside mine near Springfield. I told him I wasn't no murderer, so I guess he got somebody else to do his dirty work."

"Why do you think it was unusual for the PMA leaders to tell you you might have to shoot your way out if surrounded by armed gunmen in Coulterville?" Fitzgerald asked on cross examination.

"Why, he was telling us to use violence."

"Could he have been telling you that you might need to defend yourself if attacked?"

"Well, I suppose so, but that's not how I took it." Marshall balled his fists, then moved them quickly onto his lap.

"And if dynamite was stored at your farm, and you were indeed an undercover man, why wouldn't you immediately report that to the coal company?"

"Well, I figured it would have blowed my cover."

"Ah," Fitzgerald said, "so your cover was more important than the lives of those miners whose airshaft was about to be bombed?"

"Objection !" Eubanks said.

"Sustained," Judge Briggle said. "Strike that comment from the records.""No further questions, Your Honor." Fitzgerald returned to his seat.

"Why did he let them strike that from the record?" Vinnie whispered.

"Just because it's stricken from the record doesn't mean it's stricken from the jurors' minds," Mason said. "They'll remember it."

The next witness was a former Progressive named Ora Dabbs.

"Ray Tombazzi told me the Progressives were trying to get the Chicago and Illinois Midland trackmen to support them with a sympathy strike," Dabbs said.

"Isn't it true that unions often threaten and bully other unions to go on sympathy strikes in support of their cause?" Eubanks asked.

"Yes."

"And if you had been a member of the trackmen's union, would you have gone on strike knowing that if you didn't, you might lose your life in a bombing?"

"Objection," Fitzgerald said.

"Sustained," Briggle said.

"I withdraw the last half of that question," Eubanks said. "Would you have gone on strike if you had been a member of the trackmen's union?"

"Of course I'd go on strike," Dabbs said. "Them Progressives is vicious."

"Objection, Your Honor!" Fitzgerald shouted. "That question requires speculation from the witness."

"Sustained," Judge Briggle said. "The question is stricken from the record and the jury is ordered to not consider this line of questioning in their deliberations."

"The jury will remember that too, won't they?" Vinnie whispered to Mason.

John Westfall of Harrisburg was then called up to testify that Sheriff Nip Evans handed out guns and ammunition on the Harrisburg square just before the alleged gun battle.

"So you are another former Progressive who became an undercover man for Peabody Coal Company?" Fitzgerald asked on cross examination.

"Yes, sir."

"And did you get paid by Peabody to take on this dangerous assignment?"

"Yes," Westfall said.

"And did you get paid PMA relief money when you posed as a Progressive?"

"Well, sure," Westfall shifted his weight in the hard, wooden chair. "I had to take it or that would look suspicious."

"Ah, but I suppose buying that new Ford coupe last spring didn't make you appear suspicious?"

"Objection," Eubanks said.

"Sustained."

"I withdraw the question," Fitzgerald said and returned to his seat. "No further questions, Your Honor.

"It seems like half the stuff that will influence the jury has been stricken from the record," Vinnie told Mason after court that evening as they walked to their cars.

"That's often the way it works," Mason said.

* * * * * * *

That evening, the three Vacca boys found an old shovel while walking through the timber behind their house.

They promptly found an area of softened dirt and began digging a hole.

"I'll bet if we dig deep enough, we'll reach China," Tony said when it was his turn to dig.

"That's silly, Tony." Willie stood over the hole, whittling on a piece of driftwood he'd found in a creek. "We would reach Pellucidar first."

"What's Pellucidar?" Sid sat down in the grass and began thinking.

"It's a world deep underground where dinosaurs live," Willie said. "I read about it in a book Edgar Rice Burroughs wrote."

"I thought he only wrote Tarzan books," Sid said.

"Ah, no," Willie said, "he's written about people who go to Mars and Venus and all sorts of places."

"I think we should make it a swimming pool." Tony handed the shovel to Sid and stepped out of the shallow hole. "We could pour concrete into it and stock it with crawdads."

"Why would we want crawdads in it?" Sid asked as he took his turn digging.

"To keep girls out, of course." Tony said.

Sid dug harder. He wasn't sure he liked the idea of keeping girls out of their pool. He had been playing with a tomboy named Rosemary Donovan lately. She reminded him of his mother. She liked to wear dungarees and ball caps, and she wasn't afraid of spiders and snakes like most girls.

Then his shovel struck something mushy. It felt like clay, so he put the point down in the dirt and stood on the flat handles. When it still didn't budge, he bounced up and down like it was a pogo stick. The black liquid that shot up out of the hole squirted onto his face. He couldn't stop his mouth from tasting it, even as he screamed and swiped it immediately from his lips. Willie was suddenly at his side lifting him back into the grass. Sid spit and spit while Tony and Willie jumped onto all fours and began moving dirt with their hands to see what their cousin had found. When the brothers screamed in unison and jumped out of the hole, Sid looked down and saw the outline of a human face.

The dead man's eyes were closed, but his mouth was open. He had been screaming as he was buried alive.

21

Vinnie didn't go to the trial the next day. He stayed home
with Sid, who was very shaken over being the one to find
the body. His son took turns sitting on his mother and father's lap until Angie Eng walked into the house. When he
saw her, Sid jumped up and ran into her arms.

"My young hero," Angie said as she stroked the back of
his head. "You must feel like Huckleberry Finn did when
he saw Injun Joe kill the man in the graveyard."

"I cried, Angie," Sid said. "I didn't mean to, but I
couldn't help myself."

"Of course you did, my dear. My goodness, even the
most courageous soldier in the world would have shed
tears after something like that."

"You're a mighty brave young man," Corporal O'Sullivan said from the doorway.

Sid hadn't seen the soldier walk in and wasn't sure he
liked having him there. At that moment, Sid hated everything to do with the mine war. The guardsman, with his
pistol tucked smartly away in his side holster, was a grim
reminder of the death that seemed to be everywhere, especially since the day of his Grandma Vacca's murder. He
buried his head in Angie's shoulder and shut his eyes.

When Sid began sobbing, Angie picked him up and carried him over to the rocking chair. They sat there in silence
for a long time.

"Who was he?" Sid finally asked without raising his head.

Angie looked at Sam, who nodded. "He was a strike-breaker from southern Illinois," Angie said.

"Did he have children?" Sid asked.

"Yes, he did. But they are grownup."

"I wouldn't want that to happen to my daddy, even if I was grownup."

"No, I wouldn't either."

Sid looked up at his father. "Pa, would you ask the Progressives to stop killing people? Please, Pa? Then maybe the coal company and the United Mine Workers will quit too."

Vinnie nodded. His eyes were glazed and watery. "I surely will, son."

* * * * * * *

Court began the next morning with Ira Jacobs, another former Progressive, called by the prosecution to identify guns and ammunition that were used by the Progressives at the Harrisburg gunfight. On cross examination, Fitzgerald quickly poked holes in his testimony.

"Why, them's the bullets that Nip Evans gave us at Harrisburg," Jacobs said.

"Oh?" Fitzgerald said with a smile. "Well, that's very interesting." He held a bullet out to the defendant. "Is this one of the bullets that Evans handed out also?"

"Well, I don't rightly remember," Jacobs said.

"Oh, but you do recognize these other bullets that the State showed you?" Fitzgerald said. "Your Honor, I think it's clear there is no way to prove that these weapons and ammunition that the State has produced were passed out by Sheriff Evans."

"I would agree," Briggle said. "Are you through with the witness?"

"Just a few more questions, Your Honor." Fitzgerald turned back to Jacobs. "And were you also an undercover agent for the UMW?"

"Well, yeah," Jacobs said, then added, "'Cause I wasn't so sure the Progressives were honest."

"Did you report PMA activities to the UMW representatives?"

"Well." Jacobs squirmed in the chair. "Sometimes, sure."

"Did you or did you not make attempts to urge the Progressives to more violence by telling them stories that you fabricated about abuses by Peabody officials?"

"No, I didn't do that," Jacobs said, half-rising in his chair.

"Remembering that you are under oath," Fitzgerald said. "Did the UMW pay you to leave the Progressives and come back to their ranks?"

"Well, they paid me some compensation for lost time, yeah."

"And how much was that compensation?"

"Two thousand dollars, big man!" Jacobs shouted, "and that's more money than you'll make for this whole, lousy trial."

The next witness was Andrew Sakalas, a Lithuanian miner who had come to America in 1921 after working in Scotland.

"That son-of-a-bitch must have changed over to the UMW," Vinnie whispered to Mason. "He was recently charged for murdering his wife."

"What do you want to bet those charges will be dropped after today's testimony?" Mason asked.

"What?" Vinnie shook his head. "They can't do that."

He paused and looked at Mason, his eyes growing wide. "Can they?"

"Progressive Officer Dan McGill said to me," Sakalas testified, then changed his voice to a deep authoritative one. "'We can't stop men from working by bombing their homes, so we've got to take action against the railroads for pulling the coal out.'" Sakalas chuckled, clearly amused by his own performance. "He offered me thirty dollars for a bombing job and told me to see Schneider, the paymaster. Then, when the FBI got involved, McGill told me, 'Keep your records away from government investigators.' Then later he said, 'The government is getting too close, so go change your books.' There were seven boxes of dynamite along with groceries for relief clients. I helped unload them into the PMA headquarters basement. Four days later, the food and dynamite was gone. I went to McGill's house and told him I was concerned about the railroad bombings and someone might get hurt. McGill gave me one-hundred-fifty dollars to keep me from complaining at meetings about the use of relief funds for other purposes."

"Oh, I see, Mr. Sakalas," Fitzgerald said, "so you kept your mouth shut when they let you get away with blackmail and mooching?"

"Objection, Your Honor!" Douglas Eubanks shouted.

"Sustained," Briggle said.

The next day charges were dropped against Sakalas for murdering his wife.

* * * * * * *

"The Progressives tried to hire me to kill John L. Lewis," Archie Norton testified the next morning. "I wouldn't do it, so they hired one of the defendants, Russell Smith of Gillespie."

Vinnie had to restrain himself from leaping out of his seat and attempting to thrash Norton. Fortunately, under detailed cross-examination, Fitzgerald discredited the witness by bringing to light the little gangster's extensive life of crime.

"Isn't it true, Mr. Norton, that you once served a prison term for assault with attempt to kill?"

"Well, that was a long time ago."

"And haven't you been incarcerated in county jails on at least ten different occasions in both Illinois and Missouri?"

"Them was simple misunderstandings and them charges was all dropped."

"And didn't you turn State's evidence in every one of those instances to ensure those charges would be dropped?"

"Them testimonies was coincidental to the charges."

"So in other words, you're a professional squealer?" Fitzgerald said. "How much were you paid to be here today, Mr. Norton?"

"Only expenses."

"How much are those expenses?" Fitzgerald asked as he walked in front of the jury and gave them a knowing smile.

"Oh, about five hundred dollars, I reckon," Norton said.

"Wow," Fitzgerald said, then let his eyes roll from the jurors back to the defendant, "you must have pretty darn good room service at your hotel."

* * * * * * *

"Yes, sir," hardware merchant Joseph Turigliatto of Benld testified, "I was in the store when three of the defendants purchased about twelve hundred pounds of dynamite, dynamite caps, six-volt batteries, telephone wires, and other items, and paid me in cash. Then on October ninth, while sitting in my rocking chair, part of my face was shot away by assassins firing through a window of my home." Turigliatto turned his face toward the jury and showed that his right cheekbone was missing. He was almost crying as he said, "Thank God for the United Mine Workers. They have had me under heavy guard ever since."

"Four United Mine Workers were arrested and released for that shooting," Vinnie whispered to Mason. "Why don't they mention that?"

"Because they were released," Mason said.

Court the next morning started with a young UMW man testifying against his Progressive brother, claiming he twice saw sticks of dynamite, fuses, and wiring in his brother's house. On cross examination, Fitzgerald showed that a family rift occurred when the men chose rival unions.

Next, former miner and Illinois and Missouri ex-convict William L. Weber testified that PMA Vice President John Fancher offered him one thousand dollars, along with fifty dollars expense money, to blow up the airshaft at the Peabody Coal Companies Capitol Mine in Springfield.

"So, tell us Mister Weber, are you also an undercover man?" Fitzgerald asked on cross examination.

"No."

"Are you on the payroll of Peabody Coal Company?"

"Of course not."

"How about the United Mine Workers?"

"No."

"Well, you have certainly renewed my faith in the rehabilitation system of convicted criminals," Fitzgerald said, bringing a smile to Weber's face. "You claim to have been offered thousands of dollars by the PMA to commit crimes, and yet you have never accepted any money to aide in the prosecution of the Progressive Miners of America. Before you answer that, remember that you are under oath, and as a felon on probation, a perjury conviction will put you right back in prison."

Weber's smile disappeared.

"Now, tell me, Mr. Weber." Fitzgerald walked over to the jurors and looked at them as he asked, "Have you ever been paid to aide in the investigation or the prosecution of the defendants?"

"Well, yeah," Weber said, "I've been paid a little to help in the investigation. But only for expenses."

"How much for these expenses?" Fitzgerald asked as he turned and moved rapidly toward the witness stand.

"Why, I don't know." Weber's eyes grew wide. "A few hundred or maybe a thousand or two. I can't rightly remember."

"That's a pretty good expense account at a time when most skilled workers are getting little more than seven dollars a day," Fitzgerald said as he turned his back on the defendant. "No more questions, Your Honor."

After the witness was seated, Fitzgerald walked over and stood in front of Judge Briggle's bench.

"Your Honor," Fitzgerald said, "before we break for lunch, I would like to point out that some of my witnesses are becoming alarmed because a Springfield city detective, a railroad detective and two UMW men have stationed themselves in the hallway outside the witness room in an effort to intimidate them. There might be violence in the building if such behavior continues."

"Duly noted, Counselor." Briggle rose to leave. "I will have Marshal Ruppel address the matter and close the corridors during recesses."

* * * * * * *

The next day began with a series of railroad workers describing how the many bombings made them afraid to work. Vinnie was surprised that after hearing three witnesses, Judge Briggle agreed with Fitzgerald that this evidence was immaterial. He struck the testimony from the records. Later, as Vinnie and Mason smoked on the courthouse sidewalk during a break, Vinnie shared his opinion that he thought the striking of the evidence was a victory for the Progressives.

"I'm not so sure, Vinnie. The wrong testimony or a slip from one of the railroad men could implicate the United Mine Workers in the bombings. That would open the door to Fitzgerald's conspiracy theory that the UMW and coal companies are in cahoots."

"So why would Judge Briggle rule the testimony immaterial?" Vinnie slowly released smoke through his nostrils. "You think Judge Briggle is on the take?"

"I don't know," Mason said. "Let's see what happens when the defense gets their turn."

The two dropped their cigarette butts and were smashing them with their feet when they heard angry shouts coming from inside the courthouse. They quickly followed a half dozen U.S. Marshals, who rushed to a fight taking place just outside the room where defense witnesses were being isolated from the court proceedings. Vinnie's father was a potential witness in that room.

Defense Attorney William Horsley was being held back by Fitzgerald and another lawyer. Horsley had a red burn mark around his neck where his tie had been ripped off. The front of his shirt was torn and hung at his waist.

"Those son-of-a-bitches were trying to intimidate our witnesses!" Horsley shouted.

"I was watching," Marshal Ruppel said, with a smirk. "It was you who was doing the intimidating, Counselor."

"This whole trial is rigged!" one of the Progressive spectators shouted. He was quickly escorted from the building by two U.S. Marshals.

Vinnie wanted to punch Ruppel, but would have had to fight his way through the crowded hallway to get to him. A few moments later, everyone was ushered back into the courtroom.

Fitzgerald held Horsley by the arm and had him stand beside him with his shirt torn off. Several welts were quickly forming on his bare chest and neck.

"What is the meaning of this?" Judge Briggle said when he entered and saw Horsley.

"It would seem," Fitzgerald said, "that your U.S. Marshal failed to restrain Springfield Detective Austin Jones and O.G. Chapman, a special agent for the Illinois Central railroad. As you will recall, Your Honor, both Jones and Chapman were witnesses for the prosecution, and I told you yesterday they had been loitering near the room used by defense witnesses."

"Marshal Ruppel," Briggle addressed the lawman who quickly rose to attention, "why were these men outside the witness room?"

"They had to pass it on the way to the courtroom, Your Honor," Ruppel said. "I saw them and they made no attempt to look in the room."

"Your Honor," Horsley said, "I saw Chapman turn the doorknob, and then Jones kicked it open."

"Marshal Ruppel," Briggle said, "for the duration of this trial, I want a guard standing in front of that witness room anytime it is occupied. Mister Horsley, go get a fresh shirt. Court is in recess until you return."

* * * * * * *

"After reviewing the evidence that the defense is prepared to produce," Judge Briggle told the attorneys after the recess and before the jury entered the courtroom, "I am ruling that you are not to discuss the UMW/PMA dispute, nor are you to explore the possibility that the UMW and coal companies conspired to use the bombings as a way to force the governor to send troops in to keep the mines open."

The courtroom erupted with jeers from the Progressives' side and laughs and cheers from the UMW and company side. Briggle pounded his gavel and threatened to empty the courtroom.

"On what grounds are you suppressing this evidence, Your Honor?" Fitzgerald asked.

"On the grounds that it is immaterial to the guilt or innocence of the defendants," Briggle said.

An old miner in the back of the room stood and hurled a barrage of swear words at the Judge. Immediately, a burly U.S. Marshal put a choke hold on the man, lifted him off his feet, and carried him out of the room. When the spectators rose to protest, a half dozen other lawmen stepped forward and put their hands on their night sticks.

"Bailiff, bring in the jurors," Judge Briggle said as if nothing had happened. "Mr. Fitzgerald, call your first witness."

The first witnesses for the defense stated that many of the prosecution's witnesses were testifying in an attempt to get the ten-thousand-dollar reward offered by the coal company if that testimony lead to a conviction in the railroad bombing in Saline County.

Another witness, a mine payroll clerk, showed that three of the defendants were working in the mine at the time of the bombing they were accused of. One other defendant was bartending. As the alibis stacked up, it became more and more apparent to Vinnie that Fitzgerald was leading up to a conjecture that only the coal mine company and the UMW had the means and opportunity to blow up the trains and tracks.

"What is your occupation?" Fitzgerald asked the next witness, a muscular man in his early thirties.

"I'm a former associate of Mr. Al Capone," Vernon Vickery testified. "I served time for my indiscretions but I'm stronger for it. In fact, I can lift more than any man I ever met, and I have the prowess of a world champion boxer."

"Were you hired by Peabody Coal Company in 1933?"

"Yes, sir," Vickery said. "Peabody brought me in to strong-arm the Progressives."

"Well," Fitzgerald said, "I know you are a world class boxer, but there were over five thousand Progressives in Christian County. Were you expected to strong-arm them with only your fists?"

"Ah, hell no," Vickery said, cracking his knuckles as he spoke. "The coal company had an extensive arsenal, which included dynamite, machine guns, high-powered rifles, revolvers and ammunition. Peabody District Superintendent W.C. Argust wanted someone who could dish it out, and directed me to beat up men who Argust thought might try to break up the UMW. Argust organized five heavily-armed cars of five men each to patrol roads in the vicinity of Peabody mines."

"What role did you have in dealing with the weapons you mentioned?" Fitzgerald asked.

"Argust put me in charge of the whole shebang," Vickery said. "He told me to handle the machine gun myself, but to hand out dynamite and arms to the boys who wanted to go out and raise things up."

"Didn't you worry that working for Peabody this way might get you in legal trouble again?"

"I asked Argust about that one day when I saw the sheriff nosing around the munitions room. Argust said to hell with the sheriff and his deputies. He said he was running Christian County, not the sheriff."

"So the law never gave Peabody any trouble?"

"Why should they? Hell, Peabody had the sheriff and about a hundred-to-one-hundred-fifty deputies on their payroll by the end of 1932."

"Objection," Eubanks said, "requires speculation."

"Sustained," Briggle said quickly. "Counselor is instructed to refrain from going into accounts of violence other than listed in the bill of particulars."

"What personal knowledge did you have of the bombings that took place in Christian County?" Fitzgerald asked.

"Well," Vickery said. "I know that one so-called bombing of a cable at Peabody Mine 58 at Hewittville was only a short circuit."

"Objection!" Eubanks shouted. "Speculation."

"Sustained," Briggle said as he slowly stood and banged the gavel onto his desk. "Okay, gentlemen, I am adjourning this court until tomorrow morning at nine o'clock."

* * * * * * *

Felina Phelan knew her beauty was beyond comparison with anyone else in the room. The envious gaze of the women and the lustful eyes of the men made her doubly aware of the method she would use to enter this class of wealth and power.

The dinner party at the lakeside mansion included members of the United Mine Workers as well as coal company executives. She thought it strange that the one man that she found most appealing was the fat, obnoxious lawyer, Douglas Eubanks. Eubanks was, at that moment, gloating over his accomplishments in the courtroom.

"But what about the testimony of Vernon Vickery today?" one of the immaculately dressed businessmen asked. "He certainly offered powerful evidence."

Eubanks threw down another glass of Scotch and laughed. "Don't worry. When I present my witnesses, I'll make Vickery look like he just got out of a lunatic asylum. That boy's family would kill their own grandmother for five dollars and a mule."

Felina had seen Eubanks in court in Taylorville and had never given the man a second thought. But, now that he wielded power over the lives of thirty-six men, he appeared interesting. Her husband was down by the boat dock smoking with a busty fourteen-year-old girl he had taken a fancy to. Since it was the young ladies first experience smoking, she wouldn't know until she awoke that it wasn't tobacco she was filling her lungs with—nor would it be perspiration oozing down the inside of her thigh.

When Eubanks caught sight of Felina Phelan, he lost all interest in discussing the most important trial of his career. The beautiful blond woman wore a strapless red dress that fit tighter around the waist than was considered modest for this type of evening event.

It took Felina less than ten minutes to manipulate Eubanks into taking her to one of the mansion's many bedrooms on the third floor. She wanted to be a part of the affluent man's future—even if as his private mistress. With the Eubanks' fortune, he could provide her with the luxurious lifestyle she deserved. Still, she knew she would have to train him, as she had so many men before him.

"Lay still and quit gruntin' like an old pig, you fat son-of-a-bitch," Felina ordered after ripping the attorney's clothes off his body. Naked, she straddled the gigantic man, despite the fact that her knees didn't even touch the bed.

"W-w-what?" Eubanks said through a mouthful of spittle as he tried to sit. His short arms flailed above him, giving the impression of a turtle attempting to roll itself off its own back.

"Play dead!" Felina violently raised his right leg up to his stomach, reached down and slapped the lawyer's hairy, bare ass. "You be a good boy and lay there like you just got shot, and I'll play the grieving widow that wants one last ride before her man expires."

"How, how can I make love if I'm dead?"

"Don't you know that a man comes into this world with a stiff one and he gets another when he goes out?" Felina whispered seductively, then lowered her head to where he couldn't see her below the massive mountain of his own belly fat. "You play dead, Counselor, and I'll play the demon that makes Hell feel like Heaven!"

Eubanks, eyes wide open, quit moving.

22

"Maybe if they put everyone in jail the killing will stop," Little Sid said that evening when he overheard his father and grandpa in the living room discussing the trial.

Sam came out of the kitchen in time to see her son scurrying back up the stairs to his bedroom. He did so by putting first his left foot then his right foot on each step, something he had not done since he was three years old. Despite all the love and attention he received from his family and Angie Eng, little Sid was clearly sinking deeper and deeper into despair. He seldom left his bedroom and hadn't played with Willie and Tony since the day they discovered the body in the woods.

It surprised everyone that Sid wanted to talk to Dr. Hiler.

"Grandpa said that Grandma and your wife looked a lot alike," Sid said to Hiler one day when the doctor came to visit.

"They sure did."

"How did your wife die?"

"She fell off a little hill and landed wrong," Hiler said.

"Did that make you scared of hills?"

"For a little while I was. But then I got to thinking. It's a strange thing, Sid. She probably could have fallen off that hill a million times and never done more than break an arm or a leg, but she just happened to land wrong that one time."

"That's kinda like Grandma," Sid said. "That bullet just happened to come down in the exact spot she was standing."

"Did that make you scared of guns?" Dr. Hiler asked.

"It sure did," Sid said. "I still am."

"That's probably not a bad thing," Hiler said. "Sometimes when a person is scared of guns, they think of better ways to handle problems."

One day Mary Kate told Sam that Pancho Barnes was going to be in an airshow at Lambert Airfield in St. Louis. The two mothers immediately began making plans to take their sons to see the famous female aviator. Sid, especially, had always loved airplanes. On the rare occasion when one passed overhead, he would stop whatever he was doing and hurry to get in a position to watch it.

Lena Eng was just as excited by the news. She offered to drive the two mothers and their sons the hour and a half to the airshow.

Once on the highway, Mary Kate read aloud an article so the boys would know something about the great lady.

> *When Florence Barnes lived in Mexico, she had dressed as a man to hide her identity and avoid being arrested as a revolutionary, thus earning the nickname* Pancho. *Born to wealth and privilege, Barnes attended the finest private schools in San Marino, California, but loved the outdoors and was an accomplished equestrian.*
>
> *At the age of twenty-seven, she learned to fly and went solo after just six hours of instruction. In 1930, she won the Women's Air Derby and, in the process, broke Amelia*

Earhart's world women's speed record with a speed of nearly two hundred miles per hour. That year she moved to Hollywood to be a stunt pilot in the many air-adventure movies that were being produced. Her most famous film was millionaire Howard Hughes' movie Hell's Angels. *During filming, three pilots lost their lives and several were injured, prompting Barnes to organize the Associated Motion Picture Pilots, a union of film industry stunt fliers that promotes safety and standardized pay for aerial stunt work.*

"I know you boys are mostly interested in seeing the airplanes," Lena said as she drove, "but I am excited to meet Pancho Barnes because she's a union organizer."

"I heard that Howard Hughes himself crashed an airplane during filming of *Hell's Angels*," Willie said, emphasizing the swear word, then giggling.

"If you think swear words are so funny, young man, I'll not be taking you to anymore movies," Mary Kate scolded her son. "That film had entirely too many bad words. I wish they would give parents a warning when movies are inappropriate for children."

The size of the crowd at the airfield was much smaller than Sam expected. The grandstand was barely half full when the program began. The emcee was Archie League, a celebrity in his own right as the world's first air traffic controller.

"Ladies and gentlemen," League said into a hand-held megaphone, "please turn your attention to the eastern sky and feast your eyes on the Five Blackbirds."

As the loud roar of engines crescendoed to a deafening

level, five double-winged airplanes flew low directly over the grandstand. So low, in fact, that many of those in the audience screamed and ducked for cover. Sid, Willie and Tony were among the few who stood and reached for the planes.

The audience recovered and began applauding. The five airplanes banked sharply into one-hundred eighty degree turns that took them in front of the grandstand. While three of the planes skimmed just above the ground, two rose into the sky and, in perfect synchronization, performed a climbing loop-the-loop. For the next thirty minutes, the planes took turns doing barrel rolls, perilous drops, and even flying upside down.

"I heard those are colored pilots." Mary Kate leaned forward to tell the boys.

"That's ridiculous!" A woman in a yellow bonnet glared at Mary Kate. "Everyone knows that Negro brains are too small to learn mechanical things."

Several people screamed and pointed. Everyone looked up, and from one of the higher flying airplanes, a man stood on the wing of the aircraft. The entire audience took a deep breath. Then the man dove headfirst toward the ground. Screams followed and several spectators covered their eyes. Those that didn't saw the large white cloth that emerged from the man's backpack. Applause grew when the parachute fully opened and the man began gliding to the open area in front of the grandstand.

"Please put your hands together," Archie League shouted through the bullhorn, "for the Brown Condor of Ethiopia, Colonel John Robinson."

The skydiver rolled onto the ground and quickly unbuckled himself as several men ran out to retrieve the giant umbrella-shaped parachute. Standing before the grandstand was a dashing and extremely handsome specimen of the Negro race. He waved at the audience, some of whom quit applauding.

"Nothing but trained monkeys!" the woman in the yellow bonnet shouted. She nearly fell onto her face trying to whisk her three children out of the grandstand and back toward the parking lot. As they passed Robinson the oldest of the boys stuck his tongue out at him. The pilot smiled and continued toward the small stage in front of the grandstand.

"Thank you, ladies and gentlemen," Robinson said in a voice strong enough to carry without the aid of a megaphone. "Now it is my pleasure to give you the queen of aeronautics, Pancho Barnes."

The airplane that buzzed the grandstand did so before any of the faint of heart could even scream. Its speed was even more pronounced because it shot past the Five Blackbird planes.

"That plane must be going over three hundred miles per hour!" someone shouted as the airplane did a sharp bank and returned to the airfield. It and the Five Blackbirds landed in near perfect synchronization and taxied to within thirty yards of the grandstand.

The applause was tremendous as a round-faced woman wearing a cap, goggles, kaki knickerbockers and a leather flight jacket leapt from the cockpit and jogged to the stage. "Thank you, thank you, ladies and gentlemen!" Barnes shouted through the bullhorn. "I want you to know that aviation is no longer in its infancy. Very soon, dozens or even hundreds of passengers just like you will be traveling in bus-size airplanes from New York to Los Angeles and all over the world. In fact, I have a friend who is preparing to fly all the way around the earth," Barnes said. "Most of you have heard of her, I'm sure. Her name is Amelia Earhart.

"Today the Five Blackbirds and I are offering you the

opportunity to be among the first of the Earth-bound humans to experience what, until recently, only birds could enjoy. For just five dollars, we will show you the clouds as you have never before seen them. Come fly with us today, faster than an eagle and higher than a rain cloud."

Dozens of spectators from the grandstand rushed toward the airplanes. For the next several hours, Barnes and the Negro pilots gave fifteen minute rides to all the brave at-heart.

"I've got five dollars here if any of you three would like to take a ride," Lena told the boys as they watched one of the airplanes load a young passenger.

Willie and Tony lowered their heads and shook them as they backed a step away. Sid looked up at the airplanes that were in the sky.

"No, thank you, Aunt Lena," Sid said, "Five dollars is too much for a fifteen-minute ride."

Sam and Mary Kate sat in the grandstand talking to a group of Negro women. Lena saw Pancho Barnes walking nearby, so she went over and introduced herself.

"You're the union organizer," Barnes said. She shook Lena's hand with a firm and powerful grip. "I read about you and Agnes Wieck and that trouble with those company thugs. You coal mine folk have really had a time of it, haven't you? Do you think the Progressives will be acquitted?"

"I hope so," Lena said. Now that she was close to the great aviator, she was somewhat taken aback by how masculine Barnes was. "Those three boys looking at your air machine are with me. I'm afraid the violence is taking a toll even on our young ones. Especially that little fellow. He is named after the famous Sid Hatfield of Matewan."

"Why, my own son Bill isn't much older than those boys," Barnes said.

"What's it really like up there, Pancho?" Lena asked.

"Flying makes me feel," Barnes whispered to Lena as she leaned forward and nudged her waist with an elbow, "like a sex maniac in a whorehouse with a stack of two-dollar bills."

Lena stood with her mouth open as Pancho Barnes walked over to the boys.

"I want you to know," Barnes said as she looked directly at Sid, "that it was your coal miners in Illinois who led the way toward all laborers getting better wages and working conditions across America. You should be proud of that heritage."

Barnes shook each of the boys' hands as they introduced themselves.

"Sid Hatfield." Barnes looked at young Sid, who unlike his cousins, looked her right in the eyes. "Now that's a name to be proud of."

"Thank you, ma'am," Sid said.

"Sid, I've been wanting to take that new Ryan ST–A Special for a spin," Barnes said, pointing to a hangar where a sleek-looking silver and blue single-winged plane sat. "Would you like to join me? Free of charge."

"Yes, ma'am," Sid said. "I surely would." He took the aviator's hand and walked with her across the grassy field as if he had known her his entire life. He looked back once and saw his family watching him.

"There's a pretty bad smell around this hangar," Barnes told him. "Some boys spilled some chemicals earlier and I'm afraid it's still lingering."

Sid hadn't told anyone, but since the moment the tip of the shovel struck that poor dead fellow in the ground, he had been able to smell nothing but the putrid, gaseous odor that had escaped from the cadaver. The dark blood that had squirted across his face and clothes had washed off, but the smell always seemed to be there. He had scrubbed his body several times each day and even rubbed lye soap deep into his nostrils, but the stink always returned.

Now as Sid allowed Pancho Barnes to lift him into the open cockpit, the thought crossed his mind that if the airplane crashed, his own body might release an odor equally as horrible.

"You ever dance, Sid?" Barnes asked as she fitted a leather cap and goggles onto his head.

"I've danced with my ma," Sid said, wondering what dancing had to do with flying.

"Have you ever put your feet on top of your mama's and let her float you around the room?"

"Sure, I have," Sid said.

"Well, today, you and I are going to glide across the clouds like we are dancing on God's feet," Barnes said. "And one day we will stand before Him and He is going to ask us if we saw the beautiful sunset He made for us today. And you and I will be able to say that we sure-fire did." She looked into his eyes. "I want you to remember something, Sid. When you have a choice, choose happy!"

She buckled him in and then rolled into the rear cockpit behind him. A man ran up to the front of the airplane, held a thumb up, then grabbed hold of the propeller with both hands, lifted one leg for momentum and gave the prop a hard, clockwise spin. The next thing Sid knew, the plane was bumping faster and faster along the long, dirt runway. He wanted to raise his hand as they passed his smiling and waving family, but found both arms to be unmovable at his sides. Cool air rushed against his face and forced him to lean backwards in his seat. With eyes and mouth wide open, he turned his head to one side. They were slowly rising until they were even with the tops of the nearby trees. Then the airplane banked sharply to his left. He looked down at the people on the ground who appeared to be grow smaller and smaller.

From behind him, Pancho Barnes sang:

Off we go into the wild blue yonder,
Climbing high into the sun;
Here they come zooming to meet our thunder,
At 'em boys, Give 'er the gun!
Down we dive, spouting our flame from under,
Off with one helluva roar!
We live in fame or go down in flame. Hey!
Nothing'll stop the U.S. Air Force!

"That's a song a friend of mine wrote for a contest," Barnes shouted. "You like it?"

Sid nodded. The sound of her voice seemed hollow and far away, though she was just a couple of feet behind him. He had an urge to yawn, and when he did, he felt a little pop in his ears. The humming sound of the airplane's motor returned immediately to normal.

"You doing okay, Sid?" Barnes shouted.

Sid held his hand high above him and gave a thumbs up. The airplane had leveled out now, and he could see forward as well as to the sides. They were flying parallel to the Mississippi River. In front of him, the Missouri River arched gracefully to meet its much wider brother. He thought about Miss Eng, and couldn't wait until he could tell her that he recognized the rivers from her geography lessons.

Upon impulse, Sid raised both hands high above him. Surprisingly warm air rushed between his fingers. They were above a cloud with nothing between them and the warmth of the setting sun. He laughed aloud, and when he swayed his hands to his right, Pancho Barnes banked the airplane in that direction. Moving his hands to his left, she banked hard that way. He kept them that direction until they had made a complete three-hundred-sixty-degree turn, then he dramatically pointed them forward and downward. Pancho let the nose drop gradually, but Sid laughed again and held both hands in a thumbs down position.

"Okay, Sid," Pancho yelled, "hang onto your socks!"

The nose of the plane dropped hard and fast. For a moment, Sid lowered his hands to hang onto his seatbelt, but then gave the confederate yell he had learned from his father and pointed one finger to the sky. The plane rolled sideways, and then shot almost straight up. The force pulled him backwards into his seat, and he once again grabbed onto his seatbelt. When they were back above the clouds, Pancho leveled the airplane again and turned it back toward the south.

"There's our sunset, Sid!" Pancho shouted.

Sid thought he had never seen anything so beautiful. The vastness of the blue sky seemed to go on forever and ever. The horizon was not the hills and trees he was used to seeing from the ground, but rather puffy, white clouds that blanketed the area below the airplane. As the orange sun began its gradual descent, those clouds became tainted with tints of red, pink, purple and blue. Sid felt calmer than he had in a long time. He breathed the cool, evening air in through his nose. It brought the smell of a fresh, spring-like rain. He wanted to remember that smell. In fact, he wanted to memorize this entire experience so he could relive it every night in his dreams.

The sun began to sink below the clouds, and so too did the little airplane. Young Sid's eyes remained on the sunset as the wheels touched back down on the earth. By the time they had taxied to the grandstand, stars were beginning to take their turn as the shining light of the heavens.

When Pancho helped Sid out of the cockpit and back to the ground, he gave her a tight hug. She carried him over to where his mother stood with one hand reaching out to him and the other clasped firmly over her mouth.

"Oh, Mama," Sid said as he reached out to his mother, "now I know why birds sing."

23

As the trial progressed day after day, Vinnie began to understand the magnitude of the devastation the coal mine war had ravished on Illinois from one end to the other. Every community with a mine had experienced shootings and bombings that resulted in deaths and disappearances. In most towns, parents made their children sleep in bathtubs at night for protection from drive-by shootings. Vinnie thought about the James Hartman drive-by shooting and how easily that could have happened to his own son or nephews.

One testimony told about a little girl who had been shot to death while sitting on the window ledge in her home. When Fitzgerald tried to show it was UMW men who were arrested, although later released, for the child's killing, Judge Briggle again intervened.

"Counselor," Briggle said in court one morning before the jury was summoned. "I am going to remind you just one more time that you are not to show motive for the UMW and Coal Company committing these acts of violence themselves."

"Your Honor, the evidence is simply being presented honestly," Fitzgerald pleaded. "I can't always be responsible for where the testimony may lead."

"Uh, huh," Briggle said. "Just remember, you've been warned."

The judge's point was immediately reinforced when Vernon Vickery was again called to testify.

"What type of dynamite was used on the Midland track bombing?" Fitzgerald asked.

"The type that is bought exclusively by Peabody Coal Company," Vickery replied. "No one else."

"To the best of your knowledge, was any dynamite of this type reported lost or stolen by Peabody Coal Company?" Fitzgerald asked.

When Eubanks rose to object, Briggle shouted, "You won't have to object! No such testimony will be permitted."

Trying not to show his disappointment, Fitzgerald said, "Your Honor, I would now like to call one of the defendants, John Schneider, to the stand."

After Schneider was sworn in and seated, Fitzgerald kept up his rapid-fire questioning. "Mr. Schneider, where were you at midnight on the evening of August twenty-first last year?"

"Glenn Stufflebeam and I were coming back from Gillespie. I was driving and he was in the passenger seat."

"The prosecution has stated that you were responsible for the explosion at the Hewittville Mine that occurred at midnight," Fitzgerald said. "Do you have any proof that you were on the highway, miles away at that time?"

"Yes sir," Schneider said. "Mr. Stufflebeam's head was shattered by a blast fired from a car which pulled alongside our vehicle."

"Where did this shooting occur?"

"On Route 66 just a few miles south of Springfield."

"Were there any witnesses to this shooting?"

"Yes, the man and woman in the car behind us saw the shooting and stopped to help. They were there when the police arrived. By then, Stufflebeam was dead. I gave a report including the make of the car and license plate number of the vehicle where the shots came from."

"Did the police run the information?" Fitzgerald asked.

"Yes, the vehicle belonged to R. K. Moody," Schneider said, then turned and looked directly at the jurors. "He is a United Mine Worker's organizer and investigator."

"And was anyone arrested for the murder of Glenn Stufflebeam?"

"No," Schneider said.

"Does anyone ever get arrested for murder in Christian County?" Judge Briggle asked. "Don't answer that. Court is in recess until one o'clock."

* * * * * * *

"Your Honor," Fitzgerald said immediately after court resumed, "efforts to locate and subpoena Peabody Coal Company District Superintendent W.C. Argust have been unsuccessful. We need Argust's testimony."

"I will send out marshals to look for him, Counselor," Briggle said. "That is all I can do."

That afternoon, Fitzgerald put a half dozen witnesses on the stand to testify that Peabody Coal Company had offered them bribes for paid testimonies in the court case.

PMA President Jack Stanley testified that he had worked for Argust. "I quit because Argust wanted me to get information on the activities of the Progressives. As a result of my refusal, my home was bombed twice."

* * * * * *

"Jack Stanley is a double agent himself," a Progressive miner named Art Gramlich told Vinnie and Mason during a break that afternoon. "He's on Peabody's payroll. That's why they only blew up his porch and outhouse. Just making it look good."

"I was with Chuck Davin when Archie Norton and George Lyman shot at the Stanley house," Vinnie said. He was confused by the old miner's words and a little miffed at him implying that the Progressive President of his own local was a double agent. "Davin got his leg shot off that day."

"Yes. I know'd you were there, son," Gramlich said, "but nothing happened to Stanley, his family or his property that day, did it?"

Vinnie tried to shake away the cobwebs that were forming in his brain. If he couldn't trust the Progressive leader of his own county, who could he trust? He threw his half-smoked cigarette aside and followed Gramlich and Mason back into the courthouse.

****

"Your Honor, it is imperative that we find W.C. Argust," Fitzgerald said again when court resumed. "His testimony is vital to the case of the defense."

"May it please the court," Prosecutor Eubanks said. "I have just received a report from Dr. Arthur R. Metz testifying that Mr. Argust is seriously ill of coronary thrombosis."

"Bullshit!" Vinnie whispered to Mason. "Peabody Coal Company would kill Argust before they'd let Fitzgerald question him."

"The Harrisburg riot was a fake," United Mine Worker A. R. "Blackie" Swafford testified a few minutes later for the defense. "Peabody staged the gun battle by having machine guns on armored trucks fire into houses along the roadside. They forced their workers to stay in the mine. They wanted to create sympathy and get the National Guard to come protect the mine."

"How do you know that to be true?" Fitzgerald asked.

"Because the mine boss gave me a pistol and told me to stand in the mine yard and fire shots into the air. He said it was to make people think there was a gunfight going on so the National Guard would come in and protect the coal mine."

The next to testify was Harrisburg Chief of Police Allen Davis, who said he saw machine guns at the coal mine and reported it to Sheriff Eugene Choisser.

"Choisser told me not to bother about them," Davis said. "The Progressives didn't even have no pickets out that night. The next day, the UMW miners told me they were told to stay in the mine all evening to make it look like the picketers were shooting at them."

Corporal Michael O'Sullivan was called by the defense to testify to being part of the National Guard's efforts to restore order in Harrisburg.

"The first thing my unit did was pick up cartridges off the streets."

"How many do you suppose you collected?"

"Well over a thousand," O'Sullivan said.

"What kind of cartridges were they?"

"Machine gun cartridges."

"How many cartridges did you pick up that were not from a machine gun?"

"None, sir."

On cross examination, Eubanks stared at O'Sullivan. "Corporal, are you in love with a woman from Taylorville named Angeline Eng?"

"Objection, Your Honor!" Fitzgerald shouted. "That is irrelevant to the corporal's testimony."

"I will show that it is relevant, Your Honor," Eubanks said.

"Then make it quick, Counselor," Briggle said.

"Are you in love with Angie Eng, Corporal?" Eubanks repeated.

"Yes."

"And is she a member of the Progressives' Women's Auxiliary?"

"Yes," O'Sullivan said, "she is."

"No further questions, Your Honor."

* * * * * * *

"I was shot twice and beat up once by the Peabody thugs," Defendant Art Gramlich testified. "We didn't never do anything except peaceful picketing."

"Whoever heard of peaceful picketing?" Vinnie whispered to Mason. "He's laying it on a little thick."

"Emmitt Higgins was a United Mine Worker gunman brought up here from Carl Shelton's gang," Gramlich stated. "One night I was walking down the street when Higgins climbed out from his car with a gun in one hand and a jug of whisky in the other and started shooting. So I pulled my own gun and started firing right back at him until my own pistol was empty. Then I hightailed it home."

"So you left Higgins lying wounded in the street?" Eubanks asked.

"Why, no sir, I can't rightly say he was wounded," Gramlich said. "Least ways, last I saw he was still tipping the jug pretty good."

* * * * * * *

"We regret to inform the court that Peabody Mine Superintendent W.C. Argust died in Washington Hospital last night after surgery," State's Attorney Eubanks reported the next morning. With a smirk on his fat face, he glanced over at the shocked Arthur Fitzgerald.

After deliberating for ten minutes with his co-counsel, an exhausted looking Fitzgerald said."I have no more witnesses, Your Honor."

"Fine then," Briggle said, "the State may begin presenting their rebuttal witnesses."

It only took Eubanks two people to destroy the testimony of the defense's best witness, Vernon Vickery.

"The boy's penchant for truth and veracity has never been very good," Vickery's father testified. Mrs. Vickery testified that Vernon has a piece of metal embedded in his head. "That's the reason he has his delusions," she said. "It's caused him to be a bit pixilated, don't you know."

The crowd chuckled at Mrs. Vickery's testimony, but Fitzgerald was not laughing.

* * * * * * *

The final summations the next day were quick and to the point.

"The defendants participated in a campaign of dynamite rather than decency," Eubanks said at the end of his thirty-minute oration. "The peace and quietude of 1932 soon turned into riot, rape and rampage through the distortion of the original endeavors and intents of the Progressives by a few selfish persons.

"Evans became sheriff only because he was a Progressive miner hired to aid and abet the men in their attempt to continue their outrages of bribery and intimidation. Every man and woman in Saline County was afraid because Nip Evans was putting the finger on them. Evans wanted to stay in control because the evidence showed he received more than seven thousand dollars from the Progressives and wanted to feather his own pocket. The whole purpose behind the Progressives' bombings and shootings were to stop production and increase the cost of production in mines employing United Mine Workers."

Fitzgerald walked on egg shells when it was time for his summation, but he still found a way to get in a hint that the UMW and coal companies were in collusion.

"While the Progressives were frequently blamed for the violence," Fitzgerald said, "the UMW and the major coal operators benefited from its results. The shootings and bombings provided the impetus for the intervention of the state militia and the imposition of martial law in several key mining communities. With the military in control of these areas, Progressive strikes were broken."

Fitzgerald stared at the jury letting those final words hang in the air. Forbidden by the judge to put the blame for the violence squarely where it belonged, the defense attorney had little more he could say. The Progressives walked out of the courthouse as if they were departing a church following a sobering sermon. Vinnie talked quietly for a few moments with Steve Mason, then the men shook hands and went to their cars. Just as he was ready to turn the block, Vinnie was stopped by Art Gramlich.

"I wanted to tell you something, Vacca," Gramlich said. "I heard you were in on the assassination of James Hickey, and I just wanted to thank you for getting rid of that scum."

"It wasn't an assassination, Mister Gramlich," Vinnie said, "and Officer Schrader is the one who shot him."

"That's okay, son," Gramlich said with a wink. "I understand. Well, I'm off to make a Brunswick sandwich in my room. That is, if I have any bread left that hasn't molded."

Vinnie didn't want the man to go away thinking he had assassinated anyone. "Would you like to come to my house for dinner? My wife's a fine cook."

When Vinnie phoned to tell Sam that he was bringing Art Gramlich home for supper, she immediately sent little Sid over to have dinner at Bullo and Mary Kate's house. Sam wanted to protect Sid from hearing more stories about violence, but she also didn't want him exposed to the miner's constant swearing. She had heard Gramlich speak at several Progressive meetings and knew he was not only long-winded, but also careless with his language.

"Why, Vinnie," Gramlich said after their meal that evening as they sat on the porch enjoying a smoke, "do you remember when we blew the Capitol Mine down there in Springfield at Nineteenth and Capitol Streets? By God, it was just eighteen blocks from the capitol building. It so happened that practically every man jack was below the surface that day, which consisted of five to six hundred men on the day shift. By God, there was only one way to get the rat son-of-a-bitchin' scabs out of there, was to blow that airshaft, and, by God, they blew that son-of-a-bitch and I mean they blew it upside down.

"Them scab bastards scurried out of there like rats. They never did stop running and there was a whole hell of a lot of them that ran back to where they came from. I think we must've used about ten cases to blow that son-of-a-bitch, and when dynamite goes down, well, Jesus Christ, when it went down, that airshaft it must've knocked every son-of-a-bitch and his brother that was down there on his ass. Hell, some of them miners was probably in mineshafts that were right underneath the capitol building.

"After that, Peabody offered the Progressives the Springfield mines if we'd leave the others alone. We goddamn near had John L. Lewis whipped, but then the mine companies built fences around the mine yard and guarded it with machine guns and cannons."

"We sure did have Lewis's boys on the run," Vinnie

said, nodding, "that's a fact."

"Yes, sir, that was just before we started bombing the trains." Gramlich took a few puffs on his cigar before spitting a wad of tobacco onto Sam's clean porch.

Sam didn't take issue with the staining of her deck. She was gazing intently at Vinnie, who was struggling to avoid her stare.

"Yes, sir," Gramlich went on, "I imagine we bombed twenty-five or thirty trains along the Midland Tract that year. Hell, we weren't gonna let them deliver that damned scab coal, but at least we targeted the coal cars themselves so lives wouldn't be lost. Hot-damn, those Midland bombings were successful, but then some of our boys made the mistake of hitting the IC trains and stopped delivery of mail, and then in come the damned FBI. Those goddamn G-Men don't mess around. No sir, they don't."

Sam's face turned bright red and her eyes began to mist.

"We'd have probably been all right but we got that goddamn Charlie Briggle as a judge," Gramlich rambled on. "He's a bastard. I got a whole lot of respect for the law, but that son-of-a-bitch never was a lawman. They had all these goddamn dirty stool pigeons for the government sitting in the room and they called us in there, and then they'd call us out loud and clear. 'Art Gramlich? Is your name Art Gramlich? Is it Arthur, alias Art Gramlich?' Well, the son-of-a-bitch stool pigeon was sitting right there, and later he'd point at me and say, 'Yes, that's Art Gramlich, he's the one I saw putting the bomb on the tracks.' Hell, he never saw me. He couldn't have, 'cause I had a stocking cap pulled down over my face the whole time I set the bomb. Lying son-of-a-bitch."

* * * * * * *

After Art Gramlich left that evening, Sam Vacca found herself staring down at the dirty dishes soaking in her kitchen sink. Her hands had been shaking so violently she had stopped washing the glasses for fear she would break one. A clean conscience had been a major reason she had always enjoyed a good night's sleep. Tonight promised different.

"It's all a lie," Sam said in almost a whisper. "Everything the Progressives stand for is nothin' but a damned lie."

"Well, not everything, I reckon," Vinnie said from the doorway behind her. "I imagine the UMW and the coal companies probably did bomb a few of their own trains to get the FBI involved. Makes sense, don't it, Sam?"

For the first time since she had known him, Sam wanted to slap some sense into her husband. "Our boys lied, Vinnie. They broke the law. They deserve to go to jail."

"Did them fellas break the law when they dressed up like Injuns and threw that tea in the Boston Harbor?" Vinnie asked.

"Folks have died, Vinnie," Sam said quietly. "James Hartman was carrying firewood into his house and got his head blowed clean off. A little girl was a settin' by a window dreaming about being a woman and got gunned down."

"Now that was UMW gunmen shot that little girl, Sam."

"How do you know?" Sam said. "You thought the train bombin's was the UMW."

Vinnie sat down on the floor next to a kitchen chair. It was the same spot he and Sam had sat years before when his parents first showed the newlyweds their newly built and unfurnished home.

Sam started to sit down on the floor beside him but then took the empty chair.

"I don't know what's true anymore," Vinnie said. "Maybe Bullo is right. Maybe laborers are no better than them rich folks. Maybe we do need someone like John L. Lewis—someone who understands how to talk to mine owners and company men."

Sam said nothing the next morning when she brought the newspaper to her husband while he sat at the kitchen table with his father. She simply lay the newspaper open in front of him, put on her coat and left the house to work at Angeline's Place.

36 Defendants Are Convicted
Of Bombings in Coal Fields;
Guilty on All Three Counts

"They didn't even let me testify," Antonio said after he read the article.

"What would you have said if they'd asked about the machine gun you took off the company thug?"

"I don't know, Vinnie."

"Were we on the right side, Pa?"

"I don't know. I think we were," Antonio said, then, after a moment, suddenly sat up straight in his chair. "Yes, son, I'm sure we were. Like Agnes Wieck said. We just got a little too far ahead of our army, that's all."

24

Duffy's Tavern near Herrick, Illinois, was solidly built, both inside and out. Old Pat Duffy had grown weary of replacing chairs and other furniture every time a bar fight broke out. When the mine trouble started, he remodeled his establishment into a fortress by nailing wooden church pews to the floor with six inch spikes. He replaced the bar and tables with solid oak and set them permanently in place with nuts and bolts that ran down into the crawl space under the building. All glass bottles were kept in back rooms, and customers drank from tin cups that made fine bludgeons during the frequent melees. Even the big brick posts on either side of the driveway had been filled with rocks, gravel and concrete that enabled them to survive many an inebriated motorist.

Following the verdict of the thirty-six Progressives, Duffy experienced a surge of patrons as defeated PMA miners abandoned picket lines in Christian County and headed back to their homes in southern Illinois. Herrick was far enough away that it made a suitable pit stop. Most travelers were disheartened men who sat quietly, glumly imbibing in the spirits found within their tin cups. The United Mine Workers and the coal companies had won. Still, Duffy liked to lift the Progressive boy's spirits by reading an article that appeared in an issue of Time magazine.

The court record tells a tale of union corruption, court connivance, death, terror and double-dealing murder... Behind the government's prosecution lay the heavy face of John L. Lewis. The testimony of many a government witness was paid for, not by the government but by undercover persons, all suspected of affiliation with John L. Lewis' UMW. The Federal government as well left their footprints, blackmailing the witnesses and using perjured testimony in court. All in all, this was the most sordid trial ever witnessed in downstate Illinois.

Then came a Saturday night a week into the exodus from the picket lines. Six young men had stopped around noon and decided to play cards and get intoxicated rather than complete their journey home to their loved ones. They quickly made it clear they weren't going home with their tails between their legs.

"We sure gave those Progressives what for, didn't we boys?" The biggest of the youngsters shouted over his shoulder at two miners standing at the bar. Despite being indoors, he left his stocking cap on his head, its many holes giving it the shape of a king's crown.

The miners rolled their eyes, downed their drinks and headed for the exit. Duffy and his wife ignored the loud shenanigans of the young thugs, and as the afternoon turned to early evening began watering down their drinks. Regular weekend customers arrived and the bartenders were kept busy mixing "the usual's" the moment patrons strolled into the tavern.

Despite being busy, Pat Duffy didn't miss recognizing the transition that always seemed to occur when hard men got their fill of hard liquor. Particularly when those men had so recently been introduced to long trousers. He was pouring coffee at the bar for four older men when Stocking

Cap stumbled up behind them.

"Damn, Duff!" Stocking Cap shouted. "This joint is about to make me cry with boredom. Hurry up and give me another bottle."

Duffy continued to fill his customers' tin cups.

"Hey, old timers," Stocking Cap said to the men standing together at the bar. "Don't you want nothing with that java?"

"Why, yes, son," the shortest of the men said without turning. "I do believe we'll have a little respect with our coffee."

"Hell, you ain't gonna get no respect in these parts, you old coot," Stocking Cap said. "I know who you are. You're one of them cowards that dropped out of the PMA when things got hot, ain't you? What have you old bastards done for coal miners except make things worse?"

Though the tavern was nearly full, it suddenly became quiet. Stocking Cap's five friends whooped with delight and left their seats to form rank behind their leader. A few of the regular patrons quickly guzzled their drinks, set their empty tin cups on their table, and appeared to size up the two groups of men as if to decide which team they would stand beside when the inevitable fracas began.

An extremely handsome and well-dressed gentleman rose from a small table and donned a short-brimmed bowler cap. Carrying a silver-handled cane, he stepped between the two groups of men.

"So typical of you damned colliers," Bowler Hat said. "If you aren't fighting the coal companies, you're fighting each other."

"These ain't coal miners anymore, mister," Stocking Cap said. "Why, they's just old fuddy-duddies."

"You asked what these men have done to make life better for coal miners. Very good question, young man." The dapper gent stepped behind one of the men and pointed over his shoulder at the man's back with his thumb. "Here we have Mr. Harley Eng. Once one of the wealthiest men in central Illinois. Even as a successful capitalist, Eng was one of the rescuers at the Cherry Mine Disaster in 1909. Two-hundred-fifty-six men died down there that day, young man. Did you know that? But then Mr. Eng foolishly lost his fortune in the stock market crash of twenty-nine. He has since spent his years creating safety equipment for coal miners. Thanks to this gentleman, you boys will be wearing hard hats for the remainder of your careers."

Bowler Hat stepped behind a bespectacled, balding man who turned and leaned back against the bar, a bewildered look on his face.

"Rolfe Hiler," Bowler Hat said as if he were introducing associates at a business luncheon. "He lost his wife in Ludlow, Colorado, on April 20, 1914. Went home to Chicago and finished his medical studies. This foolish man chose a career of treating miners' asthma rather than making a decent living prescribing aspirin to the well-to-do.

"Ah," the strange narrator said, stepping behind the next gentleman. "Here we have the *coward*, as you called him. Antonio Vacca. Union organizer and one of the founders of the Progressive Miners of America. Sadly, Mr. Vacca lost his wife during the Battle of Tovey on January 3, 1933. He has since struggled to keep his family together because his only two surviving sons stubbornly chose rival unions.

"And lastly, you get to meet Mr. Joe Harrison." Bowler Hat laughed. "Hell, boys, old Joe puts the rest of these fellows to shame. He was in Pana in '98 and '99 when the United Mine Workers gave those colored scabs what for." Bowler Hat leaned into Harrison and whispered, "Want to describe what that was like, old chap?"

Joe turned and gave the man a cold, hard stare.

"Ah, well." Bowler Hat smiled. "I may as well leave you fine fellows to your pugilistic pursuits. Good day, gentlemen!"

With that, the man twirled his cane and strode from the building.

Stocking Cap turned as if to follow him. Both Antonio and Joe had enough experience with sucker punches to recognize that one was coming. When the young man turned his foot sideways and lowered his weight over his leg, Antonio started with a left hook just as Joe delivered with an equally hard right haymaker. Stocking Cap twirled directly into the two massive fists that caught him just under either cheekbone. The simultaneous blows were powerful enough that the youngster's feet were lifted high off the ground. He landed on the far side of the poker table, leaving the cards and tin cups on it undisturbed.

Two of Stocking Cap's friends tried to gain an advantage by stepping on a church pew and launching themselves at the four old miners. RJ Hiler saw the attack coming, and with lowered head, he threw a cross-body block to take the assailant's legs out from under them. The two crashed head first into the foot of the bar, the arm of one of them somehow finding its way into a pewter spittoon on the floor.

That's when the bar erupted into an all-out brawl. Every man in the place began fighting the nearest person. Pat Duffy spun and kicked a pole along the wall behind the bar. A sliding panel immediately dropped from the ceiling, providing protection for a long mirror that ran the length of the room.

For a moment, Antonio and his friends found themselves spectators. Stocking Cap and two of his allies lay unconscious, and the other three were quickly dispatched into the same condition.

"This is quite exhilarating," Dr. Hiler told his friends as he waylaid a passing drunk with his tin cup. "I've never been in a bar fight."

It took both Harley and Joe on either side of the physician to convince him to follow Antonio toward the exit. As the four stepped outside onto the outer porch, a half dozen men came rushing past them to get into the tavern before the fight ended.

Bowler Hat was leaning against a mint green Chevy Master Coach as he smoked a long pipe. "Well, this is a surprise," he said.

"How is it that you know so much about us?" Harley Eng asked.

"Well, old chap. The truth is, at one time or another my employer had each of you gentlemen on his short list of potential candidates to go bobbing face down in the South Fork River."

"So what stopped you?" Antonio asked.

"Well," Bowler Hat said, "I suppose there was always someone more important in line in front of you."

Antonio stepped forward, his fists clenched. Joe and Harley grabbed his arms just as a revolver appeared in Bowler Hat's hand.

"Now, now, Mr. Vacca," the man said with a smile as he took a quick puff on his pipe. "There's no reason to get huffy. The mine war is over. Let's let bygones be bygones." He opened his car door, got in, and a moment later was motoring out of town.

"Who was that sporty fella?" Harley asked.

"His name is Charlie Harris," Joe said. "He used to be a member of the Shelton gang. They call him Black Charlie."

"Well," Dr. Hiler said, "those Shelton boys better watch their backs with that guy around."

25

"Them Progressives are flocking back to the UMW with their damned tails between their legs," Kieran Phelan said as he hung the telephone receiver back on its hook on the wall. He clapped his hands, laughed merrily, and did a happy little jig for his wife. To his dismay, Felina scowled and crossed her bare arms over her equally bare breasts. He wondered if she was perturbed because he had performed the impromptu dance while he was still wearing her underclothes and high heels. She was getting so persnickety lately, he never knew what would please her.

"So just what the hell are you going to do for money now?" Felina got out of bed and started throwing clothes around the room as she looked for something to wear. "They aren't going to need you to bring any more of your scab buddies from down south. You promised to buy me a new car. How the hell is that going to happen?"

"I got it taken care of, baby," Phelan said. He sat down on the bed and carefully removed her high heels from his feet. "All I gotta do is, uh, I'll blackmail the coal company. Sure, that's what I'll do. They'll pay me plenty to keep my mouth shut, don't you know?"

"They'll kill you, you goddamned idiot," Felina said slowly, then went over to the dresser and pulled open a drawer. She was withdrawing her nightgown when she noticed her husband's life insurance policy tucked along the side of the drawer. She ran a hand lovingly along the top of it. Thoughts raced through her head. Her husband out of the way, money in her pocket and sugar-daddy Eubanks doing her bidding. It couldn't get better than that.

"Well," she said with a smile as she dropped the night-gown, turned back to him and began slowly moving on all fours across the bed, "come to think of it, the company probably will want to pay you a bonus for all you have done for them."

* * * * * * *

"We need to get rid of that son-of-a-bitch," Douglas Eubanks said the moment Kiran Phelan was out the door. The lawyer rested his feet on a coffee table and leaned back in his chair so that only the rear legs remained on the floor. His fingers were interlocked behind his head as he carelessly spat tobacco juice toward a wastebasket in a corner. Eubanks had been looking for an excuse to get rid of his mistress's husband. Now he had one. Plus, he was now the attorney for not only the Shelton gang, but the United Mine Workers and most of the coal companies in Illinois.

"We can't afford to be implicated in another murder," Bill Stork said. "Especially now that we've got the Progressives on the run."

"Don't worry," Stephen Eubanks said. His teeth gave a tobacco-stained smile. "We won't even be involved. I've got contacts in Chicago who will arrange things for us."

"How do you have contacts in Chicago?" Stork asked.

"The benefits of being part of the Democratic political machine," Stephen replied, a smirk of a smile on his face.

"What the hell does that mean?" Stork asked, trying to swallow without a noticeable gulp. "Are we in cahoots with Frank Netti now?"

"Let's just say that our big city allies in the north are looking to get a hold on the downstate voting," Douglas said. "With a subtle promise or two in relation to the next elections, I'm certain an exchange of favors can be arranged."

* * * * * * *

The service at the Ambassador Hotel was always impeccable, so when Garner Hamilton had to stay in Chicago, he invariably instructed his assistant, Winfield Taggart, to make reservations at that establishment. Naturally, a suite was required, since Hamilton always had important visitors who had to be properly entertained. That Sunday morning, Taggart had already ushered such guests in and out of the suite three times. The business of the Chicago political machine knew no off days for Hamilton. He had been more than pleased with the results of his first two appointments. They culminated in the procurement of nearly a quarter of a million dollars, which would be kept in secret funds for the Democratic Party's campaigns.

The third appointment had not been as pleasant. Hamilton considered his party's downstate members to be little more than country bumpkins who had to be constantly watched and pampered to make certain they remained satisfied with the meager positions they held. Therefore, when Stephen Eubanks strutted arrogantly into the room, Hamilton had to suppress a cough of amusement. Taggart, through years of experience as his boss's personal secretary, intuitively knew to provide Hamilton an early out from the meeting by lying about another appointment he had to keep in five minutes. The secretary received a satisfied smile from his employer as he bowed out of the room.

"Mr. Eubanks, so good to see you again." Before Eubanks could reply, Hamilton continued, "Sorry I haven't more time to talk with you. Business never seems to cease. Now, what can I do for you?"

If Eubanks was upset by being put off lightly, he didn't show it. "I am here about a rather delicate matter, Mr. Hamilton. As you may remember, a few years ago my family enlisted your assistance to help with a certain business rival of ours. The situation was handled very efficiently by your department, I might add. However, due to unfortunate circumstances, a similar situation has arisen, and we are once again in need of your services."

"And that would mean...?" Hamilton wanted to be completely certain of his guest's implication, and besides, he smiled to himself, he wanted to see what theatrical word Eubanks would use in place of the word "kill."

"The elimination of a certain individual in our area," Eubanks said indiscreetly as he lit a cigar. It was Hamilton's office that had handled the previous murder, and he saw no reason why they should hesitate to do the same now. Yet, there was something in Hamilton's manner that seemed contemptuous.

"I see, Mister Eubanks. I am sure that you and your colleagues have given this matter considerable thought and deem this to be the only possible solution." Hamilton sounded like a parent reluctantly consenting to his daughter's decision to marry.

Eubanks scowled, "Of course, sir. We are quite efficient at handling our affairs. My family has been successful in this state since it's very founding."

Hamilton's smile disguised his contempt for the man. If they could handle their affairs so efficiently, then why did they have to kill all their enemies? *Oh, well,* he thought. *The money is always good in the paid assassin market.*

"Very well then, Mister Eubanks, I think we can find a

suitable man to handle your case. If you will just leave the necessary information with our Mister Taggart, I will see that the matter be taken care of immediately. Good day, sir."

Without rising to shake Eubanks' hand or show him to the door, Hamilton returned his attention to the stack of papers on his desk.

Eubanks puffed his chest and stuck out his chin, then strode from the room as if an audience of thousands were watching him.

Five minutes later, Taggart reappeared in front of Hamilton's desk.

"I had Eubanks write the information out himself, as I assumed you would want, and I also collected two G's from him instead of the usual one. He bitched a little, but finally paid."

Hamilton seemed pleased. "Excellent. Now do you know of any unemployed cons needing work?"

Always ready with an answer, Taggart said, "Fellow by the name of Norton just got into town last week. Jumped bail in St. Louis and has a successful record for three jobs in southern Illinois."

"Then why was he in jail?"

"Punching a police officer."

Hamilton was satisfied. "Offer him two C's. And make it look as if he's being hired directly by the Eubanks' family."

Taggart laughed. "What is it with those farmers downstate? You'd think that Eubanks fellow would have figured out by now where his place is in the natural order of things."

Hamilton raised an eyebrow. "Don't let him know that. As long as he's willing to fork out money in the gubernatorial races, he's allowing us to put money into all the other campaigns in the state. Hamilton tapped the hand-written note Eubanks had left with Taggart. Besides, if Douglas Eubanks should ever get elected, he'll be ours, thanks to these little indiscretions. It's been quite a day. Let's go eat."

* * * * * * *

The smoke-filled pool hall only had three tables, their once flush green surfaces now grayed and scarred from years of use. The dim lighting above each table barely cast enough glow to make the badly scuffed balls visible, much less the faces of the men watching the game from barstools and chairs around the room. Most of them were regulars to the establishment, and since they each sat in their customary places, wearing their own unique styles of patched jackets and caps, they needed little light to identify one another.

The three-legged wooden chair on which Archie Norton balanced had just the day before been the ephemeral property of another ex-con. As so often happened to the patrons of the pool hall, Norton's predecessor to the seat had come into a bit of bad luck, involving the crushing of both his legs not far below the kneecaps. The news of their acquaintance's misfortune had been quite matter-of-factly told around the room that morning, and no one had given it another thought when Norton drew the chair over to a dark corner to signify his confiscated territorial rights.

Since returning to his hometown of Chicago, Norton had followed the advice of a bookie he had done a job for in St. Louis and looked up the owner of the pool hall. When Norton introduced himself, the bookie's friend had been distant but friendly to the sad-looking little man. With his help, Norton found a cheap room for rent and a night job standing guard for a gambling house that doubled as a massage parlor during the day.

Watching the intense, quiet faces of the men in the room, Norton felt as comfortable and secure as he ever had. He had a steady job, a place to stay, and the company of fellow fugitives, which most of the men in the room were. They never gave his more-than-slightly peculiar body and face a second thought. In fact, Norton thought himself to be a far sight better-looking than many of the scar-faced, heavily tattooed men around him, and, of course, what he thought was all that mattered.

Winfield Taggart had done his homework on Archie Norton, as he did with most of the underworld figures in the city. When he entered the pool hall and adjusted his eyes to the thin light and thick cigarette smoke, he was quickly able to pick Norton out of the crowd. Immediately recognizing that two hundred dollars was more than was necessary, he reached into the breast pocket of his coat, palmed half the money from the envelope, and then slid it nonchalantly beneath his shirt.

The presence of Taggart in the room drew everyone's attention, not because he was dressed in a finely tailored suit, but because they all knew a visit from Taggart meant someone in the room was about to be employed for the one thing that they could all do expertly—kill.

With the anticipating tension of beauty contestants, the men watched Taggart's searching eyes water from the cloud of smoke that hovered near his head. With the pool games stopped, the silence had turned from eerie to apprehensive. When Taggart spotted Norton in the corner, the recognition on his face caused the anticipation to change to disappointment. As the men returned to their games and conversations, the only significant transformation that had taken place in the room was their attitude toward Norton. They now each felt respect for this ugly little man who had been chosen above all others for the job he was most assuredly going to be given.

Norton seemed confused by all the attention to the stranger in the doorway. If it had not been for the relaxed atmosphere that had returned to the room, he probably would have bolted for the back door.

"Mister Norton? Archibald Norton?" Taggart's right eyebrow perked theatrically as he spoke.

"Might be." Norton played out his part in the drama to the letter. "What ya need?"

"I have been requested to offer you one hundred dollars plus expenses for your services."

"Doing what?" Norton said, sensing a setup.

Taggart handed Norton a brown manila envelope from his breast pocket. "To kill someone. All the information and the money you will need is in this. Half the money is here and you'll be able to pick up the remainder when the job is done."

"How ya expect me to do it?"

"The weapon you will require is in a box in a locker at the gym where you work. The key to the locker is in the envelope. The payment will be waiting for you in the same locker upon your return from a successful job." Taggart eyed the ugly little man seriously. "May I tell my employer that you will accept the job?"

For a moment, Norton thought about turning the job down. He had as good a job as he had ever had and he didn't want to lose it. He told Taggart this.

"It's been taken care of," Taggart said. "You'll retain your position when you return. Besides, it shouldn't take you more than a week."

Norton opened the envelope, glanced at its contents, then leaned forward in his chair, standing it on all three legs. "Tell your boss that Kieran Phelan is as good as dead."

* * * * * * *

Just moments after Archie Norton knocked the woman unconscious, her husband walked in the front door. Norton had begun humming a merry tune and felt quite giddy at the thought of what he would be able to do to the woman whose shapely figure he was able to appreciate despite the darkness of the room. The unexpected entrance of his target brought a cold shiver and caused the hair on the back of his neck to bristle.

Norton had not troubled his limited intellect with thoughts of the unexpected. When he saw the silhouette of a person standing in the doorway, he fired twice at a spot a few inches below the middle of the shadow's shoulders. The sound of two gunshots was followed by the crumpling of the man's body onto the floor. Norton took a moment to recollect his courage. He spent that calming time watching a rapid pool of blood form on the floor.

Killing Kieran Phelan, a man with whom he'd once been friendly, didn't bother Norton in the least. Ever since their collaboration in the Midland track bombing, the two had been rivals for the contractual work the UMW and coal company offered. Phelan had usually obtained the easier bombing jobs while Norton had to make his money with a gun—the latter of which required more planning for safe getaways.

Holding his weapon in one hand, he aimed a flashlight with the other into the face of the lady on the floor. He emitted two almost comical soprano-like shrieks when he saw the remarkable beauty of the woman."And now," he said as he unbuckled the belt on his pants, "you shall feel the power of the Leprechaun."

The sudden weight of the man on top of her caused the

woman to regain consciousness. A look of delight lit her eyes.

Norton tried to get up, but the lady reached up, grabbed him viciously by the hair, and rolled him off and over. Now she was on top of the little man, and for one brief moment, he thought he was going to enjoy the first consensual sex of his life. But then the woman reached toward the pool of blood on the floor, rubbed her hand in it and smeared it on her forehead and then across her eyes and mouth. Her face grew ghastly wicked.

Bile rose in Norton's throat. "Let me go!" he cried, a quiver in his voice. "This ain't fun anymore."

The crazed woman gave a shrill laugh and continued cackling as she dipped both hands in the blood and then ran the strange red shampoo through her long, blond hair and behind her ears. Her laughs turned to loud moans and her breathing turned heavy. She slapped the man hard in the face and continued gyrating her hips. Then she placed a bloody finger in her mouth and licked and sucked on it like it was the best thing she had ever tasted.

"Please let me up," Norton pleaded. "I won't tell noone, I promise I won't. I just wanna go home."

He never saw the woman reach behind her with her free hand and into her husband's boot. The last thing Archie Norton ever saw was the blur of a shiny instrument being swung down from behind the bloody and insanely evil eyes of Felina Phelan.

26

"I just can't believe you're going to be the one to deliver our boys to Leavenworth!" Angie Eng folded her arms and turned her back on Michael O'Sullivan. She looked out the school house window at her students as they played. Little Sid watched her as he seesawed with Rosemary Donovan.

"Well, someone's going to take them," O'Sullivan said quietly. "Don't you think it would be better to be me than someone who hates them and might mistreat them?"

"Oh, you just don't understand." Angie's face burned. "I just wish you hadn't come back here."

O'Sullivan's face sagged. He swallowed hard. "Well, then I wish I had never declared my love for you on the witness stand." His face reddened and he looked at his hands. "That's why Lieutenant Sebuck is making me be part of this escort. He wants to embarrass me."

Angie turned her back to him and crossed her arms.

O'Sullivan rolled his eyes, shook his head and slammed the door as he hurried out of the school house.

The young boys jumped to attention as he passed, but he ignored them and strode away.

* * * * * * *

"Tomorrow is just another work day, gentlemen," Jesse Donovan, the pit committeeman, told the miners who had been ordered to gather in the mine yard. "If any of you plan to go down to the train station in the morning, you will be immediately terminated. Further, any man calling in sick tomorrow can start looking for a different job. Now let's go mine some UMW coal."

Bullo went straight to his father's house when he got off work that night.

Antonio sat in his rocking chair next to a blazing fire in the hearth. "Those boys are going to think their brethren have abandoned them," he said with a shaking head when he heard the warning the pit committeeman had given the workers. "Corporal O'Sullivan's unit has been assigned to ride with a group of U.S. Marshals to Leavenworth. They aren't even going to allow family to say goodbye to the Progressives."

"Pa, I never wanted this," Bullo said.

"I know, son. None of us thought it would go down this way."

The two men sat in silence for several minutes, the tick of the big grandfather clock and the snapping of the burning firewood the only sounds. Bullo had a sense of what the thirty-six condemned Progressives were feeling at that moment. Five years were about to be taken out of their lives. He thought about all the things he would miss if he had to be away from his wife and boys for the next five years.

"What would you do, Pa," Bullo asked, "if you were me?"

Antonio didn't answer right away. For a moment, Bullo wasn't sure if his father hadn't heard him or if he were mad at him for asking the question.

"You're the most valuable machine operator in the mine," Antonio finally said, "and with winter coming on, the mine is operating at full force."

Bullo weighed the comment, waiting for the advice he assumed was coming. His father rose and went into the kitchen without another word.

* * * * * * *

The next morning, Corporal Michael O'Sullivan did his duty by supervising the transfer of the thirty-six convicted Progressives from the courthouse jail to the train that would carry them to the federal prison in Leavenworth, Kansas. When they arrived at the heavily-guarded train station, the prisoners were able to step directly from the bus onto the train platform.

Once in their seats, the Progressives' handcuffs were removed. Four U.S. marshals armed with shotguns sat in the back, while O'Sullivan sat next to a private in the front of the passenger car.

After the train had moved away from the city limits, O'Sullivan rose and walked slowly back along the aisle, quietly checking on the prisoners. When he came to the marshals, he nodded and started back to his seat. Some of the Progressives were just staring out the windows, creating memories of the Illinois countryside they so loved. Two of the older men, though, talked as casually as if they were waiting for their turn in a barber shop.

"What do you think of FDR's New Deal programs, Ray?"

"I'll tell you," Ray Tombazzi said, "people have a full stomach, people get different attitudes. Economy depends on the economics from any individual—that's just natural. If a man's starved, he'll go out and hustle—but if it's given to him on a platter, he'll just wait.

"It reminds me of the time the park district started putting little wooden houses up in the trees for squirrels.

They wanted lots of squirrels for the entertainment of the visitors, don't you see. Well, they kept those houses full of nuts, and those squirrels grew big and fat and lazy. On the other side of the park, the squirrels had to hustle all summer making their homes and storing up plenty of nuts. Well, sir, one year there came a particularly bad winter and the park district couldn't keep putting nuts in the houses they built, don't you see. When spring finally came along, all those squirrels that had been taken care of were dead. The ones that had hustled and provided for themselves thrived.

"That's exactly what is going to happen with all these New Deal programs. Folks who plan for their retirement and who live within their means will thrive. But a hundred years from now, those who grew up getting something for nothing won't amount to a hill of beans. By God, if you don't believe me, you just wait and see."

"That's the same idea as in the coal mine," the first miner said. "Union men used to police their own ranks. If one fella was slacking, we all yelled at him. We'd tell the slacker, 'Take pride in your work. We're union men, and if you slack it makes us all look bad.' Now the union men say, 'That's not my job.' Or, 'It's the company man's job to take care of the slacker, but, by God, them bosses better not yell at a union man or we'll wildcat.'"

"Well, sir, I like Roosevelt's New Deal," a middle-aged miner leaned across the aisle and said firmly. "My youngest boy got work with the Civilian Conservation Corps and his big brother is an electrical lineman in Kentucky with the Tennessee Valley Authority. They're both learning trades they can use the rest of their lives. Now that's smart government, I say."

The miners looked up at the eavesdropping O'Sullivan. He gave a weak smile and continued on down the aisle. As the corporal took his seat in the front of the passenger car, he thought about these Progressive miners that Angie Eng loved so much. They definitely weren't the goldbrickers he had once imagined them to be. These men didn't want something for nothing. A hard day's work for an honest wage was all they wanted.

The train conductor gave a loud series of blasts on the whistle and the slowly-applied brakes squealed. There would be a brief stop in Virden, Illinois, to unload and load a few passengers in some of the adjacent cars. The soldier sitting next to him seemed absorbed in a newspaper, so O'Sullivan closed his eyes and sat back in his seat.

A moment later, he realized the volume of mumbling coming from the prisoners had risen. He opened his eyes, stood and looked back at the Progressives just as the mumbling became shouts of joy. Every man in the passenger car opened windows. For just a second, O'Sullivan thought they might be trying to make a break for it. Then he realized they were pushing their faces up to their windows and yelling names. When the train came to a complete stop, many of the prisoners reached out the open windows to clasp hands with people on the boardwalk.

"Corporal," a young guardsmen yelled, "what do we do?"

"About what, Private?"

"The prisoners are talking to those women and children at the train station."

"Would you like to go out there and shoot a few those children who are saying goodbye to their fathers?"

"Why, no sir, I wouldn't."

"Then go back to reading your newspaper, son."

O'Sullivan didn't want to look too negligent in his duties, so he went out the back of the passenger car and stood on the end platform to watch as small children were held up to the windows to kiss the prisoners. He recognized a few of those in the crowd, including Dr. RJ Hiler. Then he saw a face that almost made him fall flat on his face.

Angie Eng squeezed through the crowd toward him, shouting something. His name, he thought. Before she was close enough to hear her words above the clamoring, the train lurched and slowly moved away from the station. O'Sullivan had to resist the urge to leap from the platform and into her arms. Then she was free of the shouting and crying crowd and was out in the open running along the train platform toward him, her hand held out.

"I love you!" her lips were saying, though her tiny lungs couldn't overcome the train noise and the crowd that followed her.

Michael O'Sullivan's baritone voice, though, had no trouble being heard above the din.

"Meet me at the St. Louis train station Monday at noon!" O'Sullivan shouted so loud the crowd on the platform came to an almost immediate quiet. "I want to marry you."

The cheers and applause that followed came not only from those behind Angie, but also from the prisoners on the train. When O'Sullivan reentered the passenger car, the prisoners met him with another loud ovation as he returned to his seat through a gauntlet of handshakes and slaps on the back.

* * * * * * *

Vinnie was the smallest, so he sat between his father and Bullo, who was driving. Four Progressives squeezed together in the backseat.

"I don't see the buses behind us," one of the men said. He was nicknamed Wart, though he had the clearest skin anyone had ever seen.

"They'll be along," Antonio said over his shoulder. "Just don't you worry."

"Well, then, what are we gonna do if they don't stop the train in St. Louis?" Wart asked. "When Bullo came down in the mine and emptied the water out of his lunch box, I sure didn't know we was wildcatting so's we could have another caravan." He stared out the car window for a few moments, then looked down at his hands. "What if they ambush us like they did at Mulkeytown? I've had dreams that Felina Phelan cornered me in a car and stabbed me with a butcher knife. What if she's with them and my dream was a premonition?"

"Why would you worry about her, Wart?"

"Why she's being hailed a hero for stabbing to death that fellow that shot her husband. You know she hates Progressives, don't you? She might take a notion to come after me."

"She's busy tending her husband, Wart." Antonio said. "I still can't believe he survived being shot twice in the chest."

"Felina a hero!" Bullo said, shaking his head. "Fiberto and Libero would sure get a laugh about that."

Several miles passed with the three Vacca men silently reflecting on happier days when the most serious things four young brothers had to worry about was how to keep their mother from knowing what mischief they were up to.

Finally, Vinnie looked at his father. "You know Wart may be right," he said quietly. "They may not stop the train."

"We could block the tracks and make the train stop," Bullo said. Both his brother and father looked over at him to make sure it was really Bullo Vacca saying that.

"You an anarchist now, big brother?" Vinnie asked with

a smile and a nudge of his elbow.

"No violence," Antonio said. "I think there's another way to say goodbye to our friends if the train won't stop."

* * * * * * *

O'Sullivan heard hisses coming from the prisoners, and when he looked back, Lieutenant Sebuck came down the aisle toward him.

"The t-t-train will not make its scheduled stop in St. Louis," Sebuck said. "Apparently, they don't want another situation like we just had in Virden."

"Yes, sir," O'Sullivan said. "I wonder why they would fear a problem in St. Louis."

"Quit t-t-thinking and f-f-follow orders, Corporal."

"Yes, sir."

So as to stay on schedule for future intersections and rendezvous with other trains, the train began to slow well before St. Louis. The prisoners were quiet as they neared the tall buildings of the city. In another few hours they would be arriving at a place they would not leave for five years. Seeing their families in Virden had, of course, been bitter-sweet.

Still, something was missing.

These men felt abandoned by the friends and colleagues beside whom they had fought so hard for the rights of working men and women everywhere. Right or wrong in methodology, their passion for the rights of laborers was honest and sincere. Now this group was taking the fall, being made scapegoats for laws that were broken by some of their own, that was true, but also for sins done by members of both the United Mine Workers and the coal companies.

When the men saw the train station approaching and realized there would be no stopping, any happiness there may have been seemed to be suddenly sucked from the entire passenger car. Heads drooped. Still, there was no crying, not even a sob or a pat on the cheek to dry an eye. As demoralized as these proud men were, they would not give up.

Then, one of the men gave a loud whoop and stood at his window. Once again, O'Sullivan and the thirty-six prisoners jumped into positions to look out the windows. Only this time, they were able to look out whichever side of the passenger car they wanted to.

As the train went slowly through the train station and then picked up speed, both sides of the railroad tracks were filled with coal miners dressed in work clothes, standing tall and proud.

"There's hundreds of them, Corporal," the young private said.

More like thousands, O'Sullivan figured. The train passed miner after miner paying tribute. He recognized many of the faces of Progressives, including Antonio and Vinnie Vacca, Joe Harrison and Harley Eng. He was surprised, however, by how many United Mine Workers were in the ranks, including Bullo Vacca and dozens of men who had never even been members of the Progressive Miners of America.

The gauntlet of miners went on for mile after mile after mile. Their salute to their comrades on the train was a simple one, but to the seasoned coal miners who would pay the price for the sins of so many others, it was a memory that would warm their hearts for years to come.

For when the passenger car carrying those thirty-six miners passed, each man extended his dinner bucket and slowly dumped water onto the ground.

END

ABOUT THE AUTHOR

After retiring from a career as an educator, Kevin Corley turned to his love of writing as a way to retell the stories he had shared with history students in his classroom. He recognized that the coal mining communities of Illinois were center-stage in the development of unions in the first half of the 20th century. From the Virden and Pana massacres of 1898-99 to the migration of miners after the Cherry mine disaster of 1909, Christian County became the rallying place for unionization.

Teaching history to many of the descendants of the coal mine wars, Corley developed a bond with the working man, a bond that was strengthened in 1986 when he was selected to research, through oral history interviews, the men and women who had lived through these powerful and often terrifying events. His research was used by Carl Oblinger to write his book, Divided Kingdom, which was published in 1991.

In addition to recording a vast collection coal miner stories, Corley discovered a wealth of old coal mining photographs dating back to 1898 in the homes of the Frank, Fritz, Otto and Max Boch family. Many of these photos are on display at the Abraham Lincoln Presidential Library and Museum in Springfield, Illinois. Taking inspiration from the Boch brothers' story, Corley loosely pattern his fictional Vacca brothers after them in *Sixteen Tons*, Corley's first novel, and *Throw Out The Water*.

TITLES FROM HARD BALL PRESS

Caring – 1199 Nursing Home Workers Tell Their Story

Fight For Your Long Day – Classroom Edition, by Alex Kudera

Joelito's Big Decision, Ann Berlak (author), Daniel Camacho (Illustrator), José Antonio Galloso (Translator)

Love Dies, a thriller, by Timothy Sheard

Manny & The Mango Tree, Ali R. Bustamante (author), Monica Lunot-Kuker (illustrator), Mauricio Niebla (translator)

Murder of a Post Office Manager, A Legal Thriller, by Paul Felton

New York Hustle – Pool Rooms, School Rooms and Street Corners, a memoir, Stan Maron

Passion's Pride – Return to the Dawning, Cathie Wright-Lewis

The Secrets of the Snow, a book of poetry, Hiva Panahi (author), Zoe Valaoritis and Hiva Panahi (translators)

Sixteen Tons, a Novel, by Kevin Corley

We Are One – Stories of Work, Life & Love, Elizabeth Gottieb, editor

What Did You Learn at Work Today? The Forbidden Lessons of Labor Education, nonfiction, by Helena Worthen

With Our Loving Hands – 1199 Nursing Home Workers Tell Their Story

THE LENNY MOSS MYSTERIES by Timothy Sheard

This Won't Hurt A Bit

Some Cuts Never Heal

A Race Against Death

No Place To Be Sick

Slim To None

A Bitter Pill

Someone Has To Die

UPCOMING CHILDREN'S BOOKS

The Cabbage That Came Back, Stephen Pearl (author), Rafael Pearl (Illustrator), Mauricio Niebla (translator)

Hats Off For Gabbie, Marivir Montebon (author), Yana Murashko (illustrator), Mauricio Niebla (translator)

Singing The Car Wash Blues, Victor Narro (author & translator)

The Garbageman's Gift, Cynthia Hernandez (author & translator)

UPCOMING GROWNUP BOOKS

Woman Missing, A Mill Town Mystery, by Linda Nordquist

Legacy Costs, an industrial memoir, by Richard Hudelson

Throw Out the Water, a novel, by Kevin Corley

98524582R00181

Made in the USA
Columbia, SC
27 June 2018